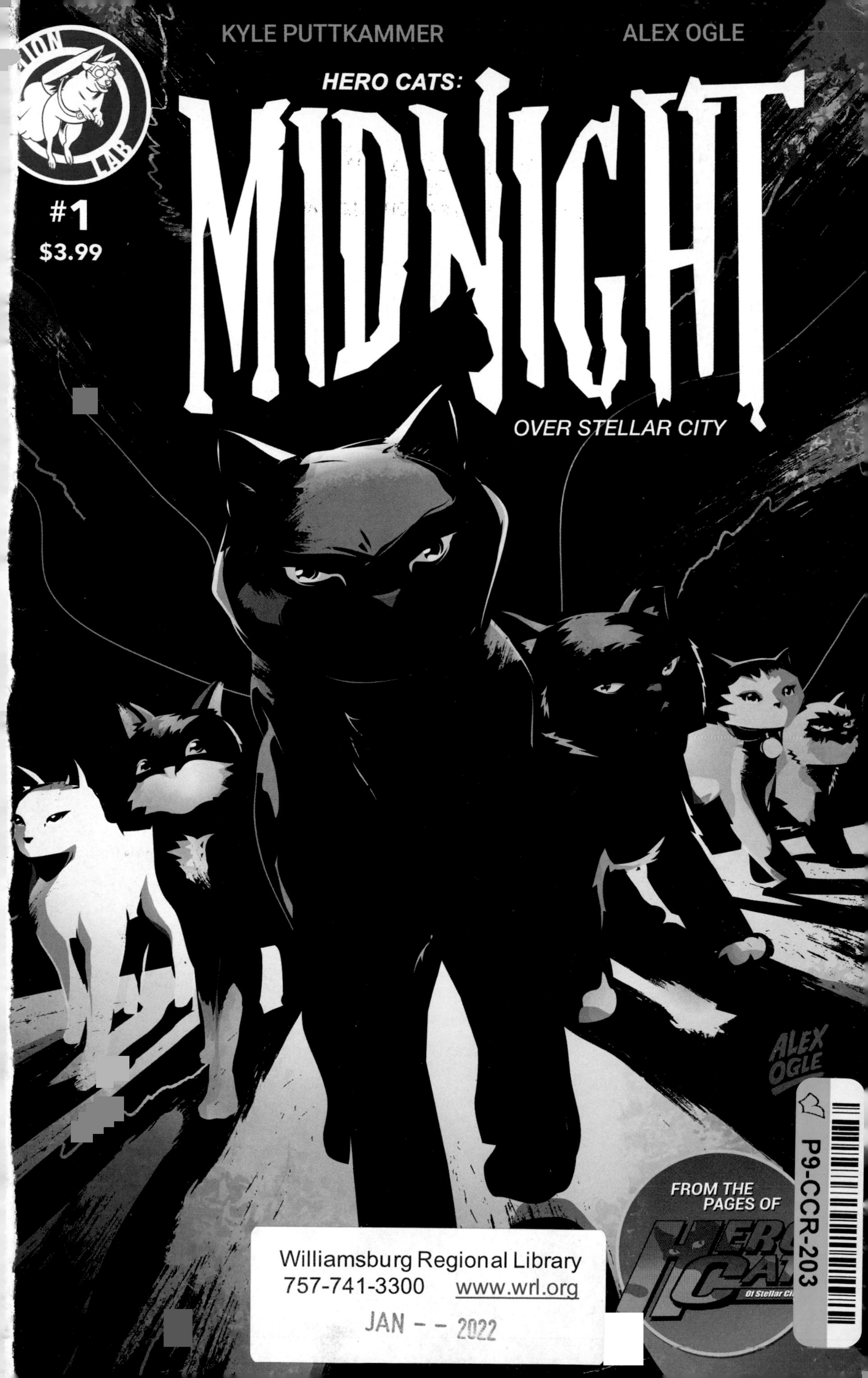
KYLE PUTTKAMMER
ALEX OGLE
HERO CATS:
MIDNIGHT
OVER STELLAR CITY
#1
$3.99
ALEX OGLE
FROM THE PAGES OF

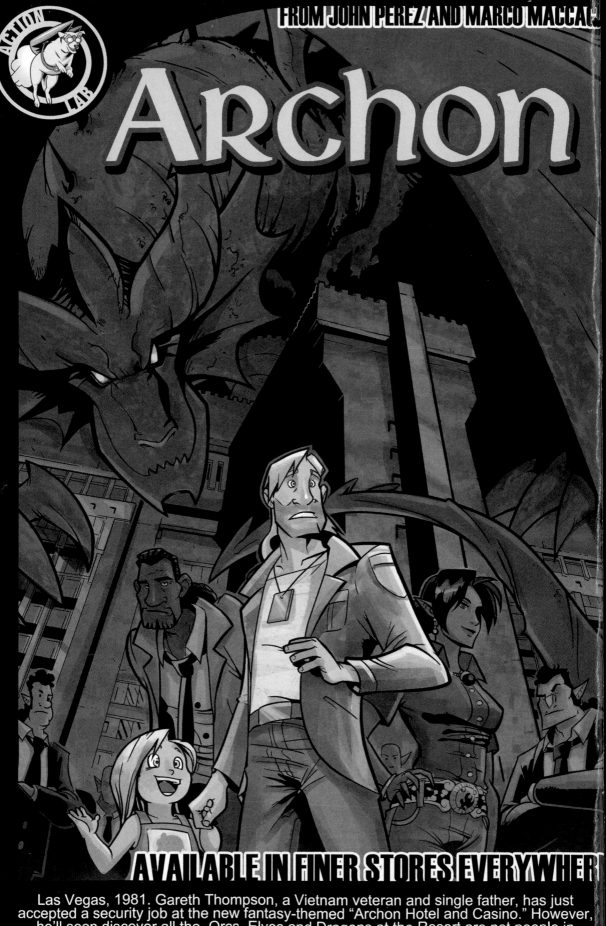

FROM JOHN PEREZ AND MARCO MACCA[

Archon

AVAILABLE IN FINER STORES EVERYWHER[

Las Vegas, 1981. Gareth Thompson, a Vietnam veteran and single father, has just accepted a security job at the new fantasy-themed "Archon Hotel and Casino." However, he'll soon discover all the Orcs, Elves and Dragons at the Resort are not people in costumes, but actual creatures of myth and legend.

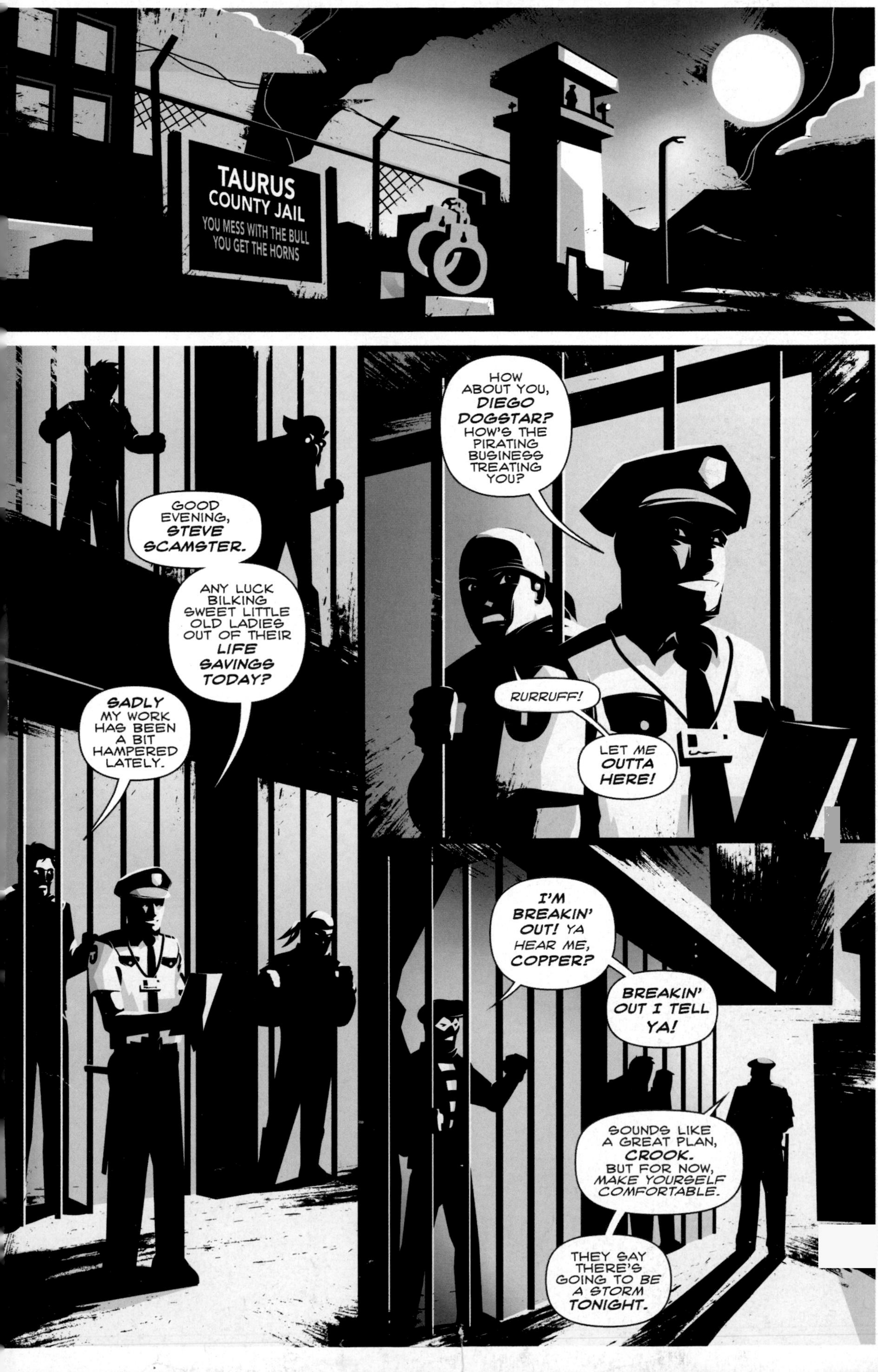
TAURUS
COUNTY JAIL
YOU MESS WITH THE BULL
YOU GET THE HORNS
GOOD EVENING, STEVE SCAMSTER.
ANY LUCK BILKING SWEET LITTLE OLD LADIES OUT OF THEIR LIFE SAVINGS TODAY?
SADLY MY WORK HAS BEEN A BIT HAMPERED LATELY.
HOW ABOUT YOU, DIEGO DOGSTAR? HOW'S THE PIRATING BUSINESS TREATING YOU?
RURRUFF!
LET ME OUTTA HERE!
I'M BREAKIN' OUT! YA HEAR ME, COPPER?
BREAKIN' OUT I TELL YA!
SOUNDS LIKE A GREAT PLAN, CROOK. BUT FOR NOW, MAKE YOURSELF COMFORTABLE.
THEY SAY THERE'S GOING TO BE A STORM TONIGHT.

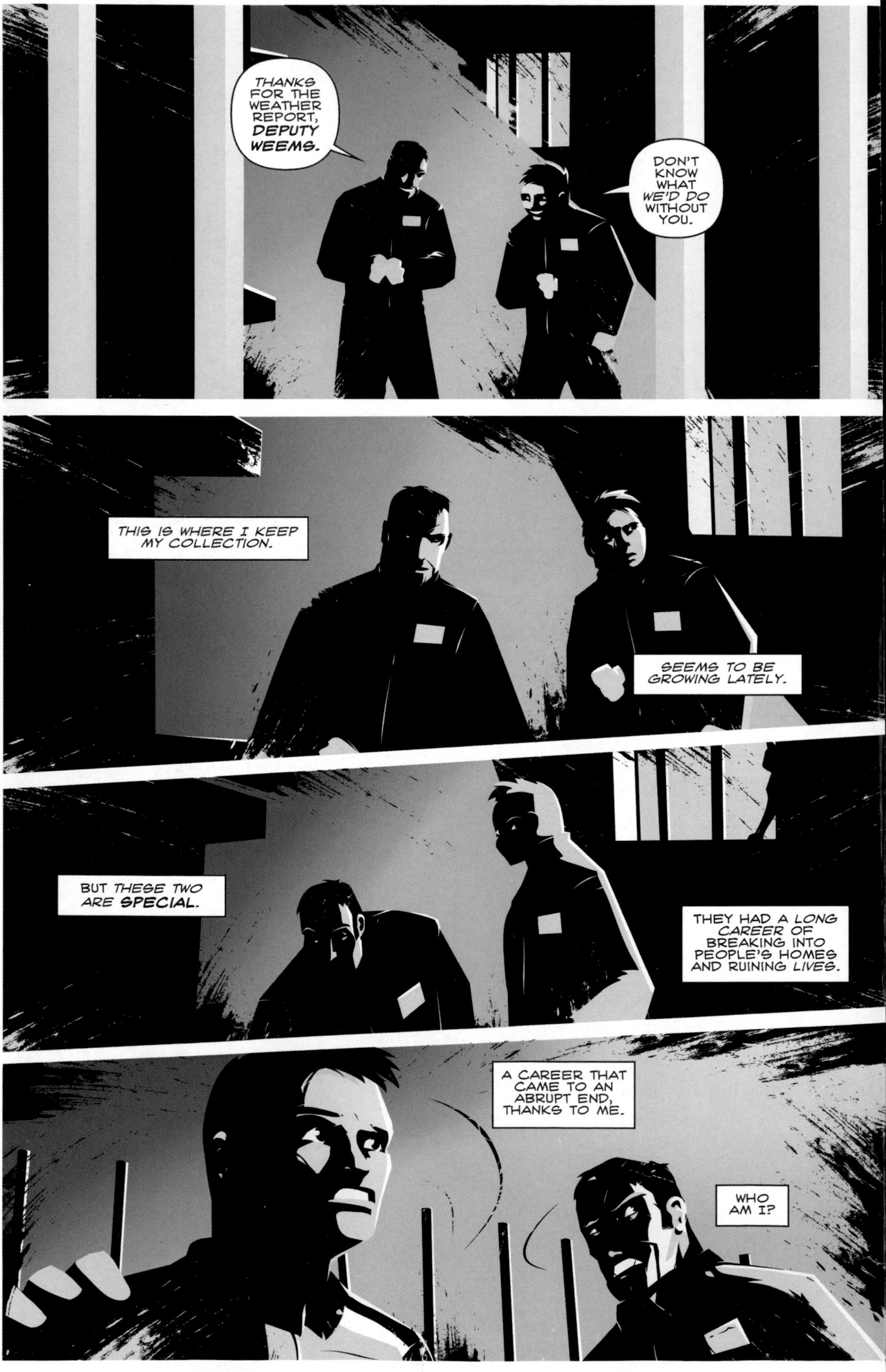
THANKS FOR THE WEATHER REPORT, DEPUTY WEEMS.
DON'T KNOW WHAT WE'D DO WITHOUT YOU.
THIS IS WHERE I KEEP MY COLLECTION.
SEEMS TO BE GROWING LATELY.
BUT THESE TWO ARE SPECIAL.
THEY HAD A LONG CAREER OF BREAKING INTO PEOPLE'S HOMES AND RUINING LIVES.
A CAREER THAT CAME TO AN ABRUPT END, THANKS TO ME.
WHO AM I?

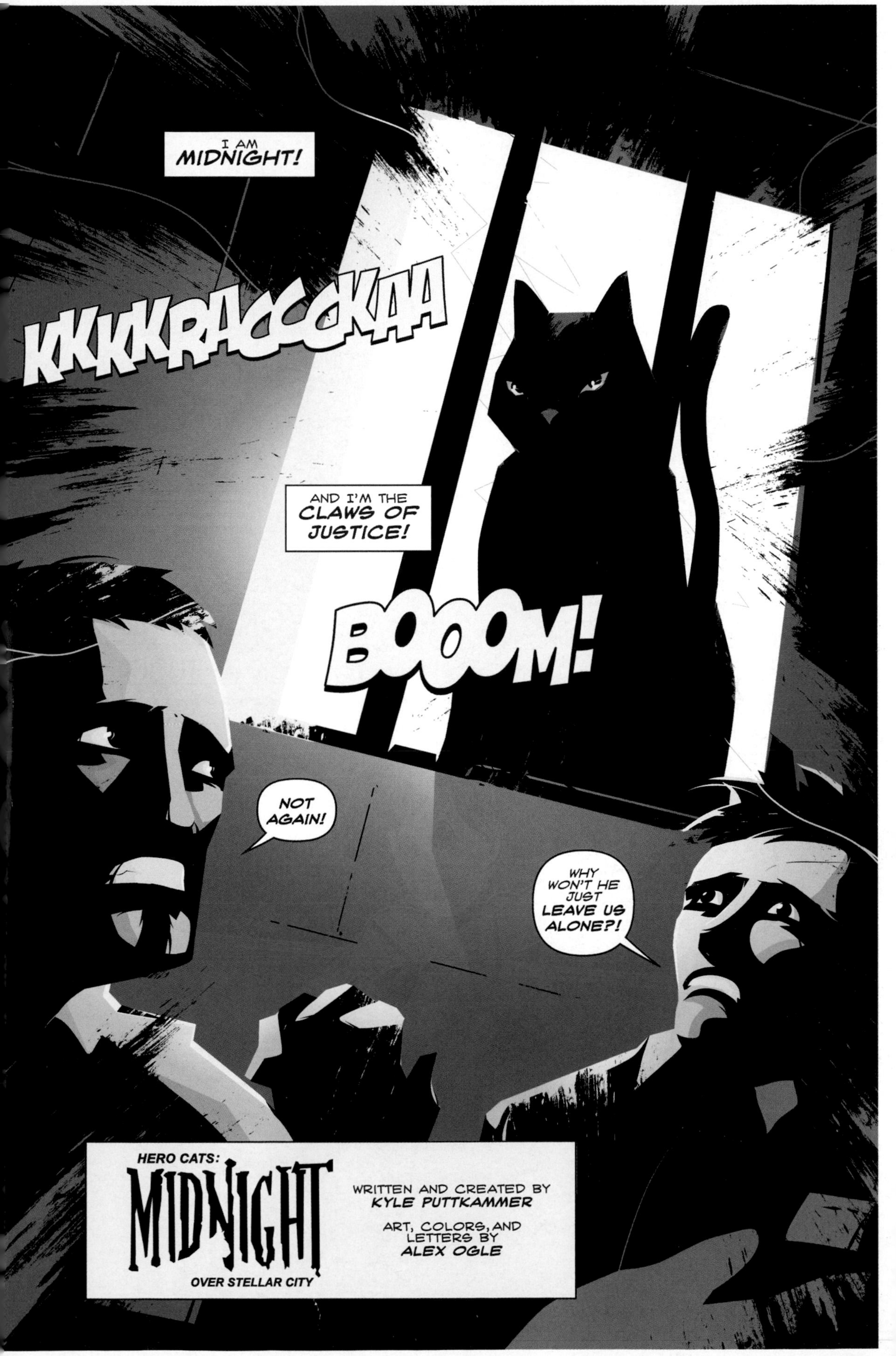

I AM MIDNIGHT!
KKKKRACCCKAA
AND I'M THE CLAWS OF JUSTICE!
BOOOM!
NOT AGAIN!
WHY WON'T HE JUST LEAVE US ALONE?!
HERO CATS:
MIDNIGHT
OVER STELLAR CITY
WRITTEN AND CREATED BY
KYLE PUTTKAMMER
ART, COLORS, AND LETTERS BY
ALEX OGLE

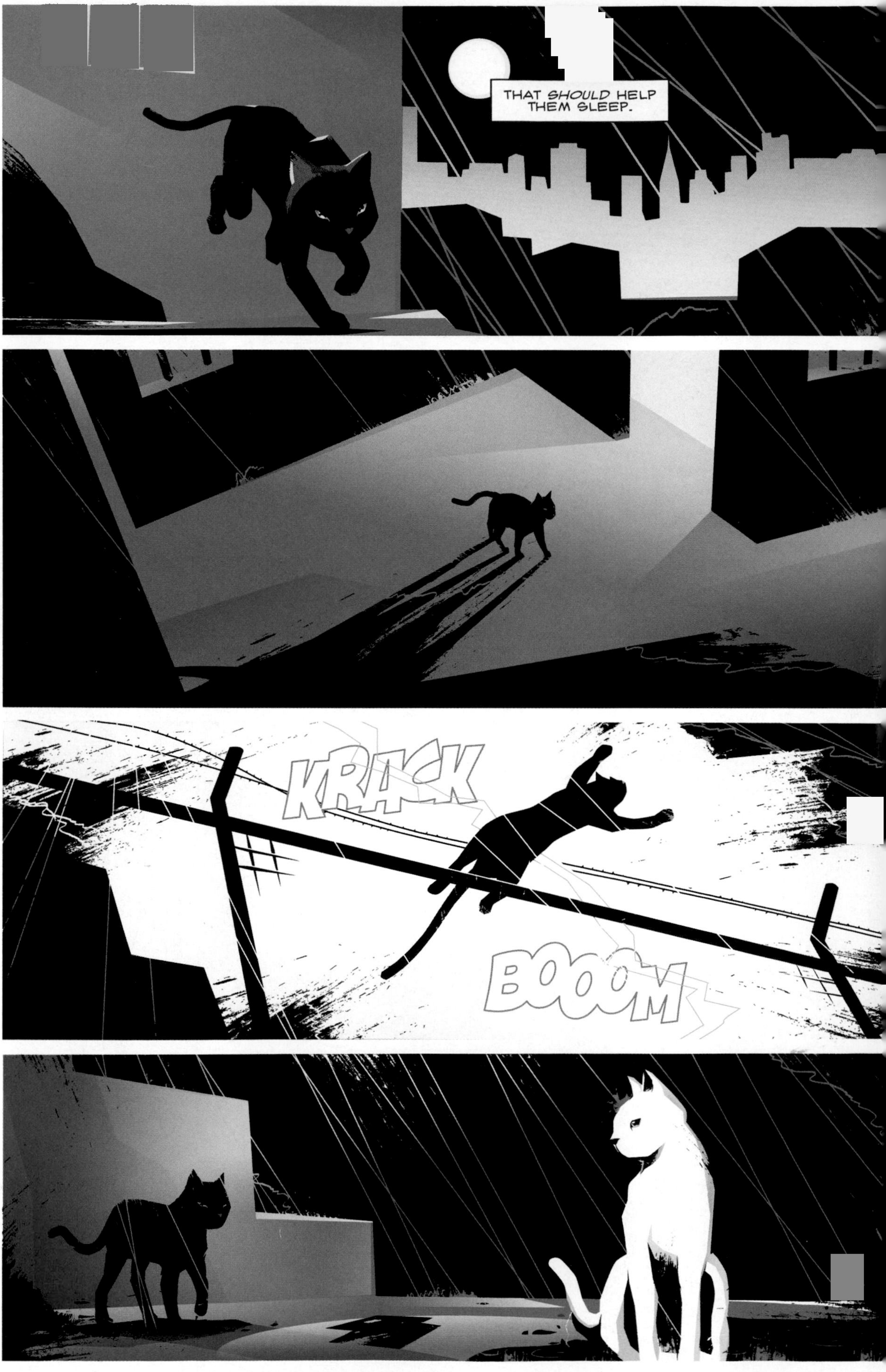
THAT *SHOULD* HELP THEM SLEEP.
KRACK
BOOOM

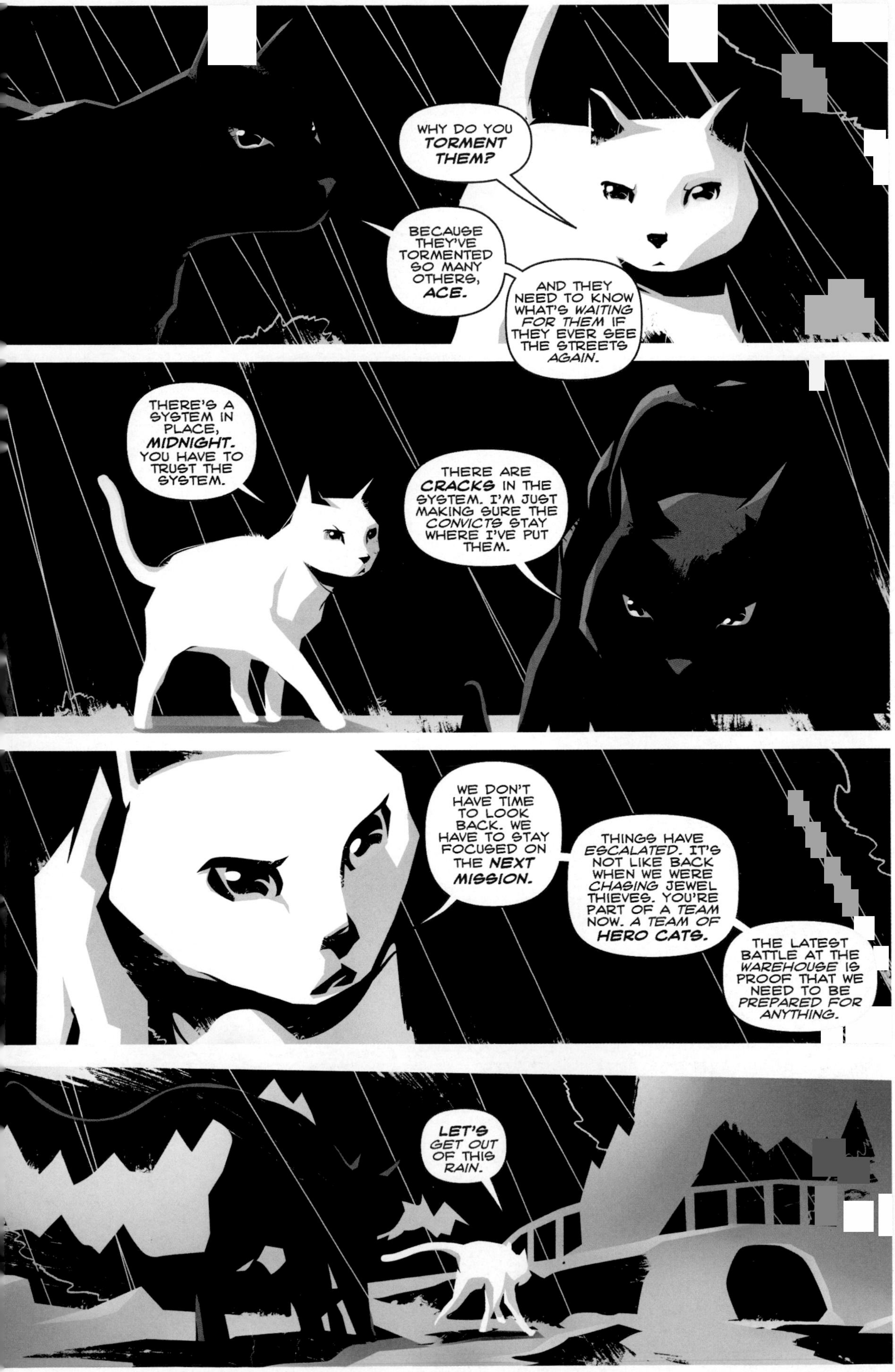
WHY DO YOU TORMENT THEM?
BECAUSE THEY'VE TORMENTED SO MANY OTHERS, ACE.
AND THEY NEED TO KNOW WHAT'S WAITING FOR THEM IF THEY EVER SEE THE STREETS AGAIN.
THERE'S A SYSTEM IN PLACE, MIDNIGHT. YOU HAVE TO TRUST THE SYSTEM.
THERE ARE CRACKS IN THE SYSTEM. I'M JUST MAKING SURE THE CONVICTS STAY WHERE I'VE PUT THEM.
WE DON'T HAVE TIME TO LOOK BACK. WE HAVE TO STAY FOCUSED ON THE NEXT MISSION.
THINGS HAVE ESCALATED. IT'S NOT LIKE BACK WHEN WE WERE CHASING JEWEL THIEVES. YOU'RE PART OF A TEAM NOW. A TEAM OF HERO CATS.
THE LATEST BATTLE AT THE WAREHOUSE IS PROOF THAT WE NEED TO BE PREPARED FOR ANYTHING.
LET'S GET OUT OF THIS RAIN.

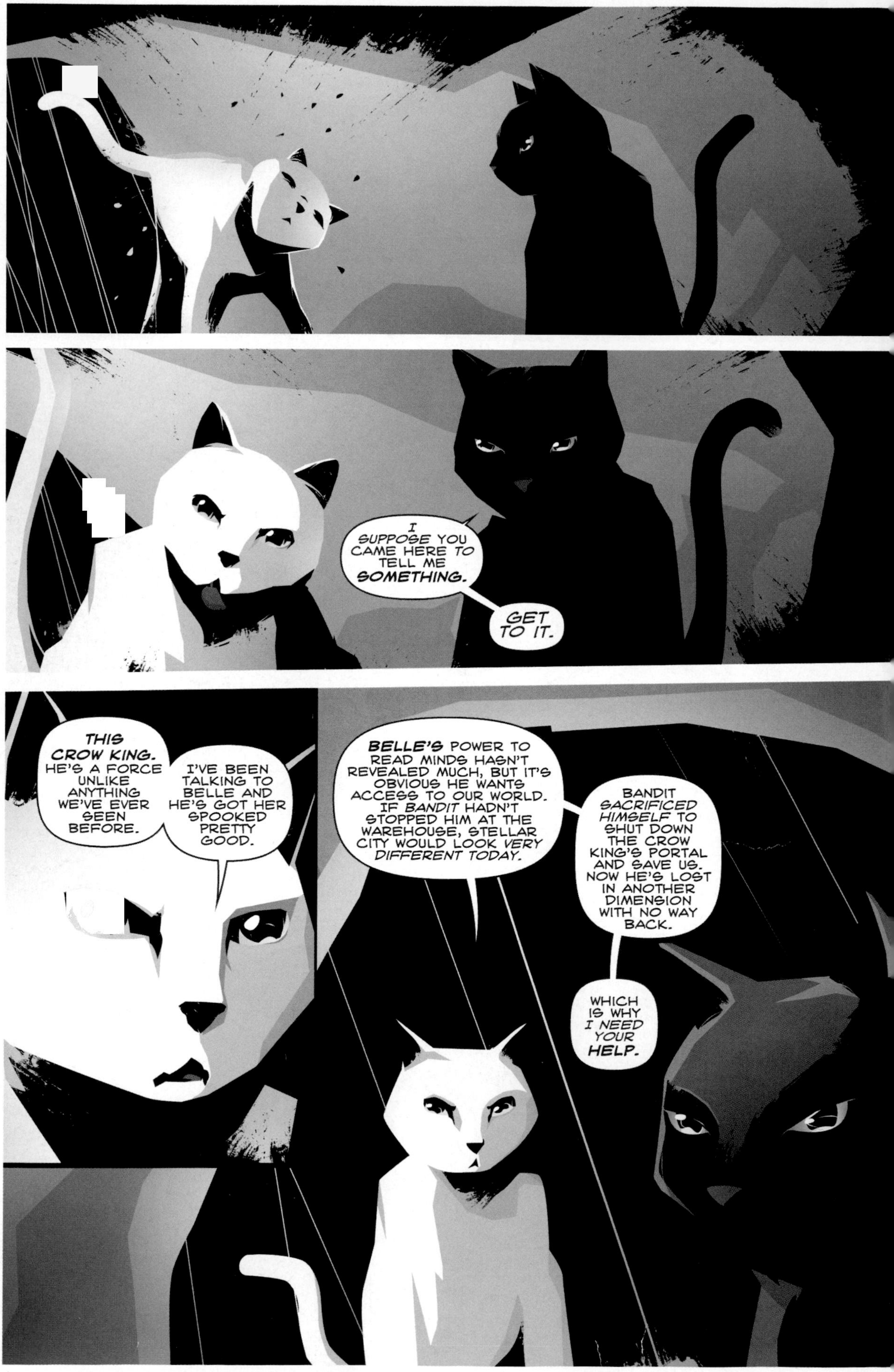
I SUPPOSE YOU CAME HERE TO TELL ME SOMETHING.
GET TO IT.
THIS CROW KING. HE'S A FORCE UNLIKE ANYTHING WE'VE EVER SEEN BEFORE.
I'VE BEEN TALKING TO BELLE AND HE'S GOT HER SPOOKED PRETTY GOOD.
BELLE'S POWER TO READ MINDS HASN'T REVEALED MUCH, BUT IT'S OBVIOUS HE WANTS ACCESS TO OUR WORLD. IF BANDIT HADN'T STOPPED HIM AT THE WAREHOUSE, STELLAR CITY WOULD LOOK VERY DIFFERENT TODAY.
BANDIT SACRIFICED HIMSELF TO SHUT DOWN THE CROW KING'S PORTAL AND SAVE US. NOW HE'S LOST IN ANOTHER DIMENSION WITH NO WAY BACK.
WHICH IS WHY I NEED YOUR HELP.

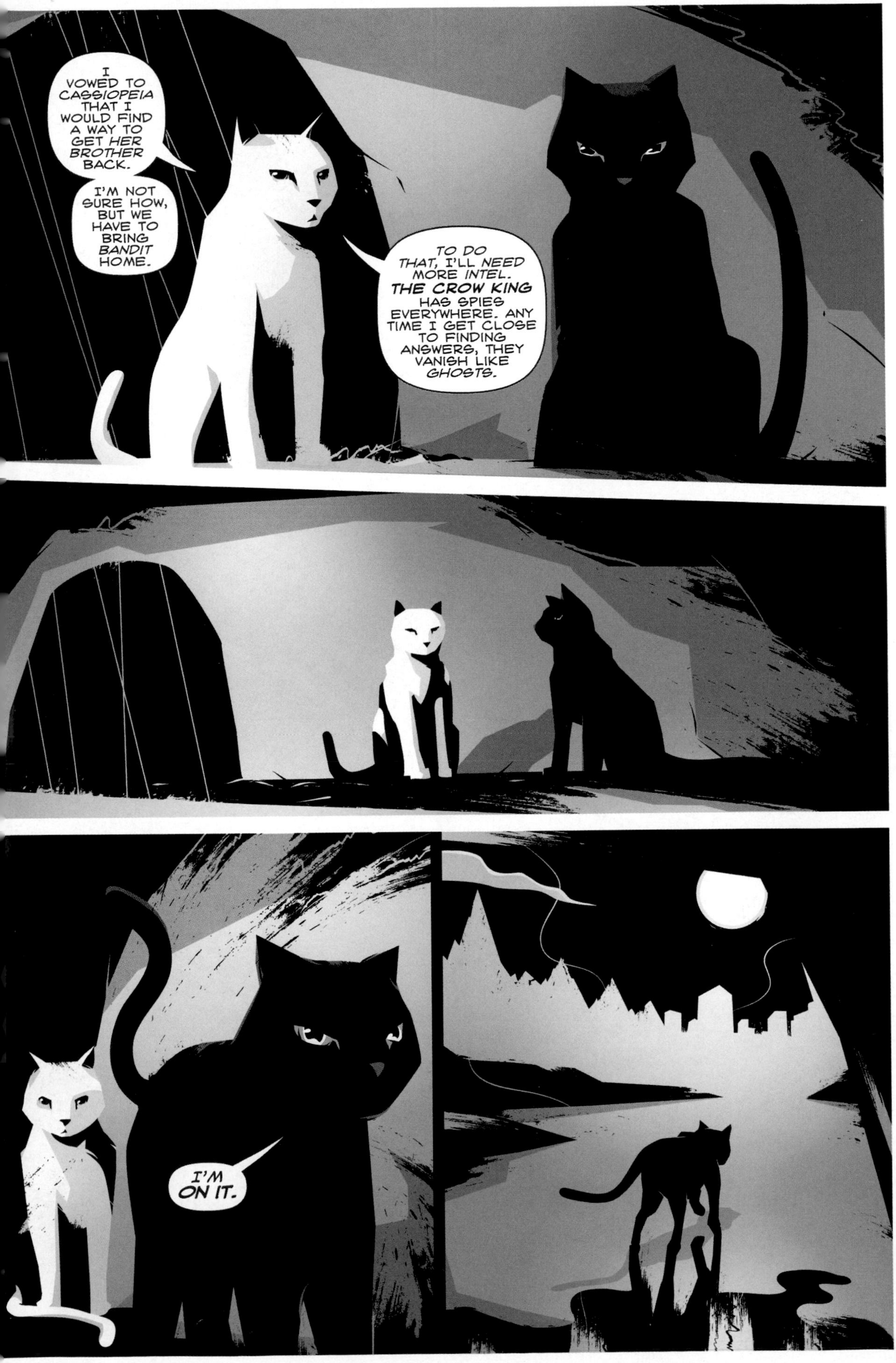
I VOWED TO CASSIOPEIA THAT I WOULD FIND A WAY TO GET *HER BROTHER* BACK.
I'M NOT SURE HOW, BUT WE HAVE TO BRING *BANDIT* HOME.
TO DO THAT, I'LL *NEED* MORE *INTEL.* **THE CROW KING** HAS SPIES EVERYWHERE. ANY TIME I GET CLOSE TO FINDING ANSWERS, THEY VANISH LIKE *GHOSTS.*
I'M **ON IT.**

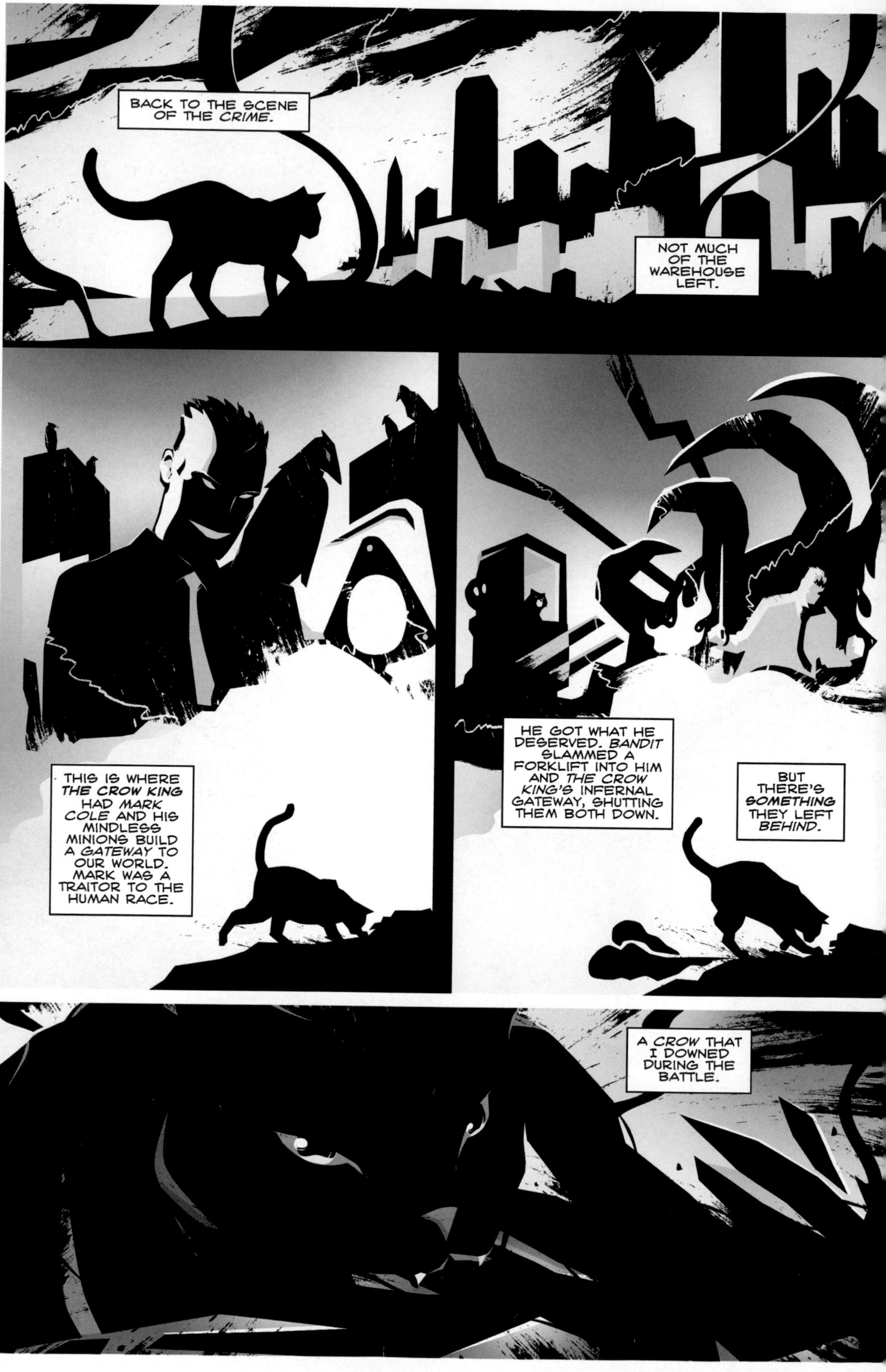
BACK TO THE SCENE OF THE *CRIME*.
NOT MUCH OF THE WAREHOUSE LEFT.
THIS IS WHERE ***THE CROW KING*** HAD *MARK COLE* AND HIS MINDLESS MINIONS BUILD A *GATEWAY* TO OUR WORLD. MARK WAS A TRAITOR TO THE HUMAN RACE.
HE GOT WHAT HE DESERVED. *BANDIT* SLAMMED A FORKLIFT INTO HIM AND *THE CROW KING'S* INFERNAL GATEWAY, SHUTTING THEM BOTH DOWN.
BUT THERE'S ***SOMETHING*** THEY LEFT *BEHIND*.
A *CROW* THAT I DOWNED DURING THE BATTLE.

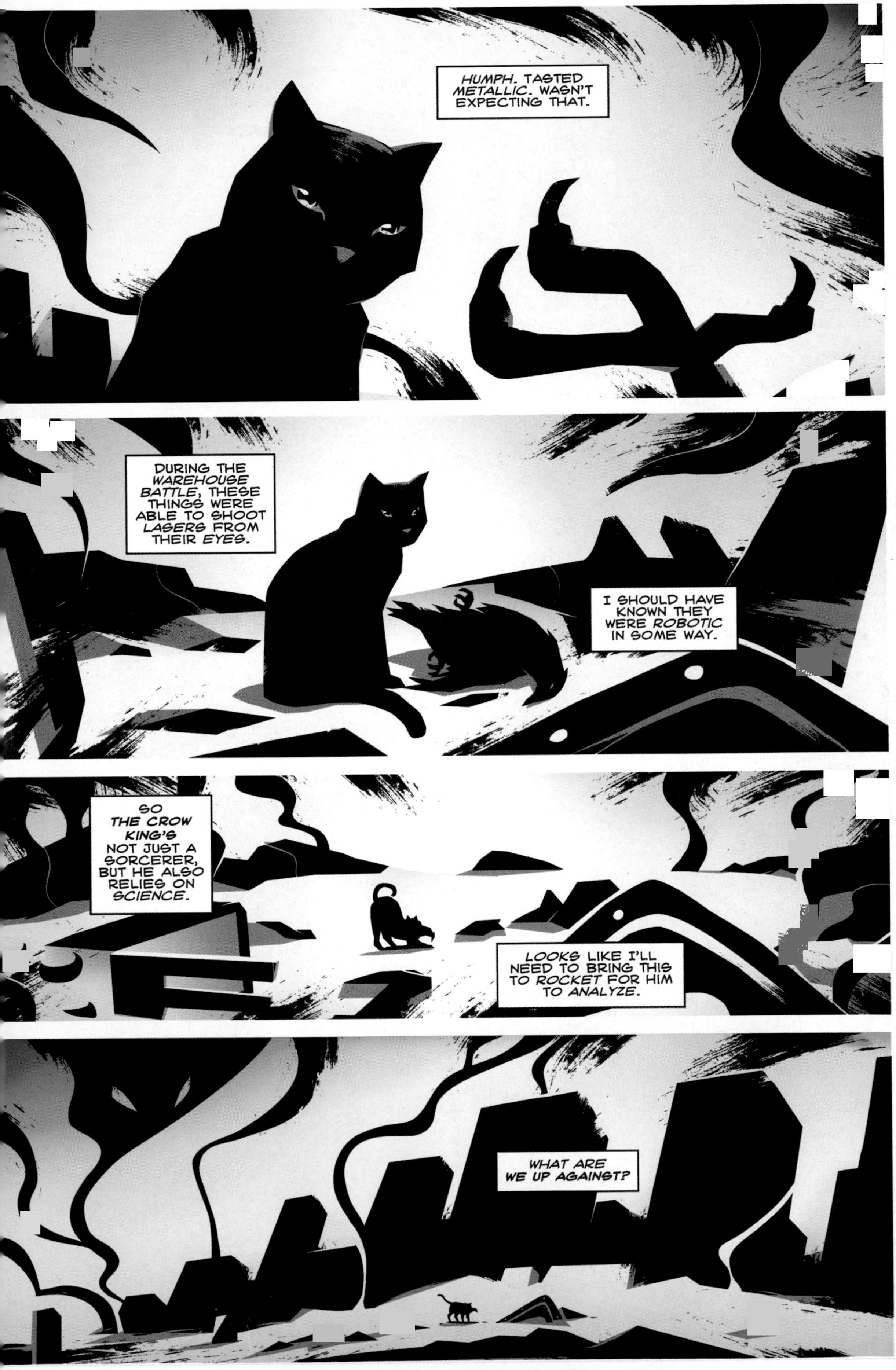
HUMPH. TASTED METALLIC. WASN'T EXPECTING THAT.
DURING THE WAREHOUSE BATTLE, THESE THINGS WERE ABLE TO SHOOT LASERS FROM THEIR EYES.
I SHOULD HAVE KNOWN THEY WERE ROBOTIC IN SOME WAY.
SO THE CROW KING'S NOT JUST A SORCERER, BUT HE ALSO RELIES ON SCIENCE.
LOOKS LIKE I'LL NEED TO BRING THIS TO ROCKET FOR HIM TO ANALYZE.
WHAT ARE WE UP AGAINST?

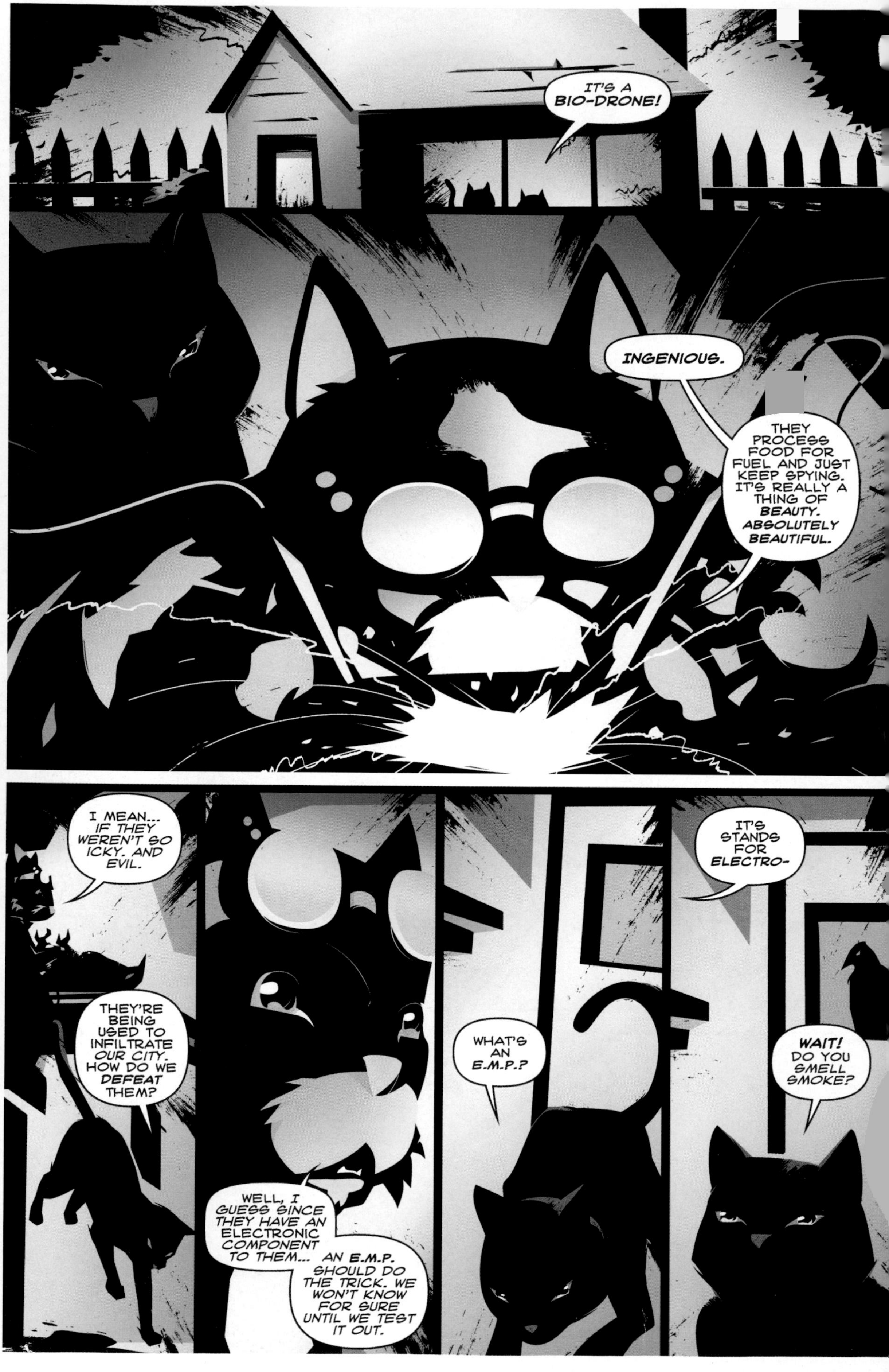
IT'S A BIO-DRONE!
INGENIOUS.
THEY PROCESS FOOD FOR FUEL AND JUST KEEP SPYING. IT'S REALLY A THING OF BEAUTY. ABSOLUTELY BEAUTIFUL.
I MEAN... IF THEY WEREN'T SO ICKY. AND EVIL.
THEY'RE BEING USED TO INFILTRATE OUR CITY. HOW DO WE DEFEAT THEM?
WELL, I GUESS SINCE THEY HAVE AN ELECTRONIC COMPONENT TO THEM...
AN E.M.P. SHOULD DO THE TRICK. WE WON'T KNOW FOR SURE UNTIL WE TEST IT OUT.
WHAT'S AN E.M.P.?
IT'S STANDS FOR ELECTRO-
WAIT! DO YOU SMELL SMOKE?

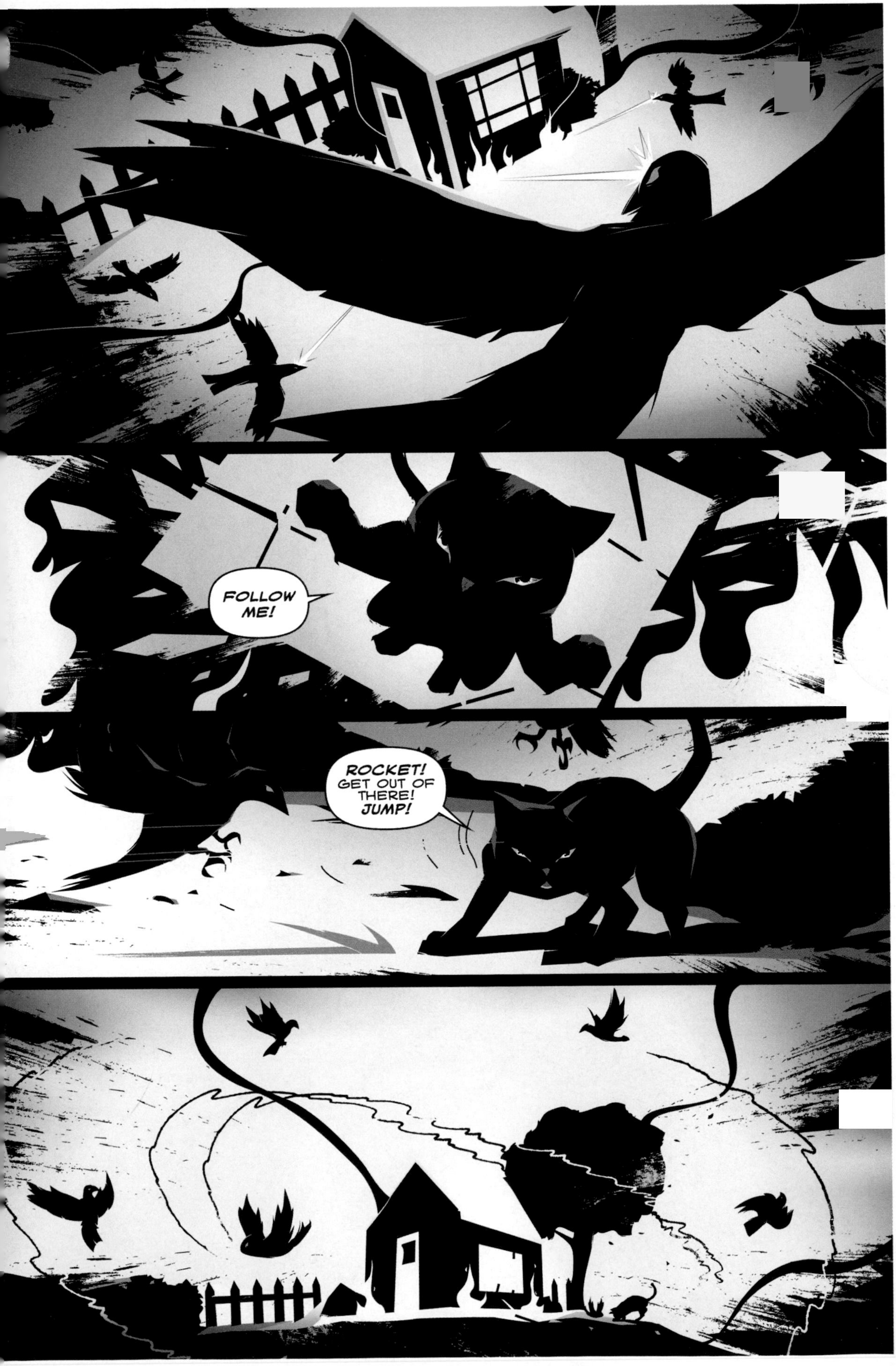
FOLLOW ME!
ROCKET! GET OUT OF THERE! JUMP!

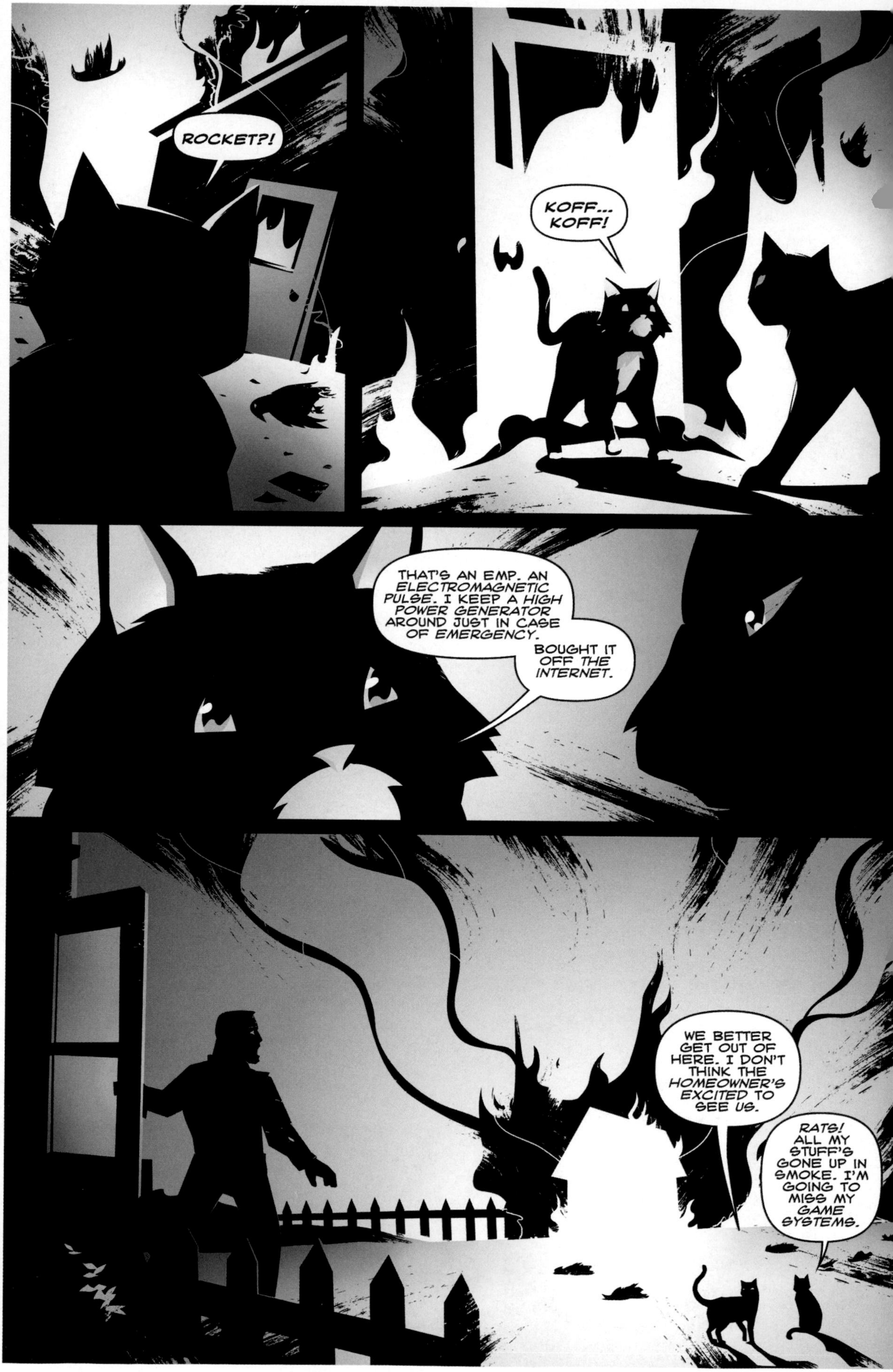
ROCKET?!
KOFF... KOFF!
THAT'S AN EMP. AN ELECTROMAGNETIC PULSE. I KEEP A HIGH POWER GENERATOR AROUND JUST IN CASE OF EMERGENCY.
BOUGHT IT OFF THE INTERNET.
WE BETTER GET OUT OF HERE. I DON'T THINK THE HOMEOWNER'S EXCITED TO SEE US.
RATS! ALL MY STUFF'S GONE UP IN SMOKE. I'M GOING TO MISS MY GAME SYSTEMS.

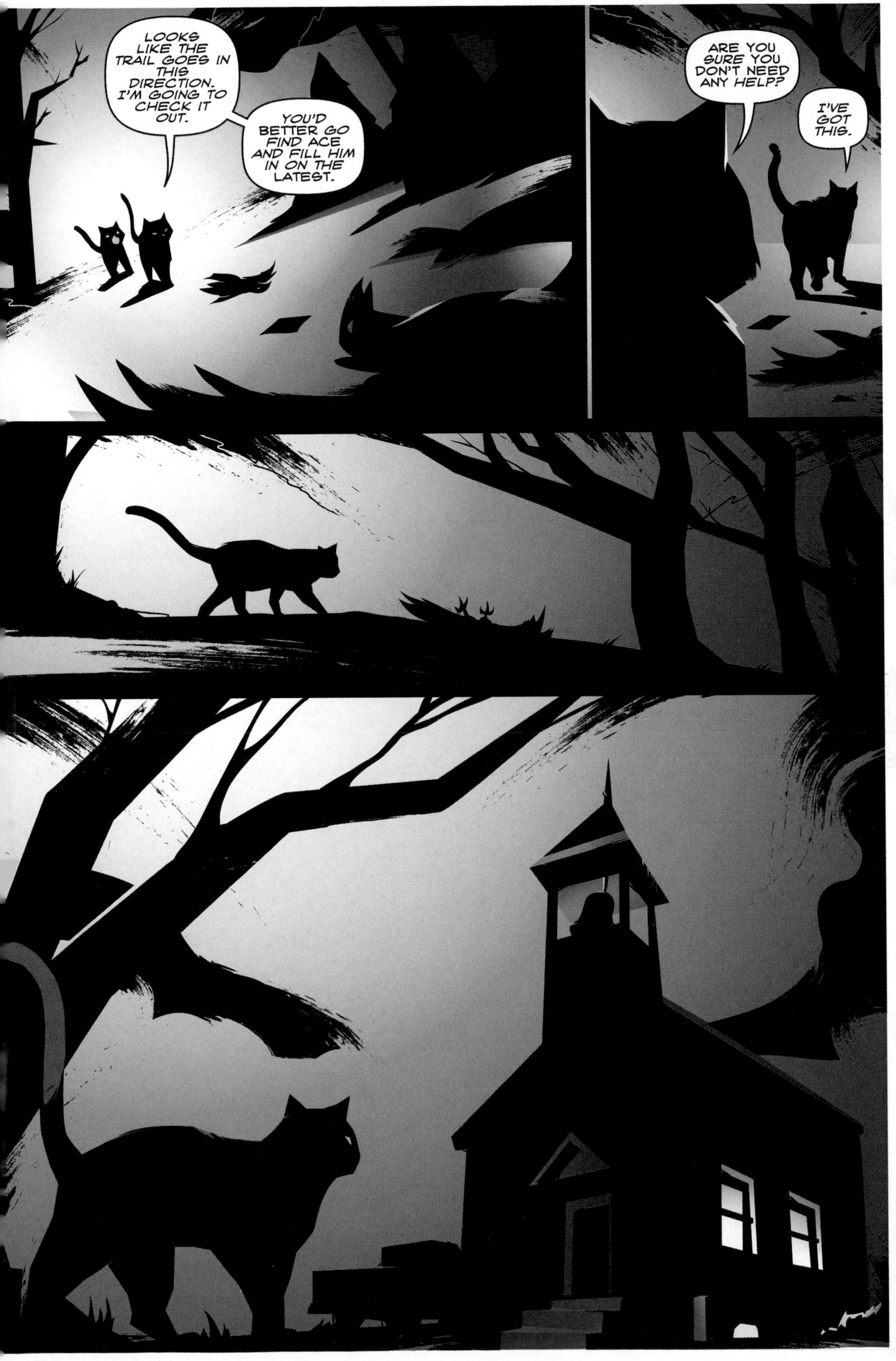
LOOKS LIKE THE TRAIL GOES IN THIS DIRECTION. I'M GOING TO CHECK IT OUT.
YOU'D BETTER GO FIND ACE AND FILL HIM IN ON THE LATEST.
ARE YOU SURE YOU DON'T NEED ANY HELP?
I'VE GOT THIS.

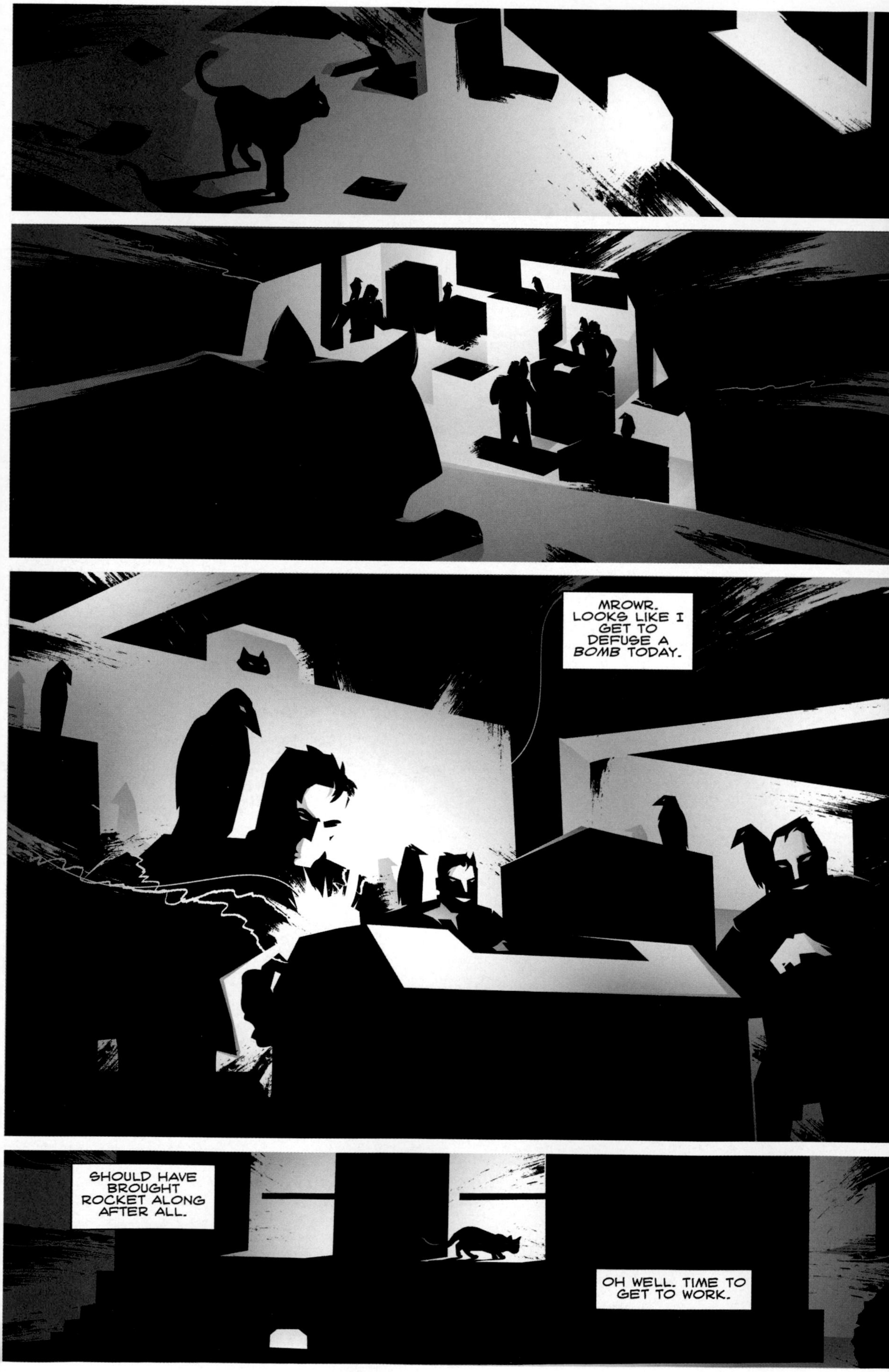
MROWR. LOOKS LIKE I GET TO DEFUSE A BOMB TODAY.
SHOULD HAVE BROUGHT ROCKET ALONG AFTER ALL.
OH WELL. TIME TO GET TO WORK.

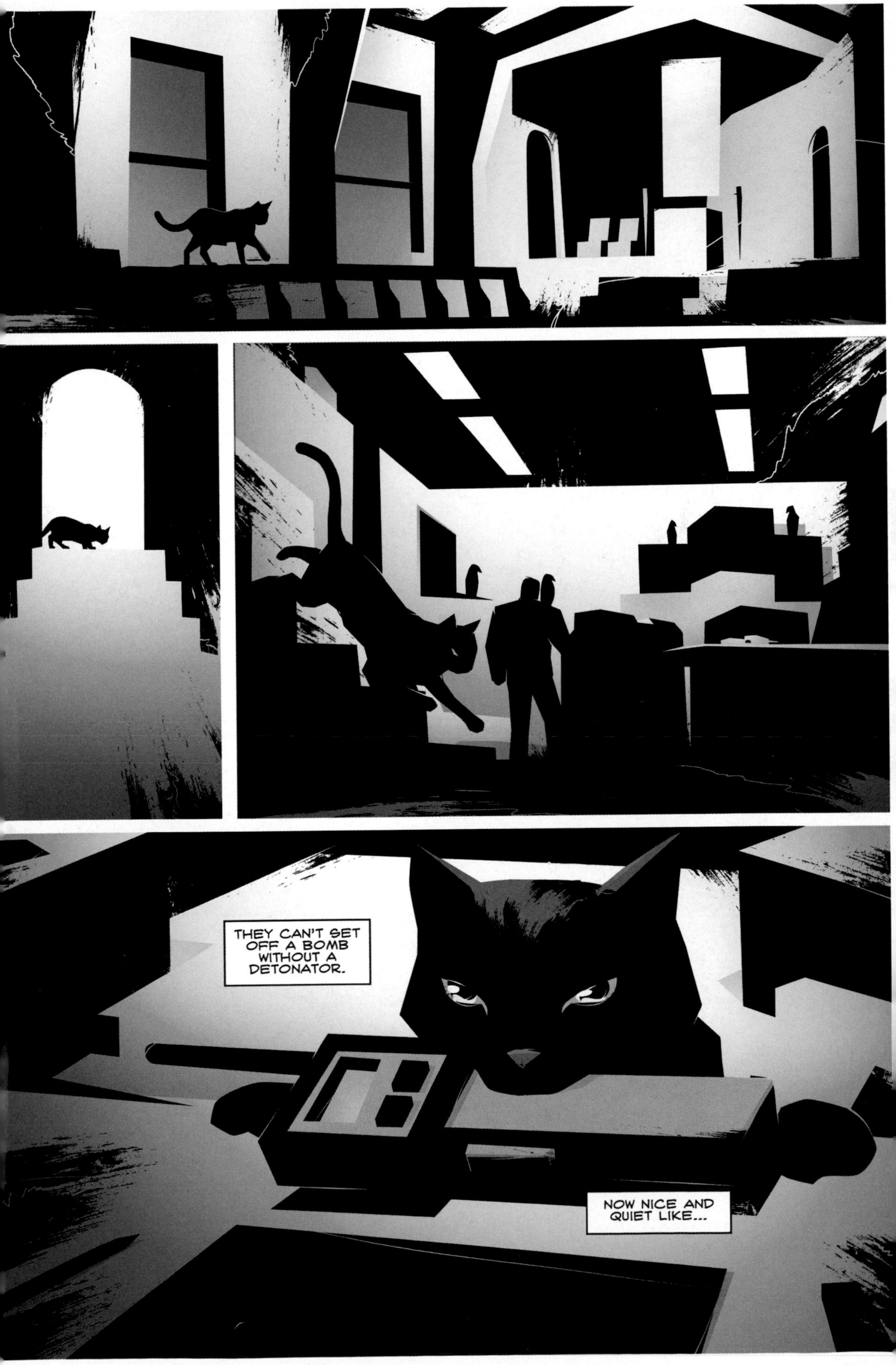
THEY CAN'T SET OFF A BOMB WITHOUT A DETONATOR.
NOW NICE AND QUIET LIKE...

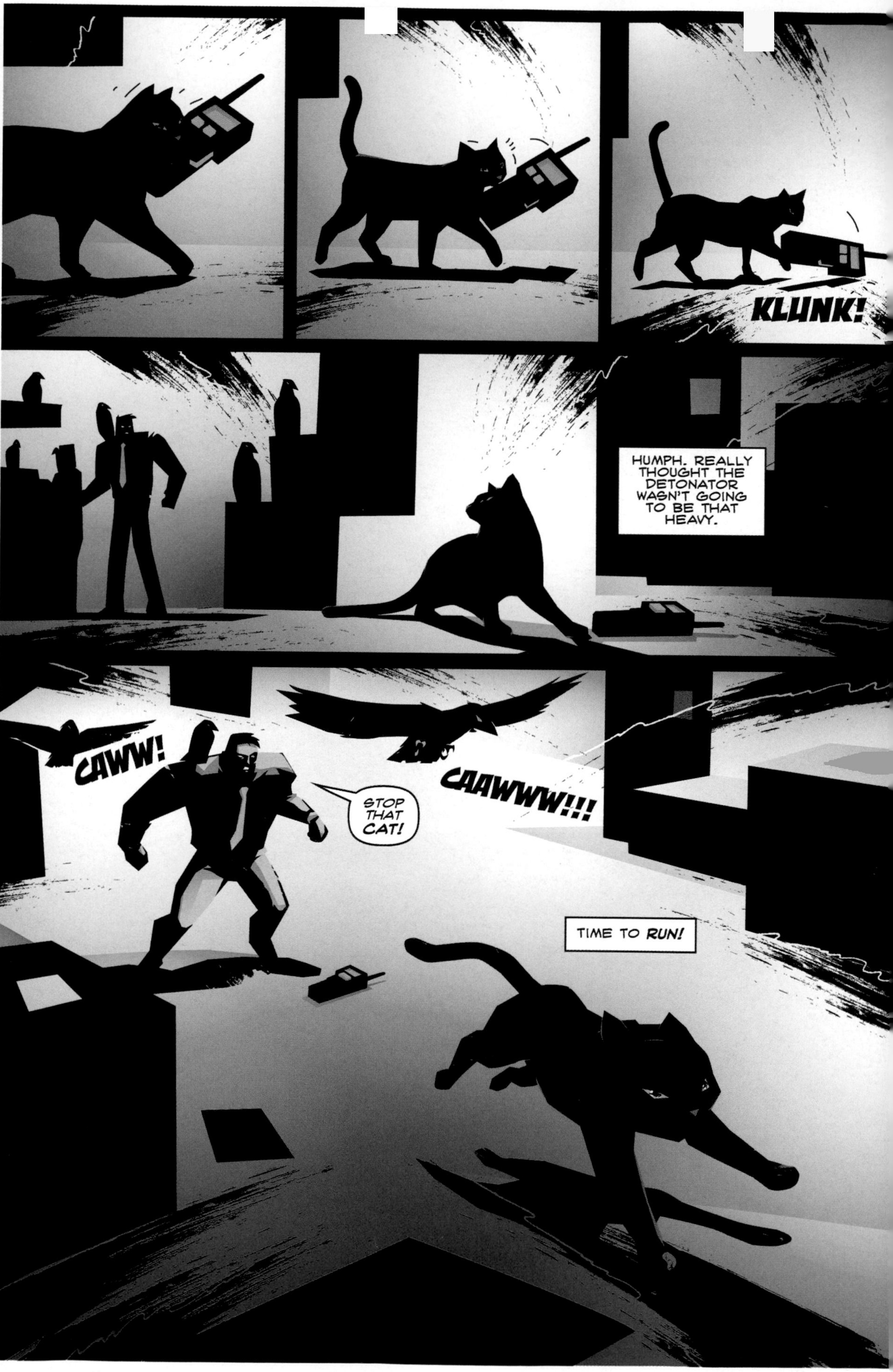
KLUNK!
HUMPH. REALLY THOUGHT THE DETONATOR WASN'T GOING TO BE THAT HEAVY.
CAWW!
CAAWWW!!!
STOP THAT CAT!
TIME TO RUN!

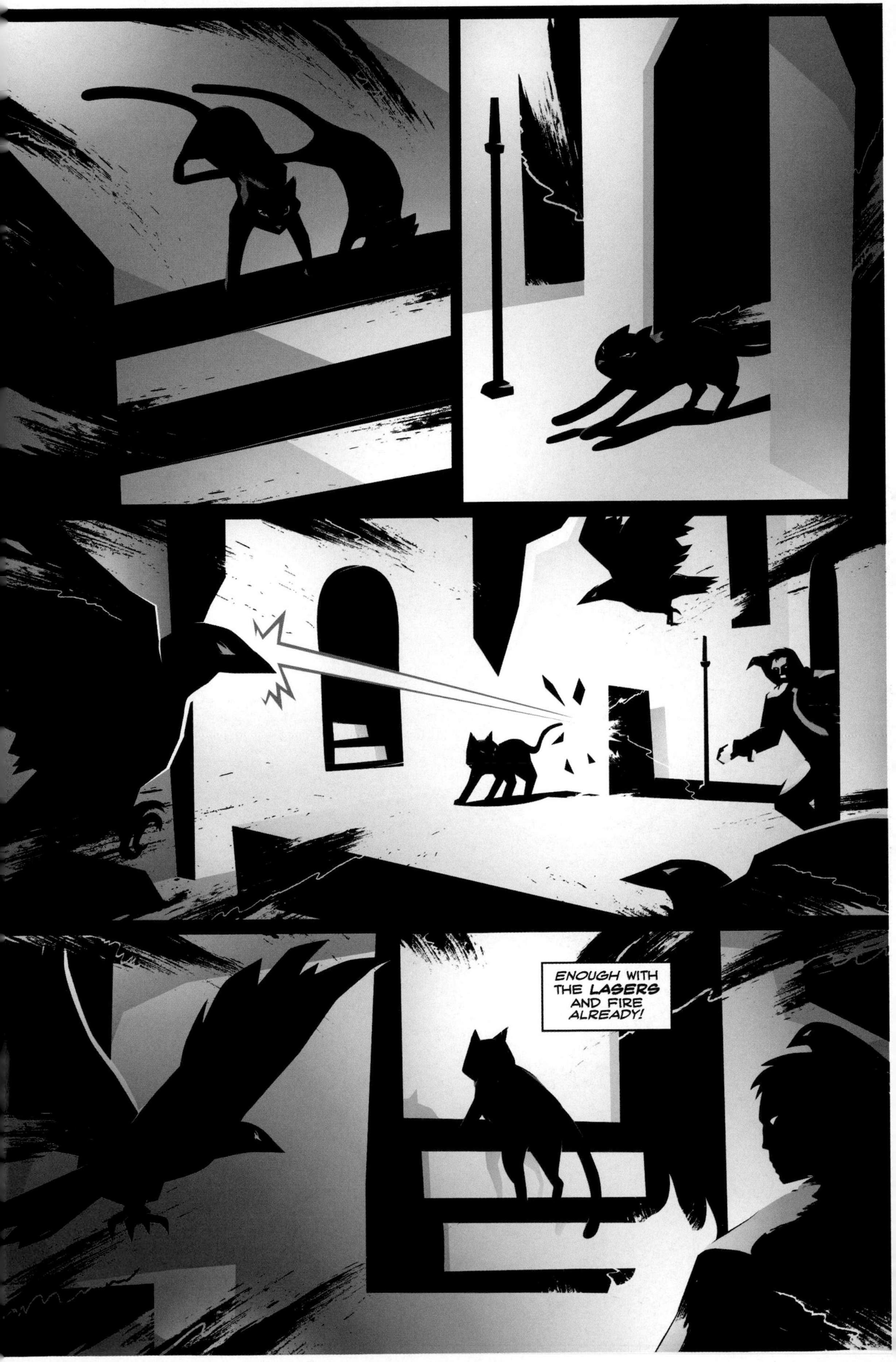
ENOUGH WITH THE LASERS AND FIRE ALREADY!

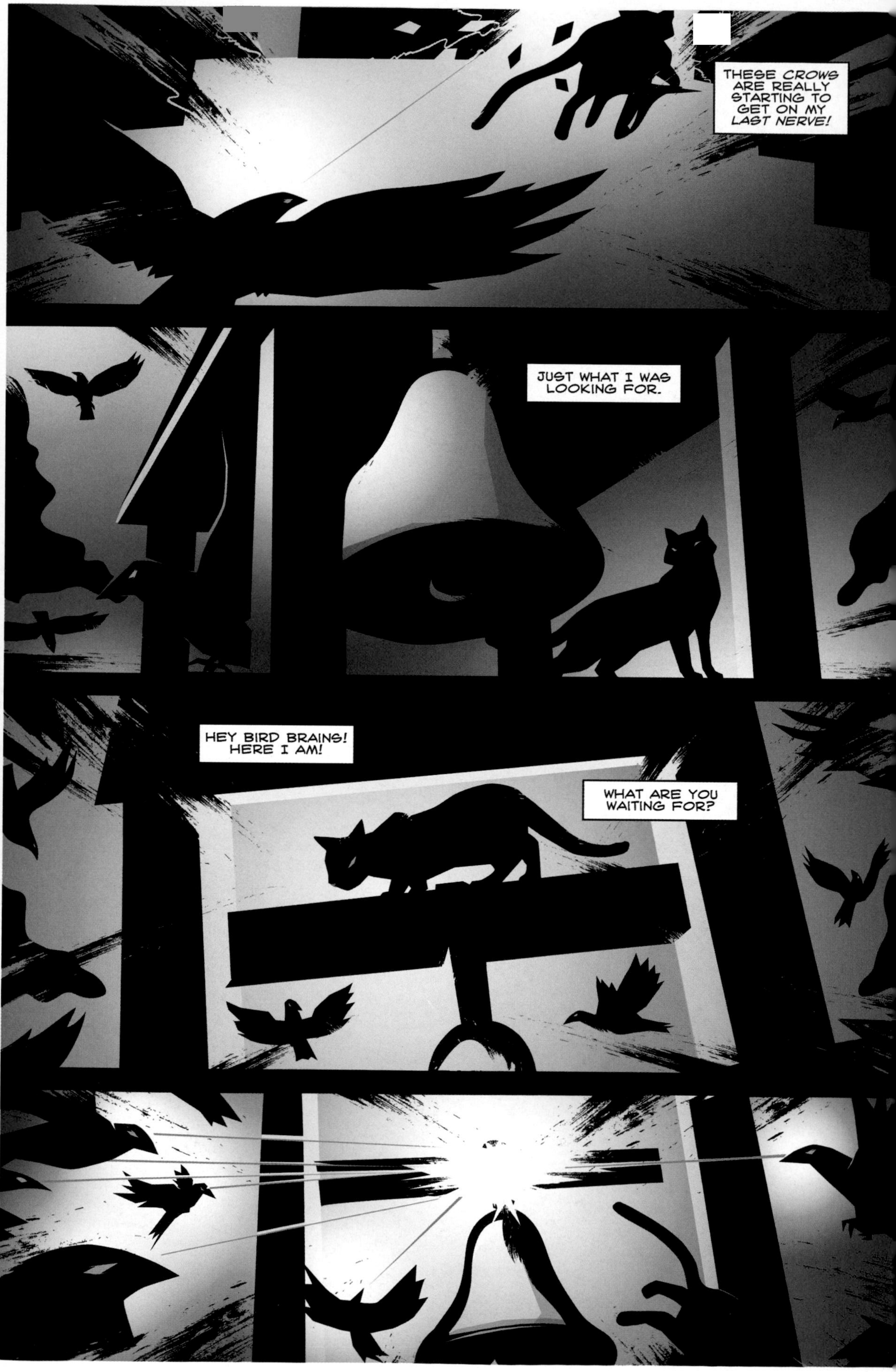
THESE *CROWS* ARE REALLY STARTING TO GET ON MY *LAST NERVE!*
JUST WHAT I WAS LOOKING FOR.
HEY BIRD BRAINS! HERE I AM!
WHAT ARE YOU WAITING FOR?

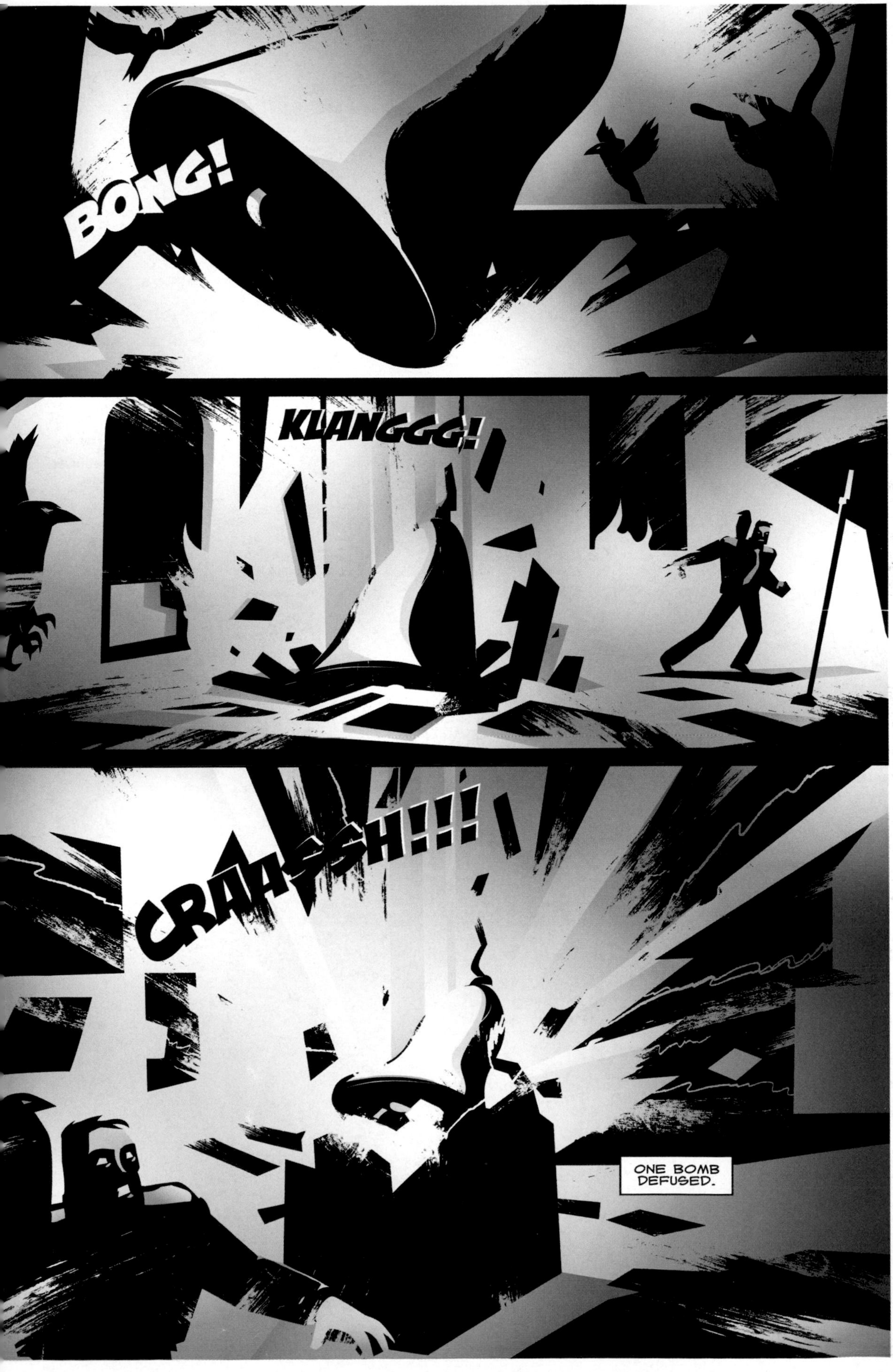
BONG!
KLANGGG!
CRAASSH!!!
ONE BOMB DEFUSED.

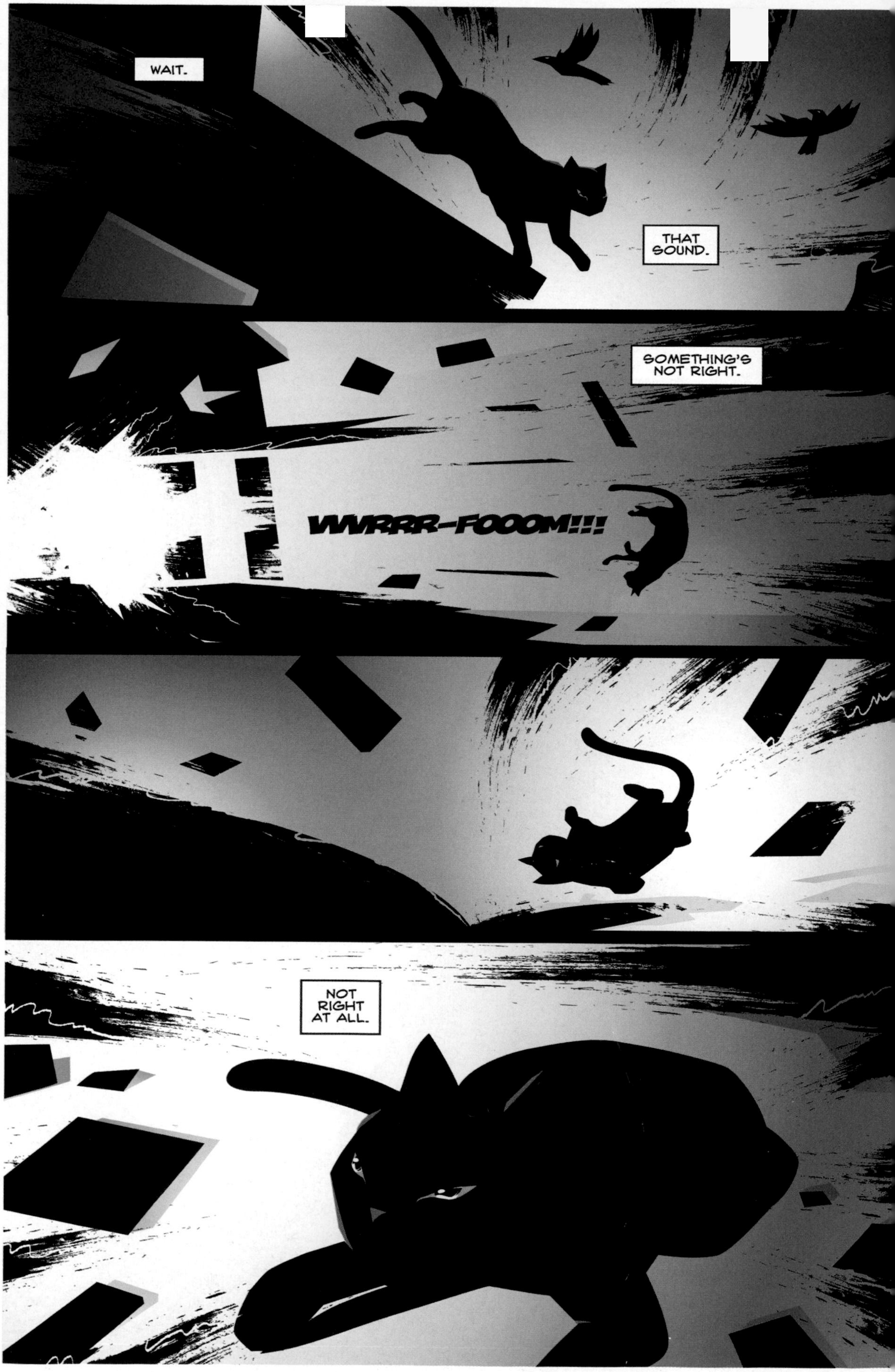
WAIT.
THAT SOUND.
SOMETHING'S NOT RIGHT.
VWRRR-FOOOM!!!
NOT RIGHT AT ALL.

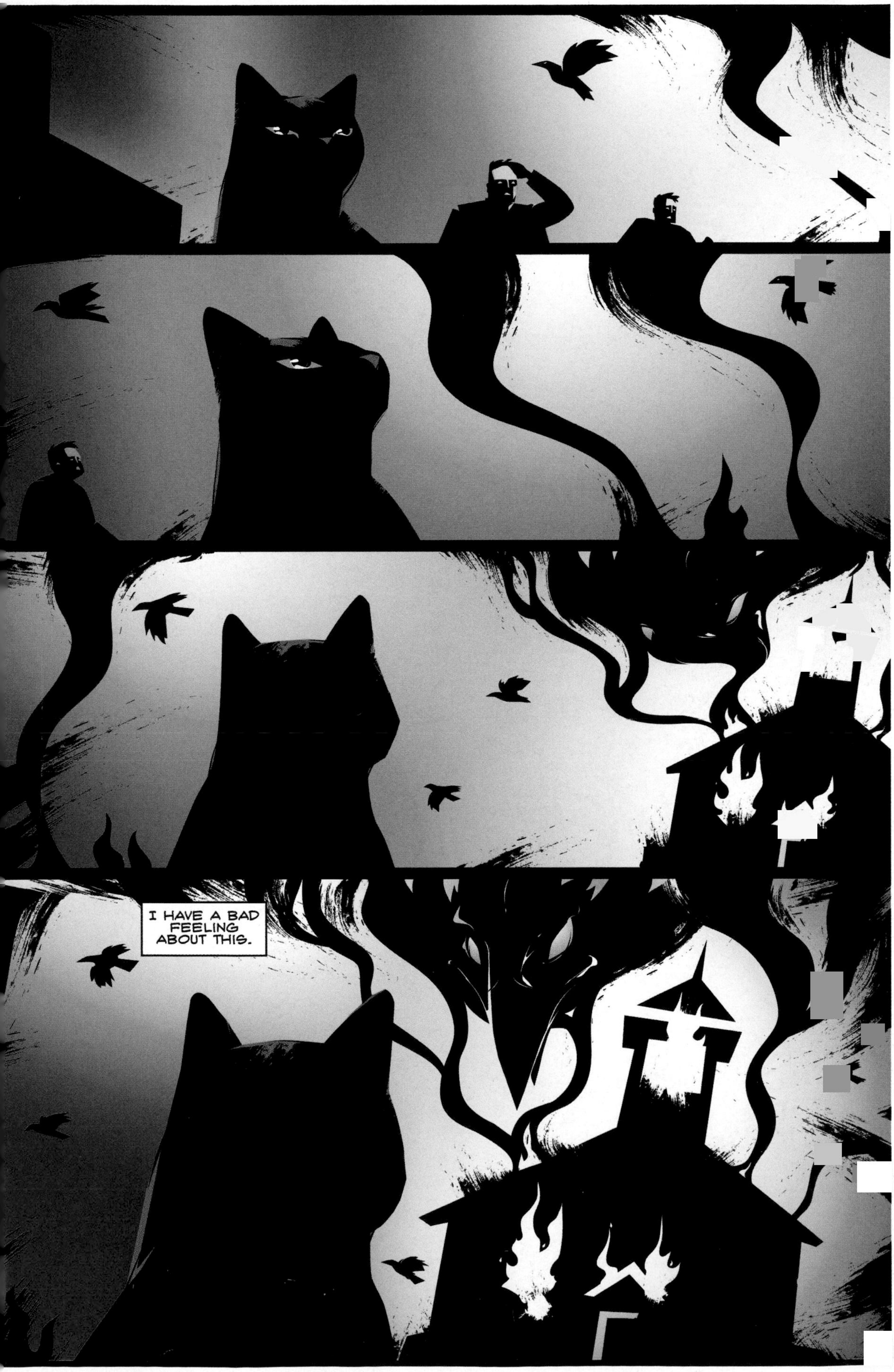
I HAVE A BAD FEELING ABOUT THIS.

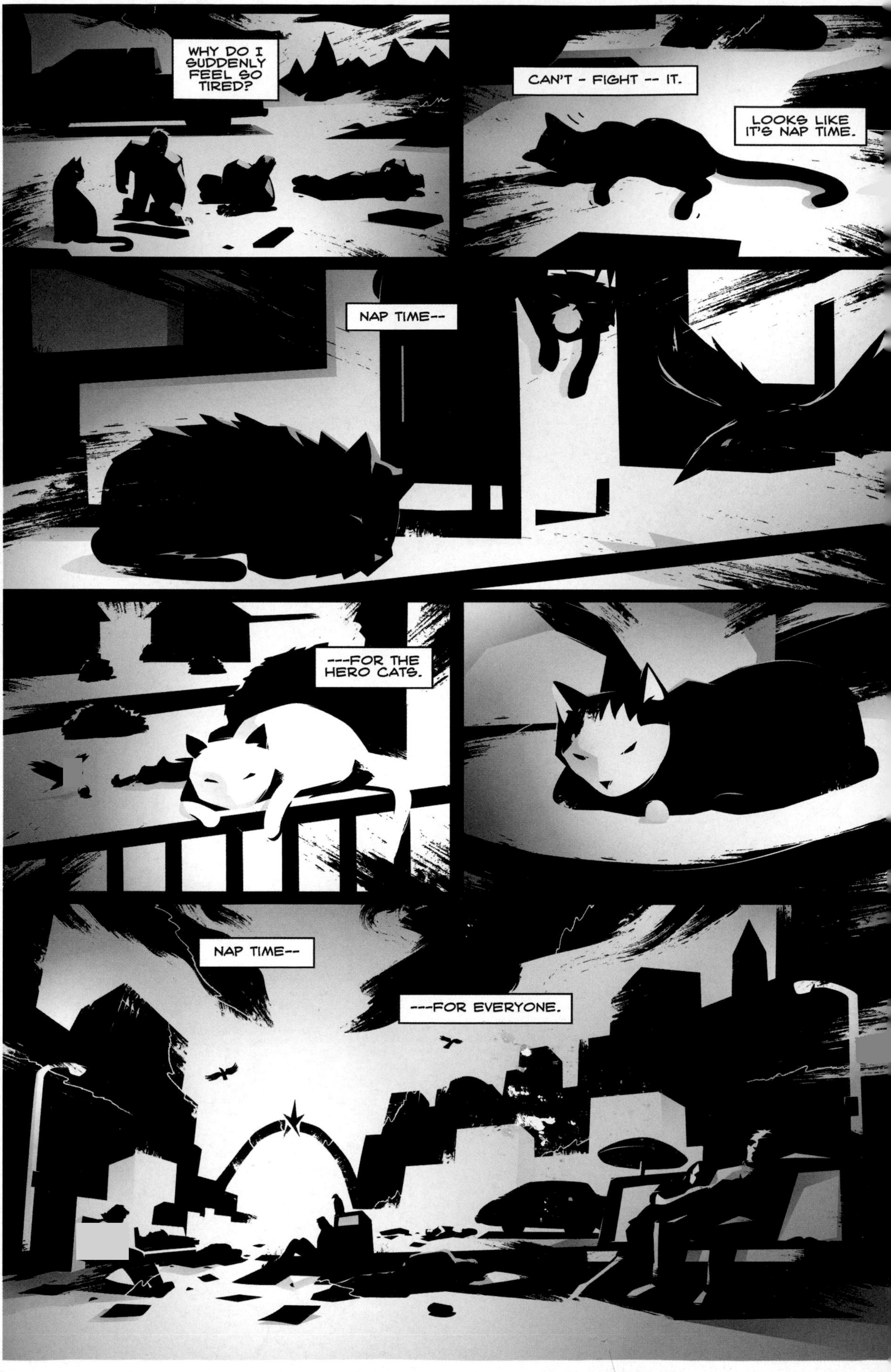
WHY DO I SUDDENLY FEEL SO TIRED?
CAN'T - FIGHT -- IT.
LOOKS LIKE IT'S NAP TIME.
NAP TIME--
---FOR THE HERO CATS.
NAP TIME--
---FOR EVERYONE.

AFTER MIDNIGHT

WELCOME TO THE WONDERFUL WORLD OF **HERO CATS!**
I AM **ROBOT**, AND WILL SERVE AS YOUR GUIDE.

MEET MIDNIGHT'S TEAMMATES!

ACE IS ALWAYS READY FOR ACTION! HIS SUPERIOR OFFICER HAS TRAINED HIM WELL. NOW IT IS HIS DUTY TO LEAD THE HERO CATS AND PROTECT STELLAR CITY.

BELLE, DESPITE HER QUESTIONABLE PAST, IS A GREAT ASSET TO THE TEAM. SHE CAN READ THE HUMAN MIND.

YOU'VE ALREADY MET **ROCKET**. HE'S THE FASTEST CAT ON EARTH AND HE WAS BORN IN OUTER SPACE. HE LOVES TO TINKER WITH TECHNOLOGY AND IS MY CREATOR.

ROCCO NEVER LOSES A FIGHT AND LOVES MOVIES.

CASSIOPEIA IS THE MOST POWERFUL OF ALL THE HERO CATS. SHE HAS THE RARE ABILITY TO READ. THIS TALENT COMES IN HANDY WHEN THEY ARE ON MISSIONS.

THE TEAM IS CURRENTLY DEALING WITH A STRANGE AND DANGEROUS VILLAIN WHO CALLS HIMSELF THE CROW KING.

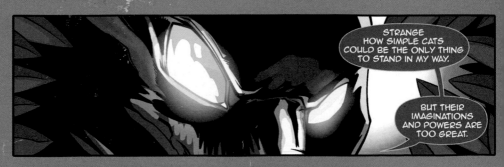

STRANGE HOW SIMPLE CATS COULD BE THE ONLY THING TO STAND IN MY WAY.

BUT THEIR IMAGINATIONS AND POWERS ARE TOO GREAT.

*SEE ALE HALLOWEEN COMICFEST 2014

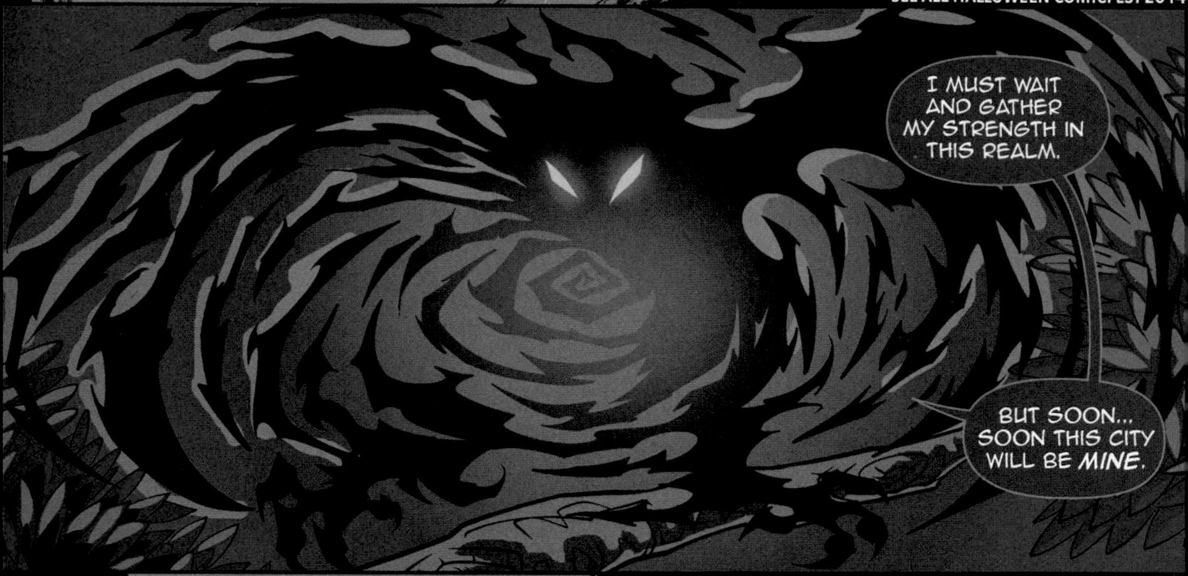
I MUST WAIT AND GATHER MY STRENGTH IN THIS REALM.
BUT SOON... SOON THIS CITY WILL BE *MINE*.

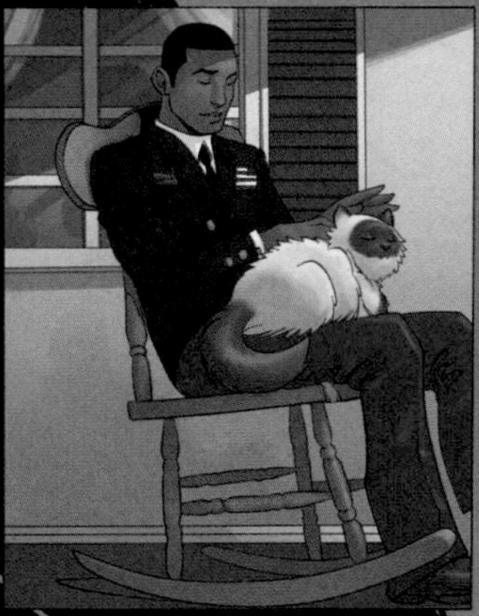

IT ALL STARTED WHEN BELLE GOT A VISIT FROM ACE'S SUPERIOR OFFICER. SHE FOUND THIS ODD SINCE DANIEL HAD GONE OFF TO WAR AND NEVER RETURNED.

HE WARNED HER OF **THE CROW KING'S COMING** AND PROMISED HE WOULD SEND **HELP**.

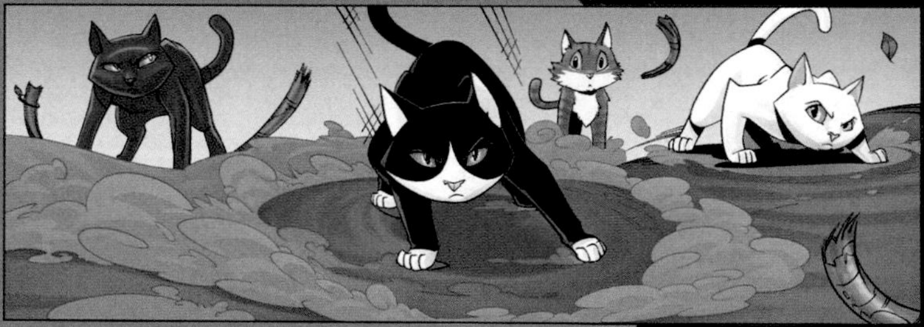

THAT HELP CAME IN THE FORM OF **BANDIT**, **CASSIOPEIA'S** LONG LOST **BROTHER**.

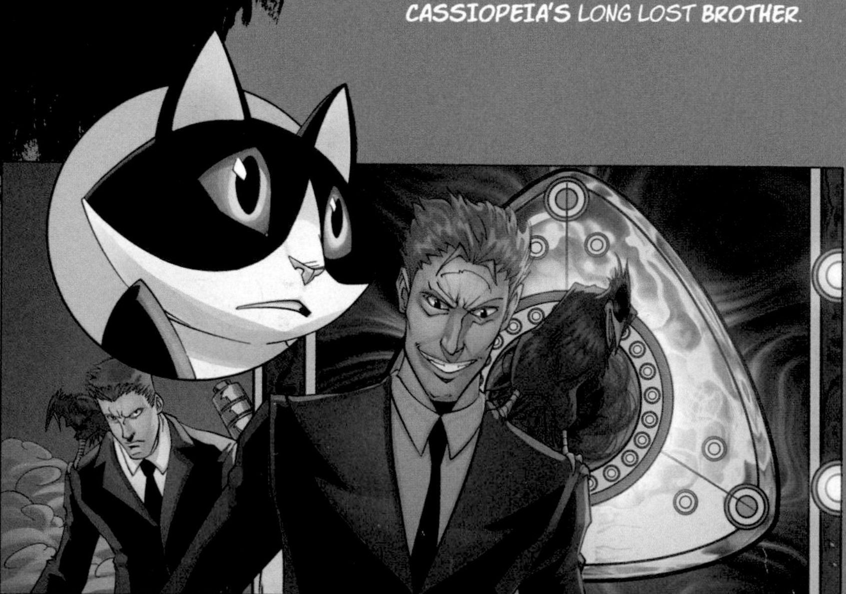

BANDIT HAD BEEN WORKING ON A CASE INVOLVING A SHADY HUMAN NAMED **MARK COLE**. MARK HAD STRUCK A DEAL WITH **THE CROW KING**. A DEAL THAT WOULD SPELL DOOM FOR ALL OF **STELLAR CITY**.

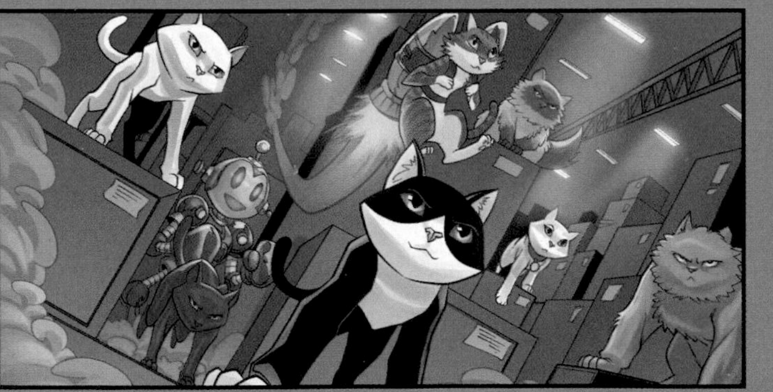

BANDIT ASSEMBLED THE HERO CATS FOR AN EPIC SHOWDOWN AT THE WAREHOUSE BY THE BAY.

THE BATTLE ENDED WHEN WE DROVE A FORKLIFT INTO THE CROW KING'S DIMENSIONAL DOORWAY. WE STOPPED HIM THAT DAY AND ROCKET GOT AWAY, BUT BANDIT AND I ARE TRAPPED.

NOW BANDIT AND I FIGHT THE CROW KING ON HIS WORLD, WHILE THE REST OF THE HERO CATS SEARCH A WAY TO BRING US HOME.

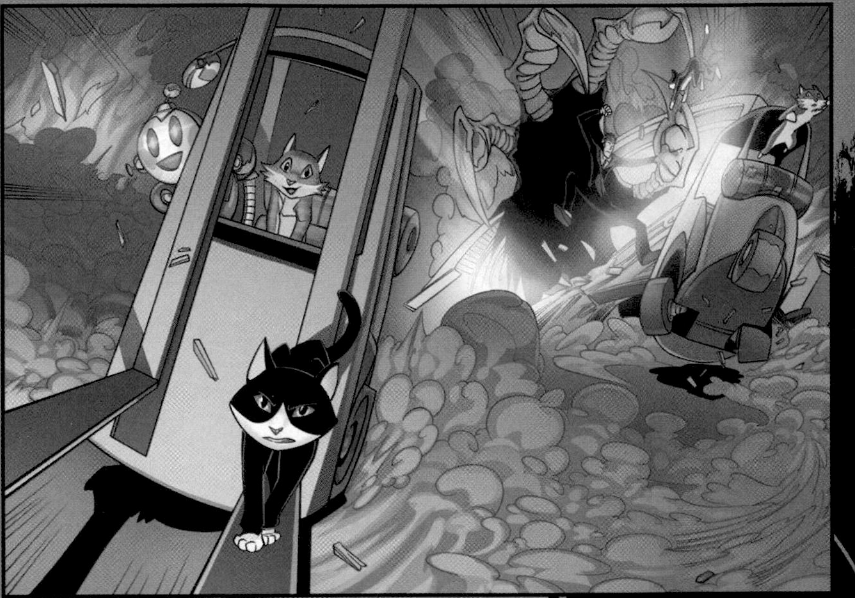

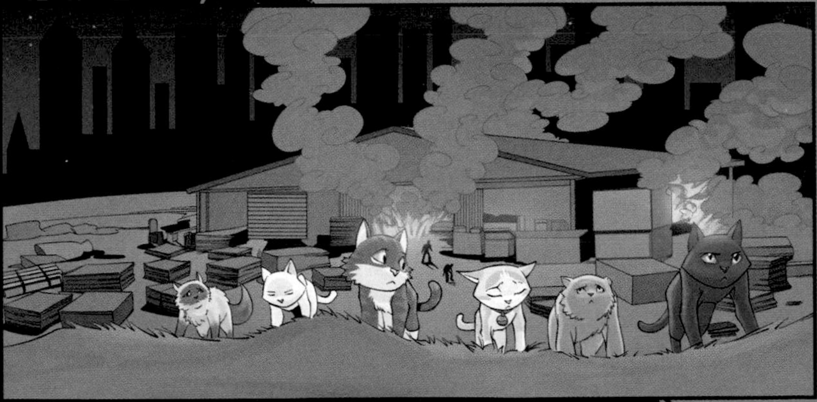

YOU CAN READ ABOUT THIS ADVENTURE IN HERO CATS OVER STELLAR CITY #7.

ACTION LAB ENTERTAINMENT
Bryan Seatan - Publisher
Kevin Freeman - President
Dave Dwench - Creative Director
Shawn Cahheron - Editor in Chief
Jamal Igle & Kelly Dale - Co-Directors of Marketing
Jim Dietz - Social Media Director
Jeremy Whitley - Education Outreach Director
Chad Cicceni & Colleen Boyd - Associate Editors

MIDNIGHT OVER STELLAR CITY #2 WILL CONTINUE OUR MISSION.

I SURE HOPE THINGS WORK OUT OKAY FOR US. **SEE YOU SOON!**

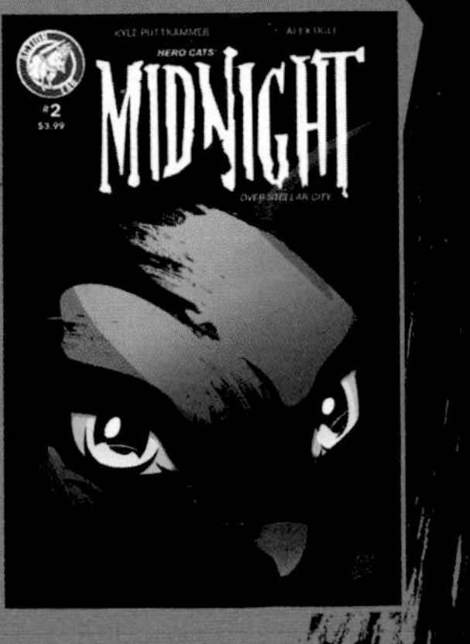
HERO CATS
MIDNIGHT
#2
$3.99

Hero Cats Midnight Over Stellar City #1, October 2015

Printed in Canada.

First Printing.

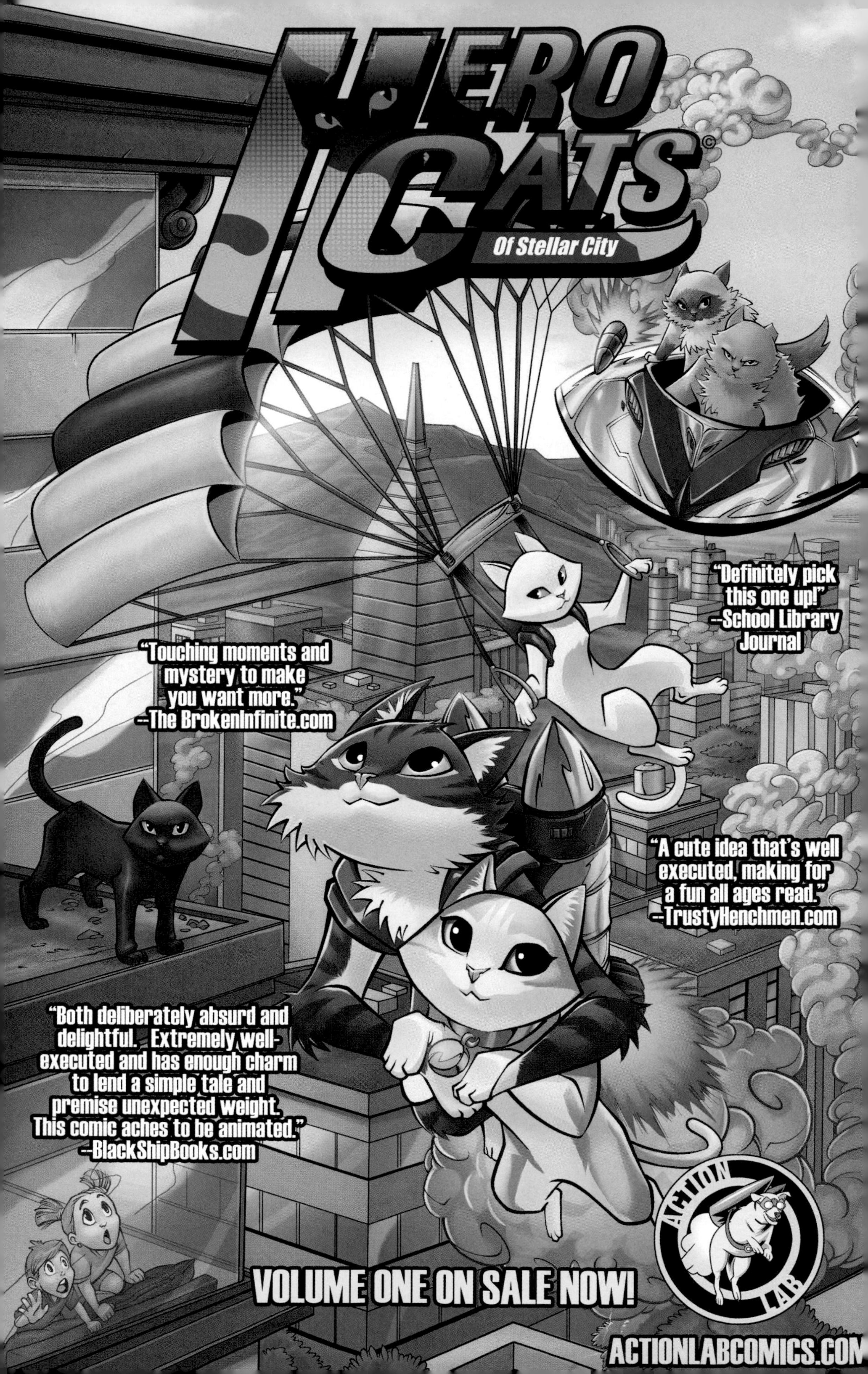
HERO CATS©
Of Stellar City
"Definitely pick this one up!" --School Library Journal
"Touching moments and mystery to make you want more." --The BrokenInfinite.com
"A cute idea that's well executed, making for a fun all ages read." --TrustyHenchmen.com
"Both deliberately absurd and delightful. Extremely well-executed and has enough charm to lend a simple tale and premise unexpected weight. This comic aches to be animated." --BlackShipBooks.com
ACTION LAB
VOLUME ONE ON SALE NOW!
ACTIONLABCOMICS.COM

FROM ANTHONY RUTTGAIZER
AND DANNY ZABBAL

the F1RSTHERO

FIGHT FOR YOUR LIFE

AVAILABLE IN FINER STORES EVERYWHERE

Jake Roth is the only man to ever manifest superpowers but not go insane. While Jake
is still trying to decide how best to use his new powers to help prevent a war between
humans and "extrahumans", an old friend reappears and draws him into direct
conflict with the local mafia who have their own extrahuman enforcer, Odinson!

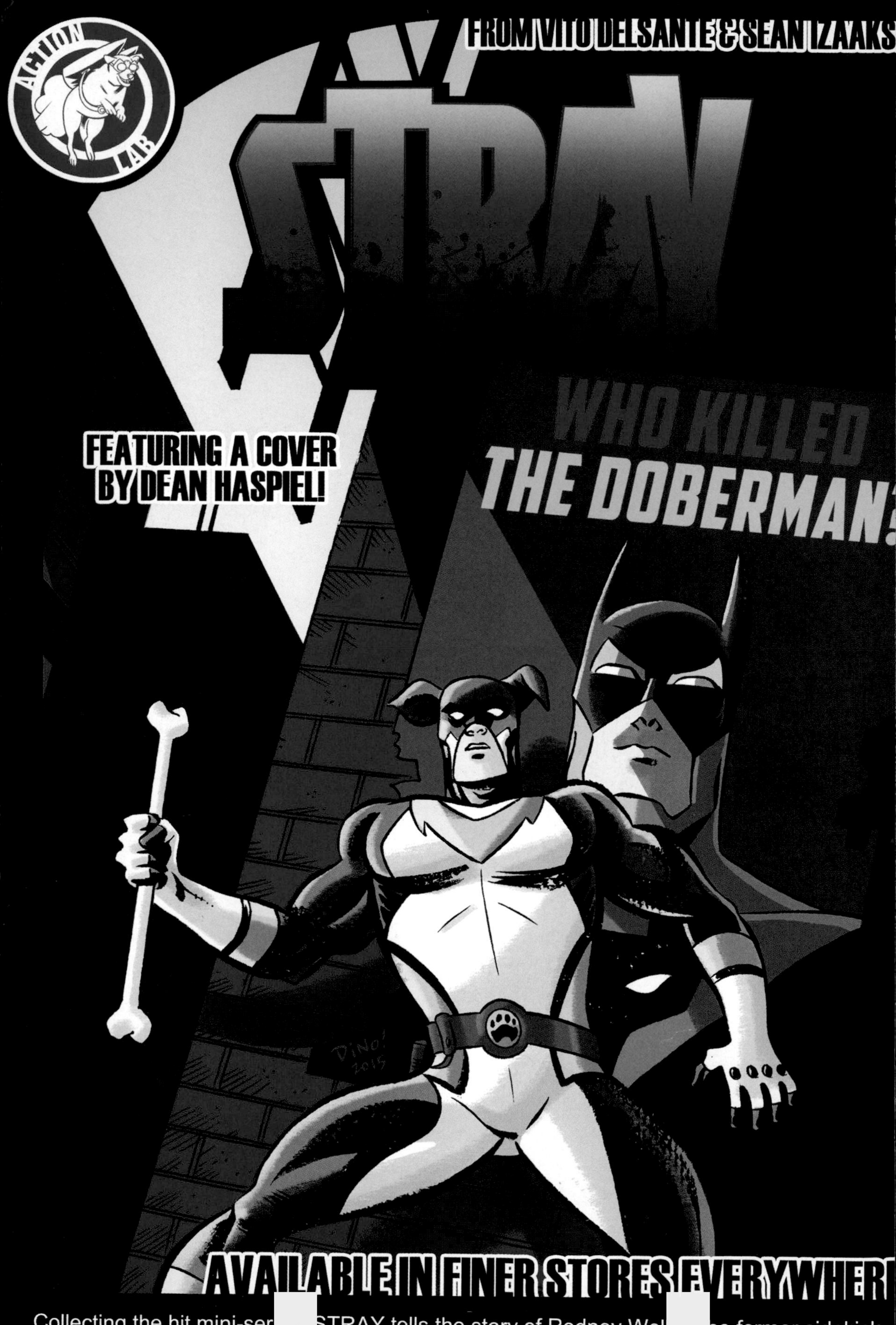
ACTION LAB
FROM VITO DELSANTE & SEAN IZAAKS
STRAY
WHO KILLED THE DOBERMAN?
FEATURING A COVER BY DEAN HASPIEL!
DINO! 2015
AVAILABLE IN FINER STORES EVERYWHERE

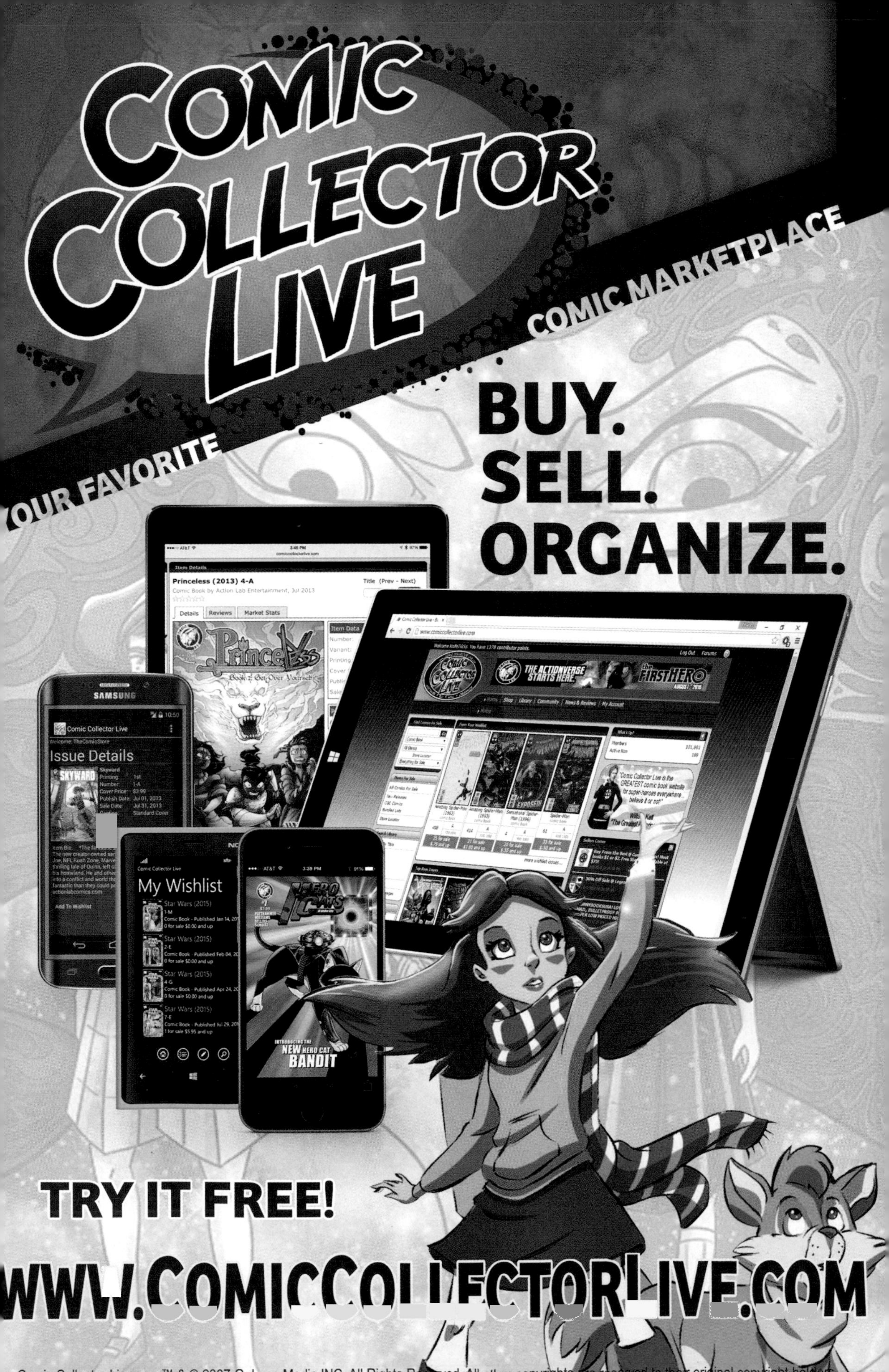

COMIC COLLECTOR LIVE
YOUR FAVORITE COMIC MARKETPLACE
BUY. SELL. ORGANIZE.
TRY IT FREE!
WWW.COMICCOLLECTORLIVE.COM

READ MORE NOW

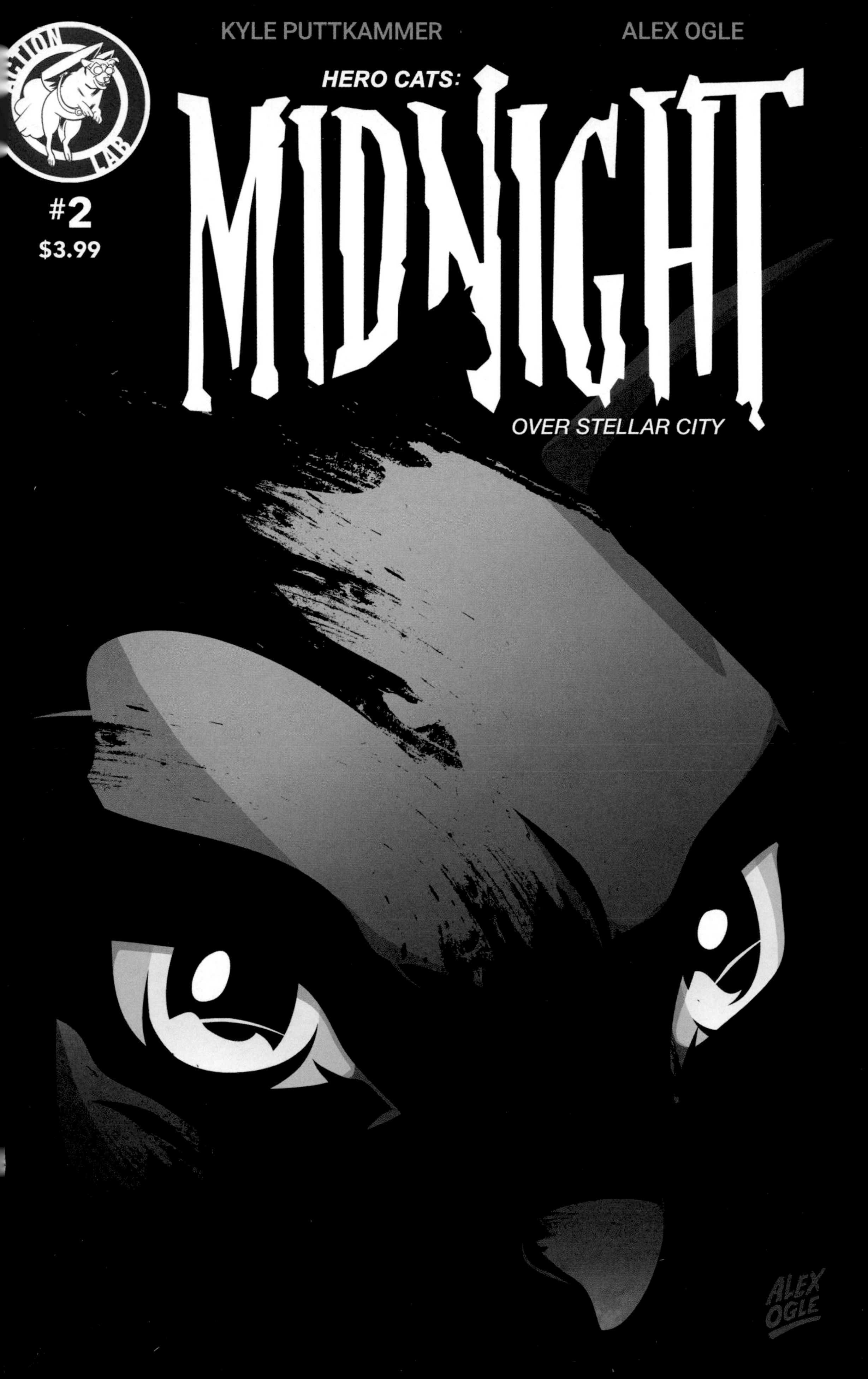
KYLE PUTTKAMMER
ALEX OGLE
ACTION LAB
#2
$3.99
HERO CATS:
MIDNIGHT
OVER STELLAR CITY
ALEX OGLE

FROM ALL-AGES TO MATURE READERS ACTION LAB HAS YOU COVERED.

 **Appropriate for everyone.**

 **Appropriate for age 9 and up. Absent of profanity or adult content.**

 **Suggested for 12 and Up. Comics with this rating are comparable to a PG-13 movie rating. Recommended for our teen and young adult readers.**

 **Appropriate for older teens. Similar to Teen, but featuring more mature themes and/or more graphic imagery.**

 **Contains extreme viloence and some nudity. Basically the Rated-R of comics.**

FIND YOUR NEW FAVORITE COMICS.

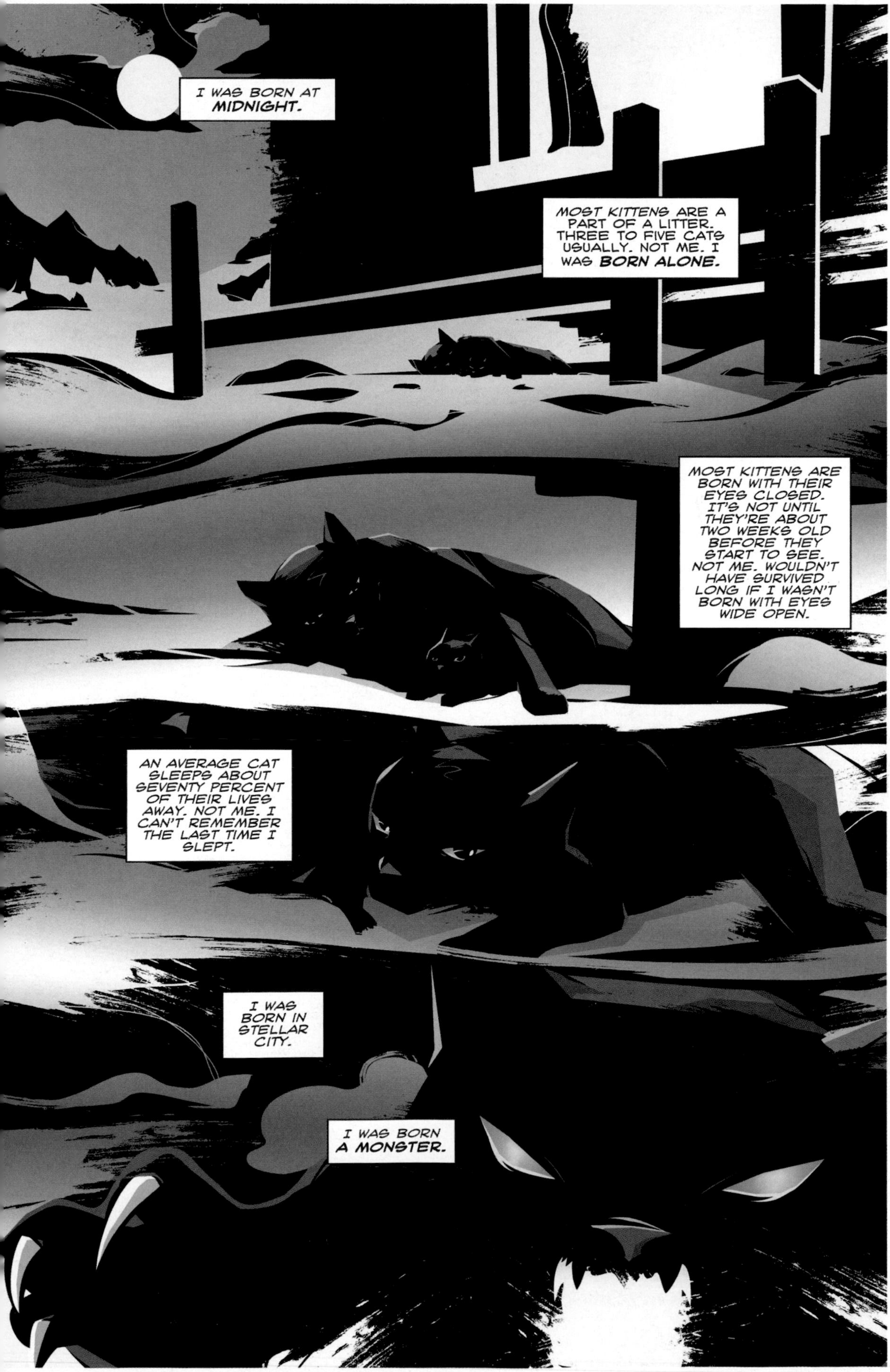
I WAS BORN AT **MIDNIGHT.**
MOST KITTENS ARE A PART OF A LITTER. THREE TO FIVE CATS USUALLY. NOT ME. I WAS **BORN ALONE.**
MOST KITTENS ARE BORN WITH THEIR EYES CLOSED. IT'S NOT UNTIL THEY'RE ABOUT TWO WEEKS OLD BEFORE THEY START TO SEE. NOT ME. WOULDN'T HAVE SURVIVED LONG IF I WASN'T BORN WITH EYES WIDE OPEN.
AN AVERAGE CAT SLEEPS ABOUT SEVENTY PERCENT OF THEIR LIVES AWAY. NOT ME. I CAN'T REMEMBER THE LAST TIME I SLEPT.
I WAS BORN IN STELLAR CITY.
I WAS BORN **A MONSTER.**

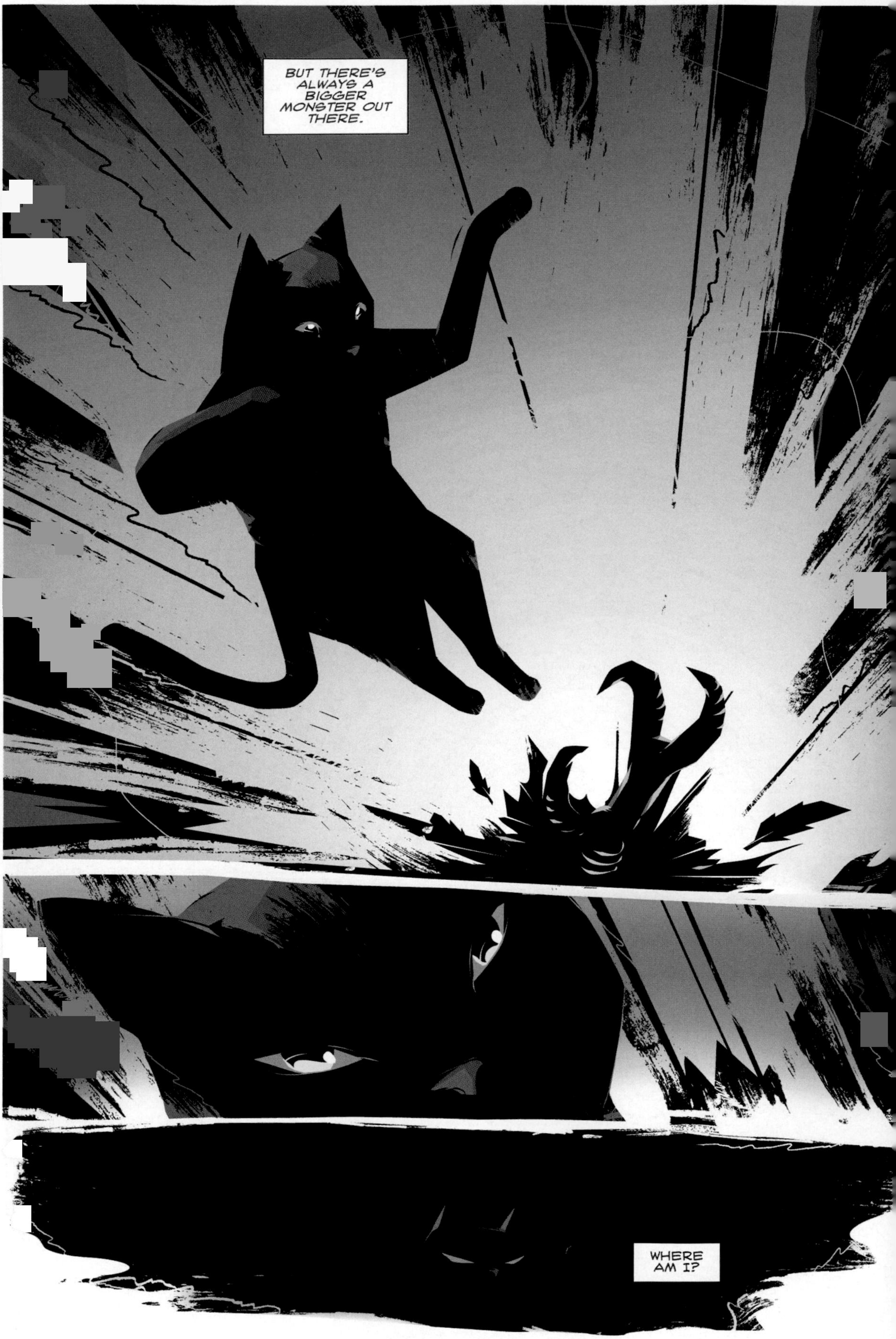
BUT THERE'S ALWAYS A BIGGER MONSTER OUT THERE.
WHERE AM I?

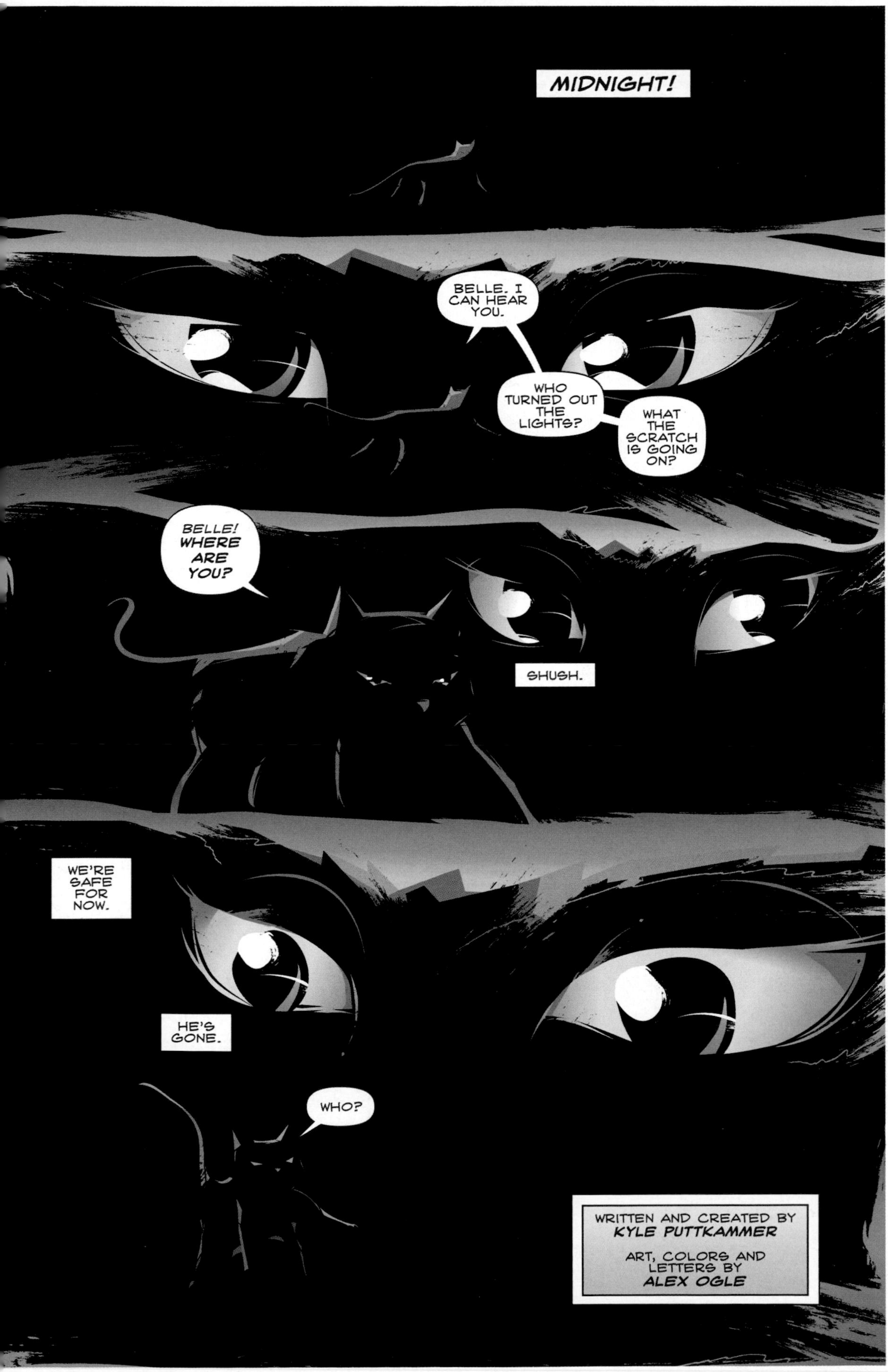
MIDNIGHT!
BELLE. I CAN HEAR YOU.
WHO TURNED OUT THE LIGHTS?
WHAT THE SCRATCH IS GOING ON?
BELLE! WHERE ARE YOU?
SHUSH.
WE'RE SAFE FOR NOW.
HE'S GONE.
WHO?
WRITTEN AND CREATED BY KYLE PUTTKAMMER
ART, COLORS AND LETTERS BY ALEX OGLE

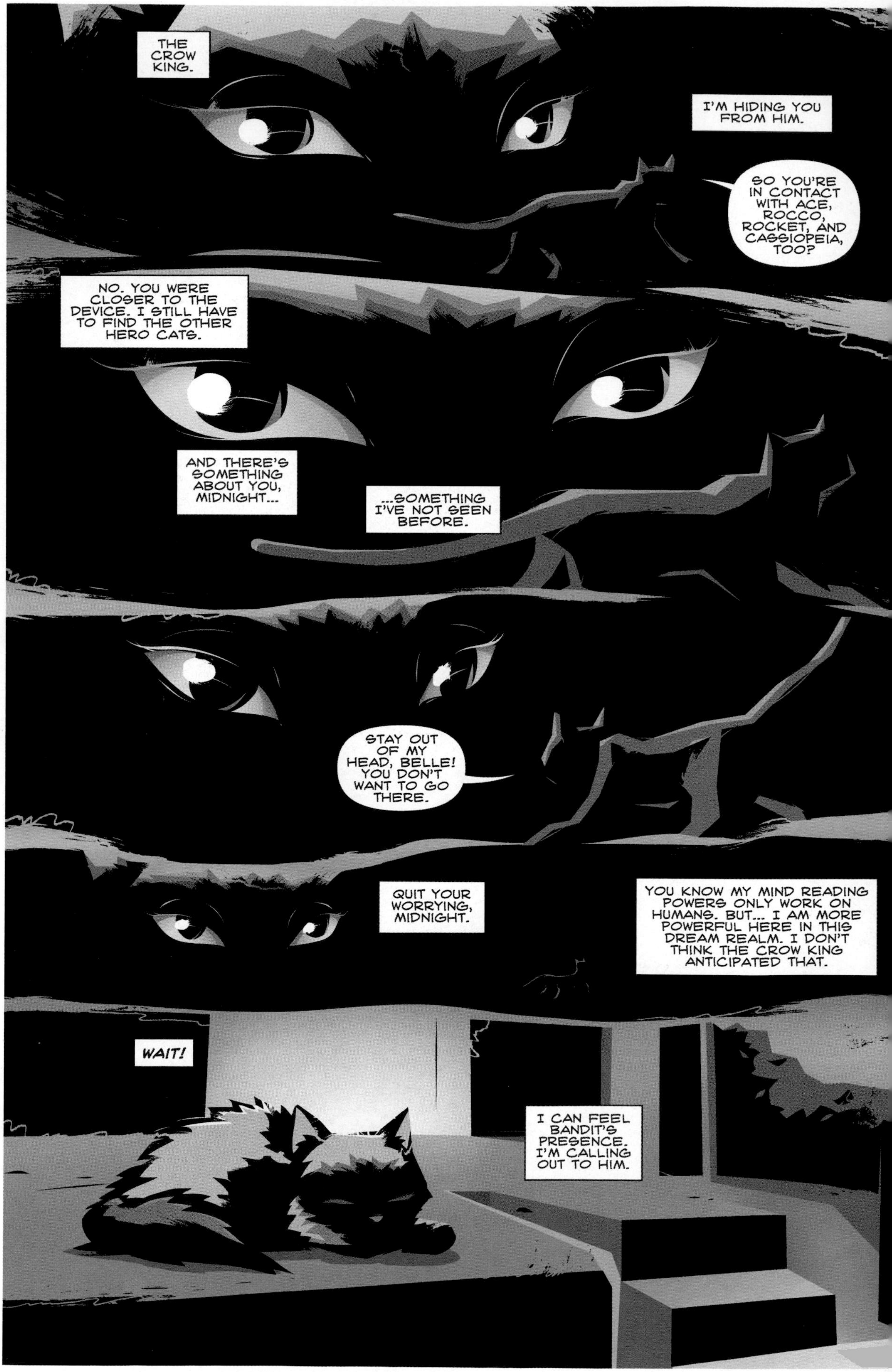
THE CROW KING.
I'M HIDING YOU FROM HIM.
SO YOU'RE IN CONTACT WITH ACE, ROCCO, ROCKET, AND CASSIOPEIA, TOO?
NO. YOU WERE CLOSER TO THE DEVICE. I STILL HAVE TO FIND THE OTHER HERO CATS.
AND THERE'S SOMETHING ABOUT YOU, MIDNIGHT...
...SOMETHING I'VE NOT SEEN BEFORE.
STAY OUT OF MY HEAD, BELLE! YOU DON'T WANT TO GO THERE.
QUIT YOUR WORRYING, MIDNIGHT.
YOU KNOW MY MIND READING POWERS ONLY WORK ON HUMANS. BUT... I AM MORE POWERFUL HERE IN THIS DREAM REALM. I DON'T THINK THE CROW KING ANTICIPATED THAT.
WAIT!
I CAN FEEL BANDIT'S PRESENCE. I'M CALLING OUT TO HIM.

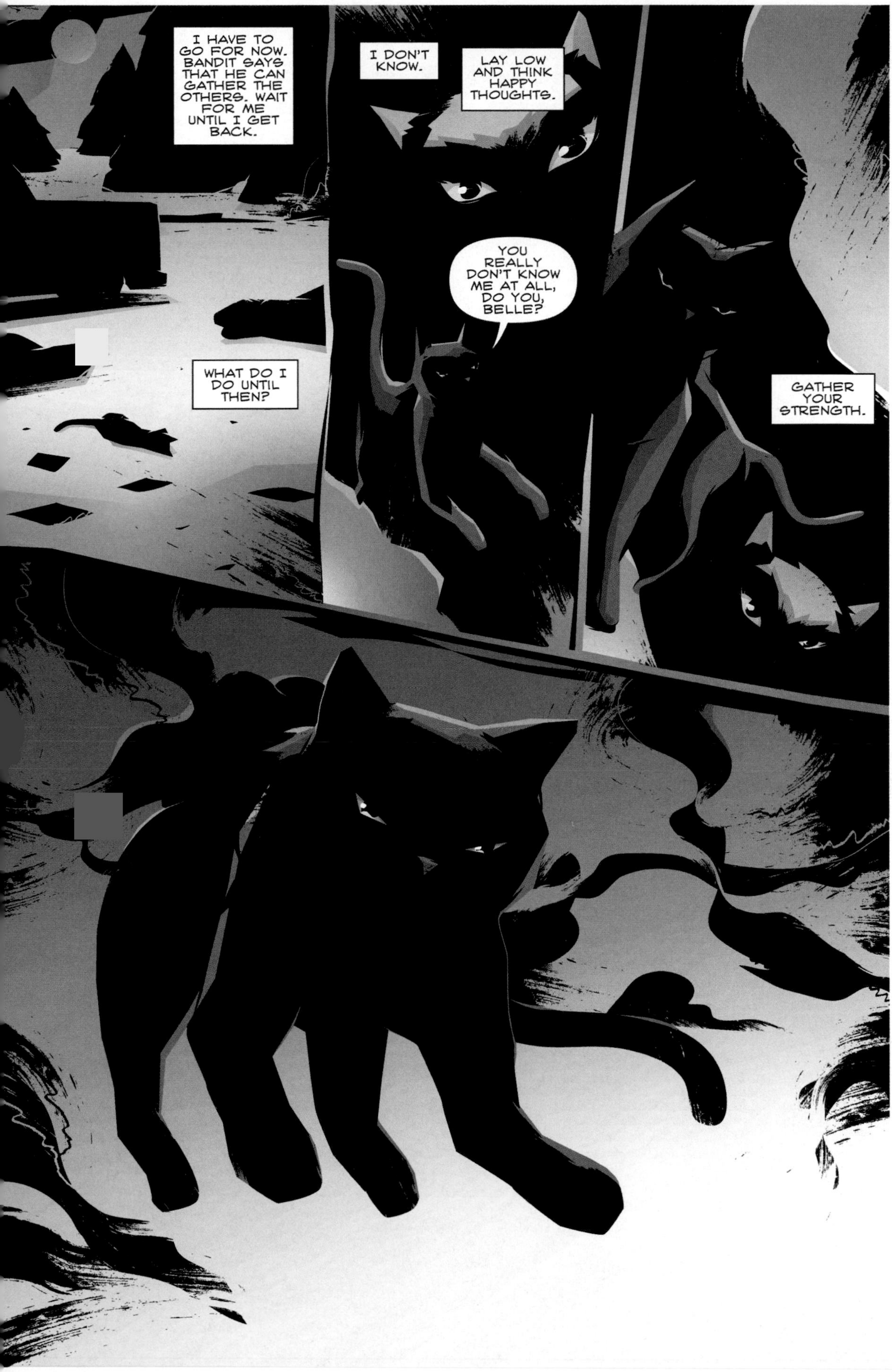
I HAVE TO GO FOR NOW. BANDIT SAYS THAT HE CAN GATHER THE OTHERS. WAIT FOR ME UNTIL I GET BACK.
WHAT DO I DO UNTIL THEN?
I DON'T KNOW.
LAY LOW AND THINK HAPPY THOUGHTS.
YOU REALLY DON'T KNOW ME AT ALL, DO YOU, BELLE?
GATHER YOUR STRENGTH.

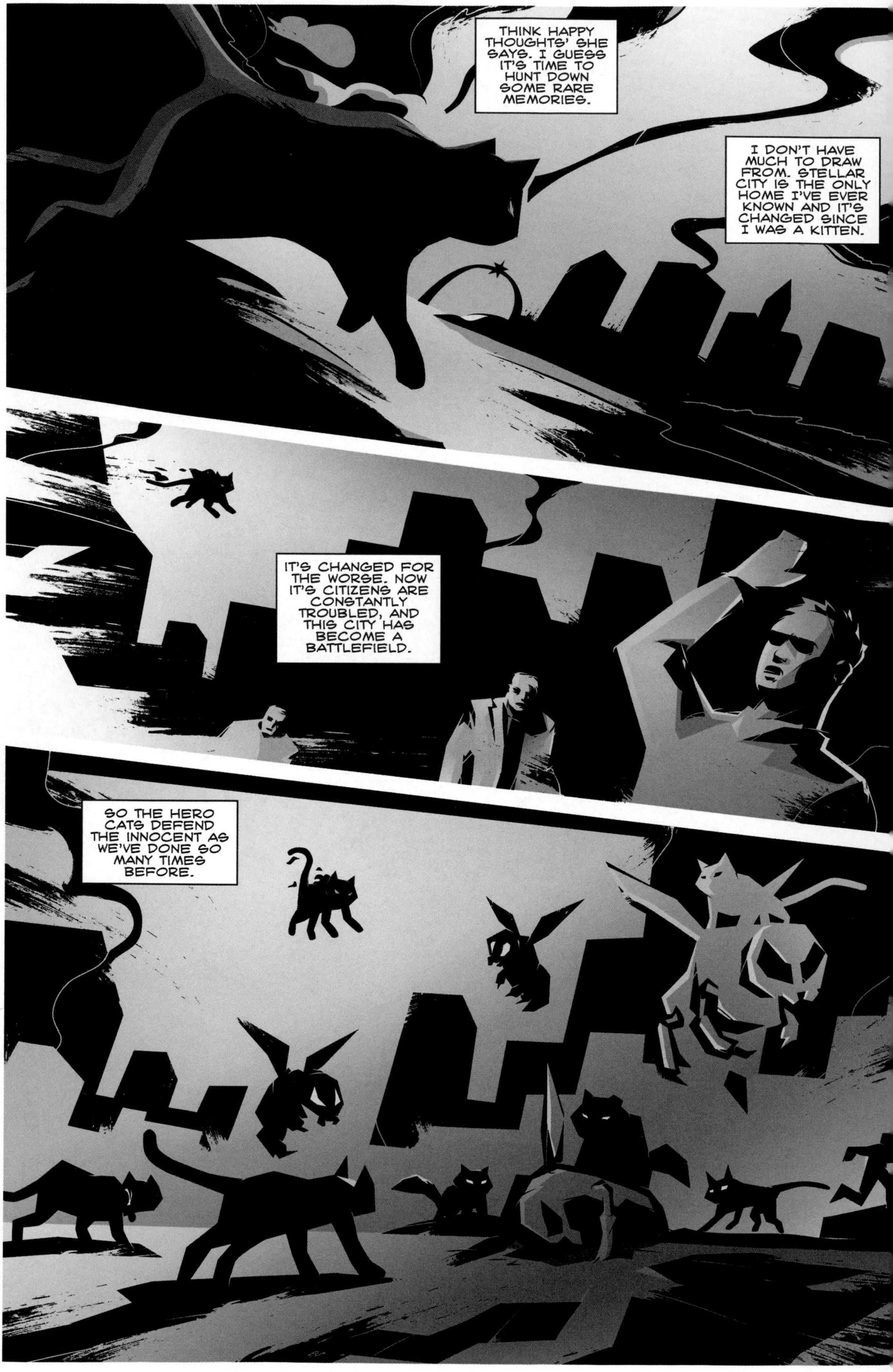
THINK HAPPY THOUGHTS' SHE SAYS. I GUESS IT'S TIME TO HUNT DOWN SOME RARE MEMORIES.
I DON'T HAVE MUCH TO DRAW FROM. STELLAR CITY IS THE ONLY HOME I'VE EVER KNOWN AND IT'S CHANGED SINCE I WAS A KITTEN.
IT'S CHANGED FOR THE WORSE. NOW IT'S CITIZENS ARE CONSTANTLY TROUBLED, AND THIS CITY HAS BECOME A BATTLEFIELD.
SO THE HERO CATS DEFEND THE INNOCENT AS WE'VE DONE SO MANY TIMES BEFORE.

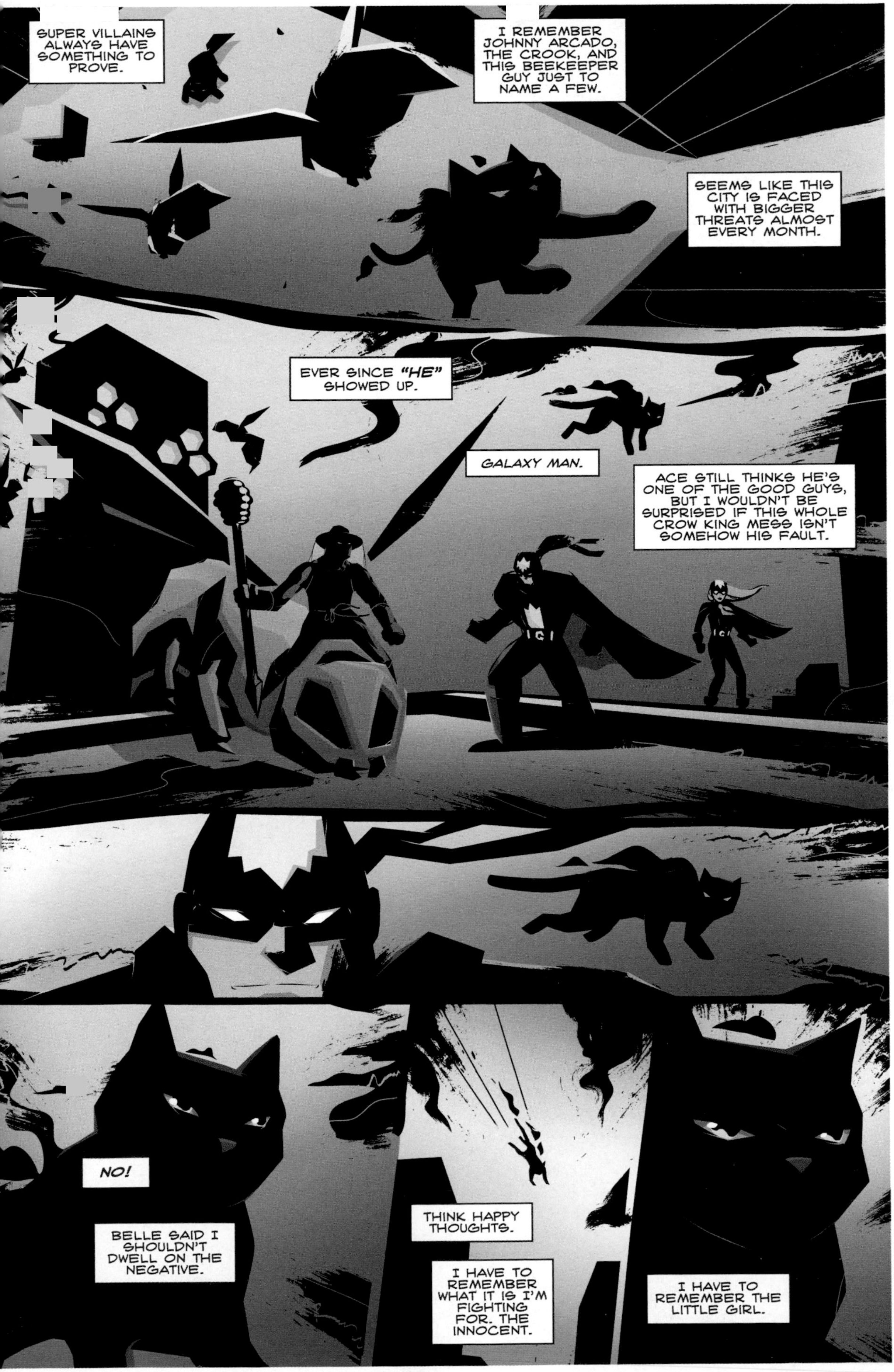
SUPER VILLAINS ALWAYS HAVE SOMETHING TO PROVE.
I REMEMBER JOHNNY ARCADO, THE CROOK, AND THIS BEEKEEPER GUY JUST TO NAME A FEW.
SEEMS LIKE THIS CITY IS FACED WITH BIGGER THREATS ALMOST EVERY MONTH.
EVER SINCE "HE" SHOWED UP.
GALAXY MAN.
ACE STILL THINKS HE'S ONE OF THE GOOD GUYS, BUT I WOULDN'T BE SURPRISED IF THIS WHOLE CROW KING MESS ISN'T SOMEHOW HIS FAULT.
NO!
BELLE SAID I SHOULDN'T DWELL ON THE NEGATIVE.
THINK HAPPY THOUGHTS.
I HAVE TO REMEMBER WHAT IT IS I'M FIGHTING FOR. THE INNOCENT.
I HAVE TO REMEMBER THE LITTLE GIRL.

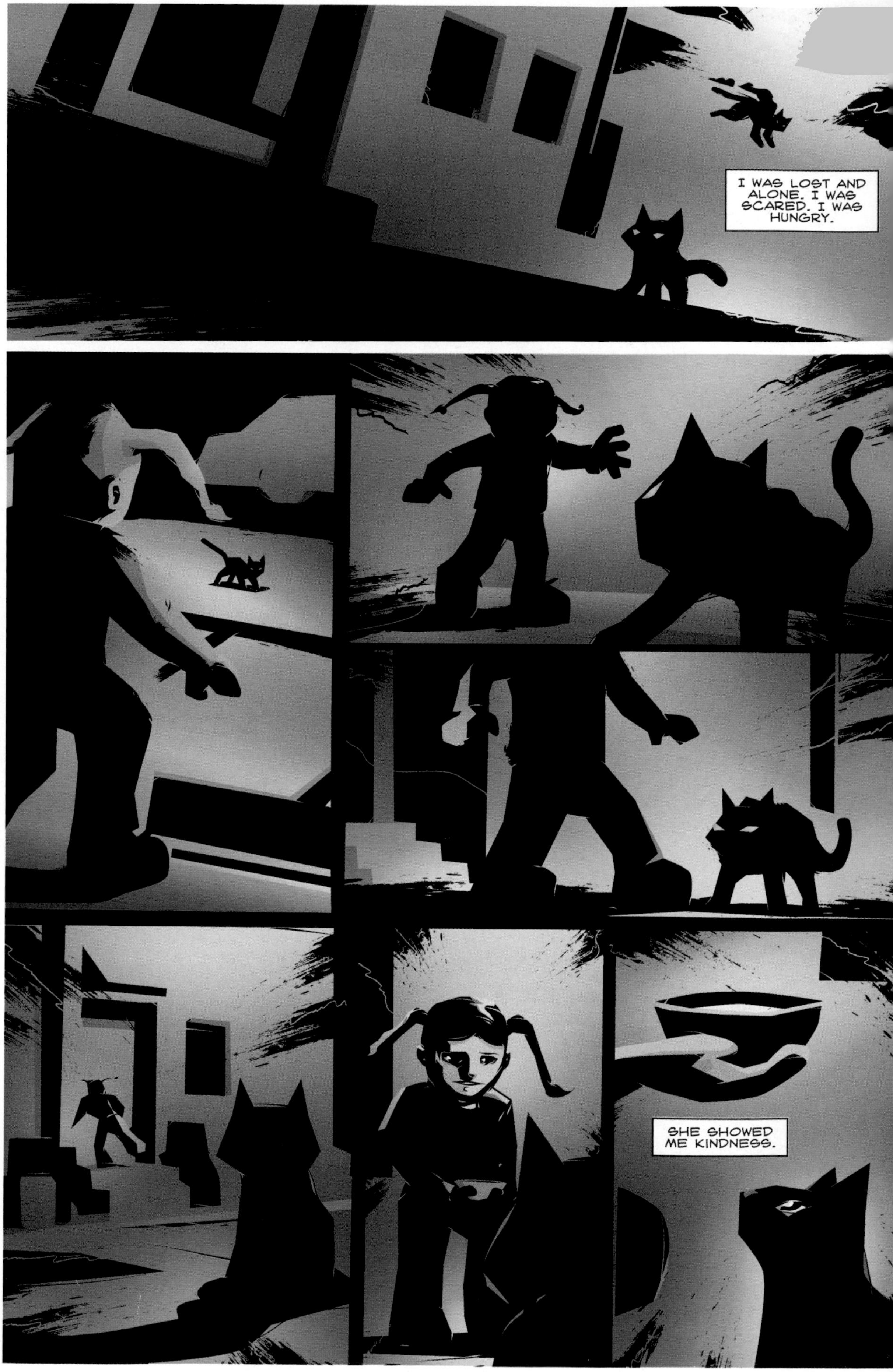
I WAS LOST AND ALONE. I WAS SCARED. I WAS HUNGRY.
SHE SHOWED ME KINDNESS.

EVERY DAY WITH HER WAS...
...WELL, I DIDN'T WANT HER TO GO AWAY.
BUT ONE NIGHT WHILE THE FAMILY WAS AWAY, CRIME MOVED INTO THE NEIGHBORHOOD.
I TRIED TO STOP THEM, BUT I WAS JUST A KITTEN. WHAT COULD I DO?
I KNEW WHEN THE FAMILY RETURNED, THEY WOULD BE DEVASTATED.
THEY HAD TO MOVE AWAY.
AND I WAS ALONE AGAIN.

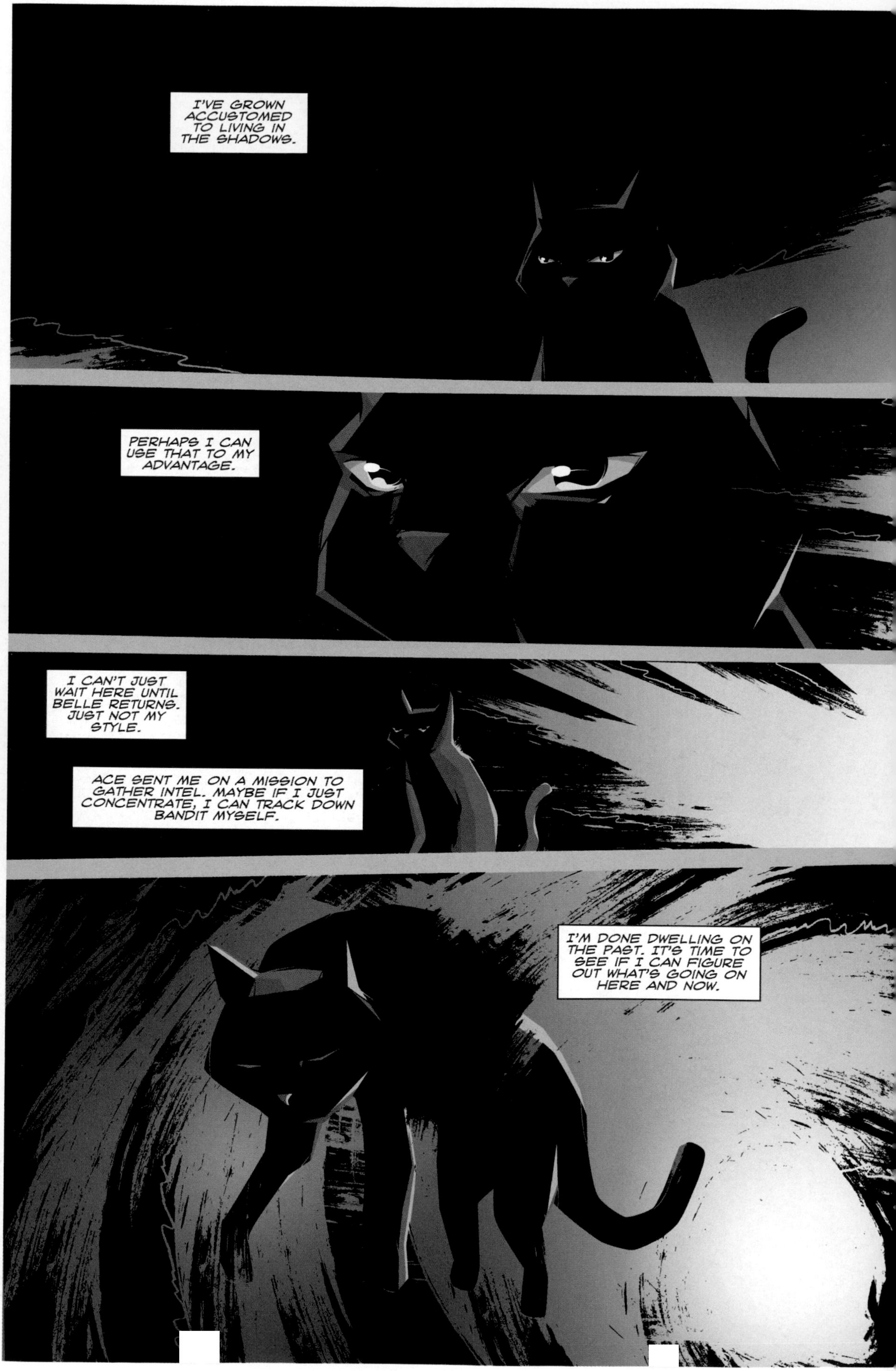
I'VE GROWN ACCUSTOMED TO LIVING IN THE SHADOWS.
PERHAPS I CAN USE THAT TO MY ADVANTAGE.
I CAN'T JUST WAIT HERE UNTIL BELLE RETURNS. JUST NOT MY STYLE.
ACE SENT ME ON A MISSION TO GATHER INTEL. MAYBE IF I JUST CONCENTRATE, I CAN TRACK DOWN BANDIT MYSELF.
I'M DONE DWELLING ON THE PAST. IT'S TIME TO SEE IF I CAN FIGURE OUT WHAT'S GOING ON HERE AND NOW.

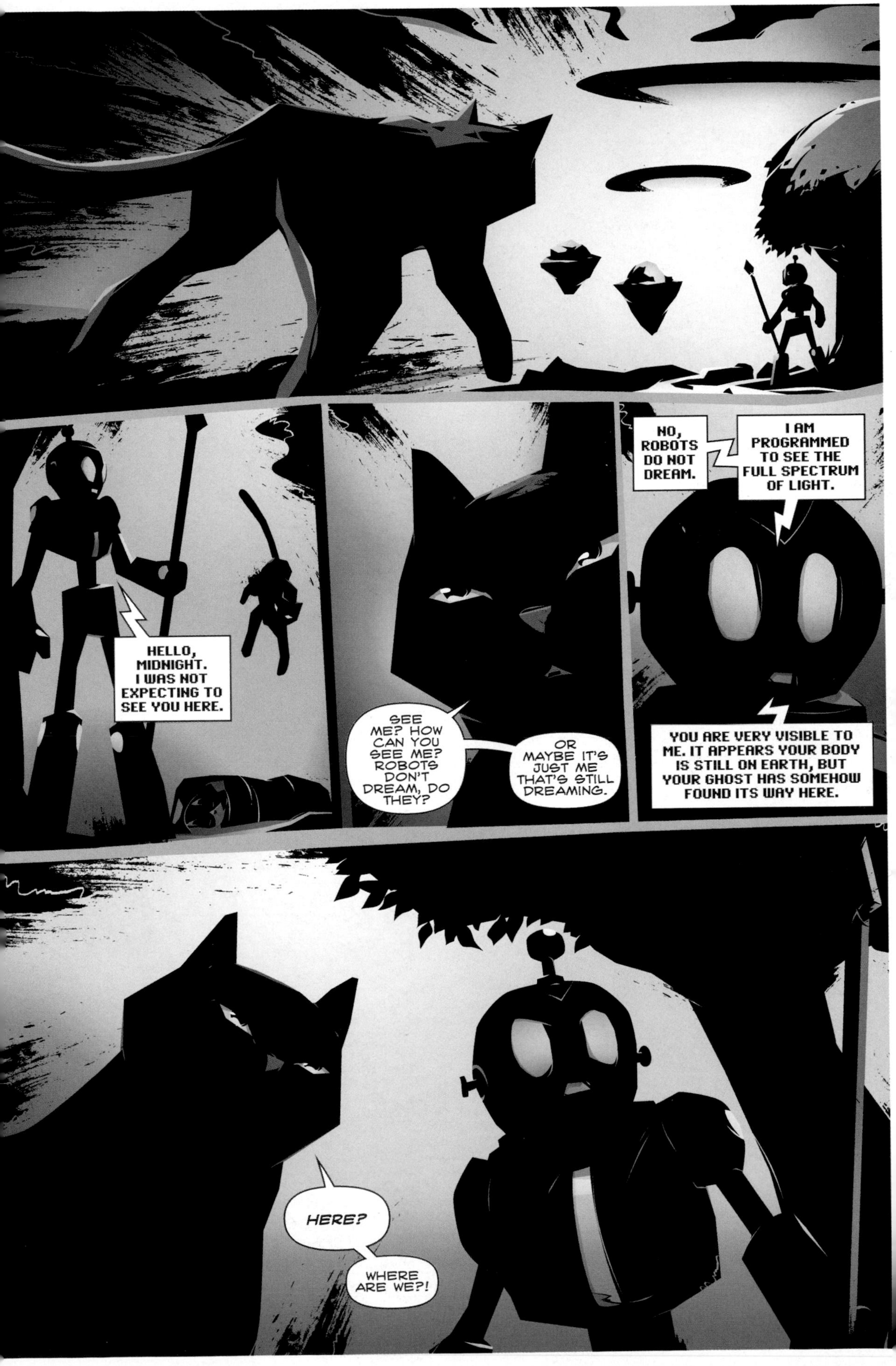
HELLO, MIDNIGHT. I WAS NOT EXPECTING TO SEE YOU HERE.
SEE ME? HOW CAN YOU SEE ME? ROBOTS DON'T DREAM, DO THEY?
OR MAYBE IT'S JUST ME THAT'S STILL DREAMING.
NO, ROBOTS DO NOT DREAM.
I AM PROGRAMMED TO SEE THE FULL SPECTRUM OF LIGHT.
YOU ARE VERY VISIBLE TO ME. IT APPEARS YOUR BODY IS STILL ON EARTH, BUT YOUR GHOST HAS SOMEHOW FOUND ITS WAY HERE.
HERE?
WHERE ARE WE?!

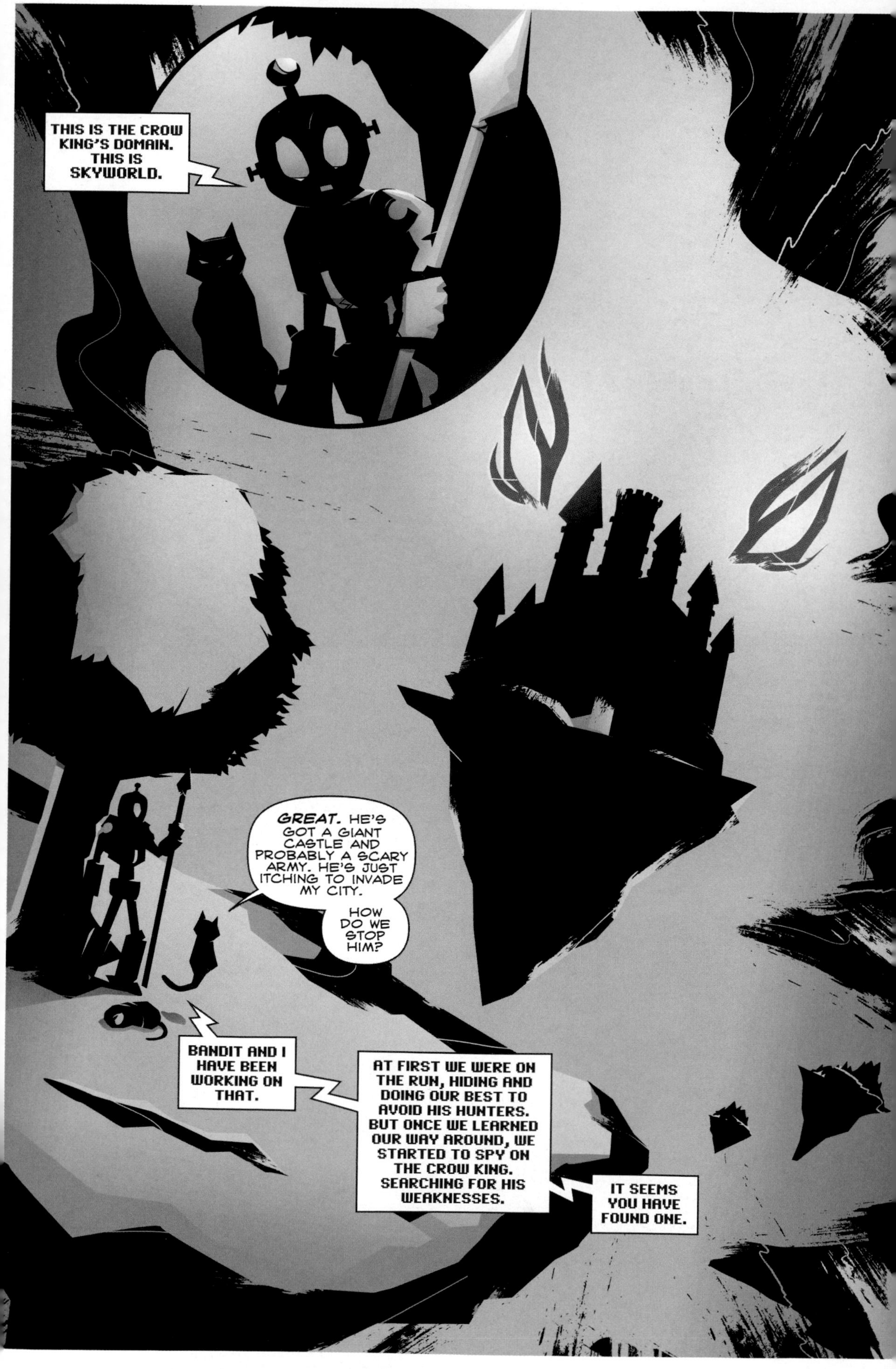
THIS IS THE CROW KING'S DOMAIN. THIS IS SKYWORLD.
GREAT. HE'S GOT A GIANT CASTLE AND PROBABLY A SCARY ARMY. HE'S JUST ITCHING TO INVADE MY CITY.
HOW DO WE STOP HIM?
BANDIT AND I HAVE BEEN WORKING ON THAT.
AT FIRST WE WERE ON THE RUN, HIDING AND DOING OUR BEST TO AVOID HIS HUNTERS. BUT ONCE WE LEARNED OUR WAY AROUND, WE STARTED TO SPY ON THE CROW KING. SEARCHING FOR HIS WEAKNESSES.
IT SEEMS YOU HAVE FOUND ONE.

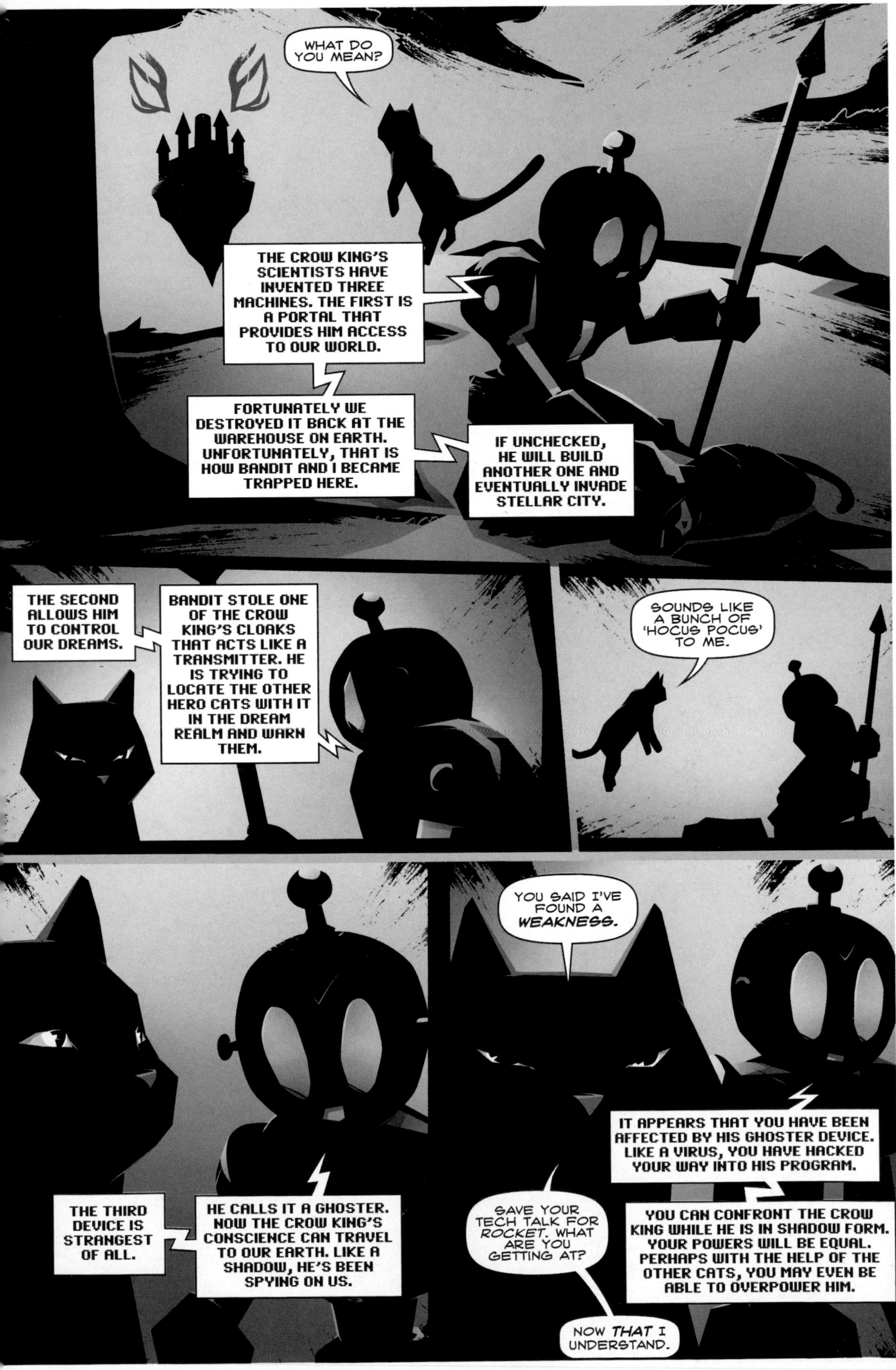
WHAT DO YOU MEAN?
THE CROW KING'S SCIENTISTS HAVE INVENTED THREE MACHINES. THE FIRST IS A PORTAL THAT PROVIDES HIM ACCESS TO OUR WORLD.
FORTUNATELY WE DESTROYED IT BACK AT THE WAREHOUSE ON EARTH. UNFORTUNATELY, THAT IS HOW BANDIT AND I BECAME TRAPPED HERE.
IF UNCHECKED, HE WILL BUILD ANOTHER ONE AND EVENTUALLY INVADE STELLAR CITY.
THE SECOND ALLOWS HIM TO CONTROL OUR DREAMS.
BANDIT STOLE ONE OF THE CROW KING'S CLOAKS THAT ACTS LIKE A TRANSMITTER. HE IS TRYING TO LOCATE THE OTHER HERO CATS WITH IT IN THE DREAM REALM AND WARN THEM.
SOUNDS LIKE A BUNCH OF 'HOCUS POCUS' TO ME.
THE THIRD DEVICE IS STRANGEST OF ALL.
HE CALLS IT A GHOSTER. NOW THE CROW KING'S CONSCIENCE CAN TRAVEL TO OUR EARTH. LIKE A SHADOW, HE'S BEEN SPYING ON US.
YOU SAID I'VE FOUND A *WEAKNESS.*
IT APPEARS THAT YOU HAVE BEEN AFFECTED BY HIS GHOSTER DEVICE. LIKE A VIRUS, YOU HAVE HACKED YOUR WAY INTO HIS PROGRAM.
SAVE YOUR TECH TALK FOR *ROCKET*. WHAT ARE YOU GETTING AT?
YOU CAN CONFRONT THE CROW KING WHILE HE IS IN SHADOW FORM. YOUR POWERS WILL BE EQUAL. PERHAPS WITH THE HELP OF THE OTHER CATS, YOU MAY EVEN BE ABLE TO OVERPOWER HIM.
NOW *THAT* I UNDERSTAND.

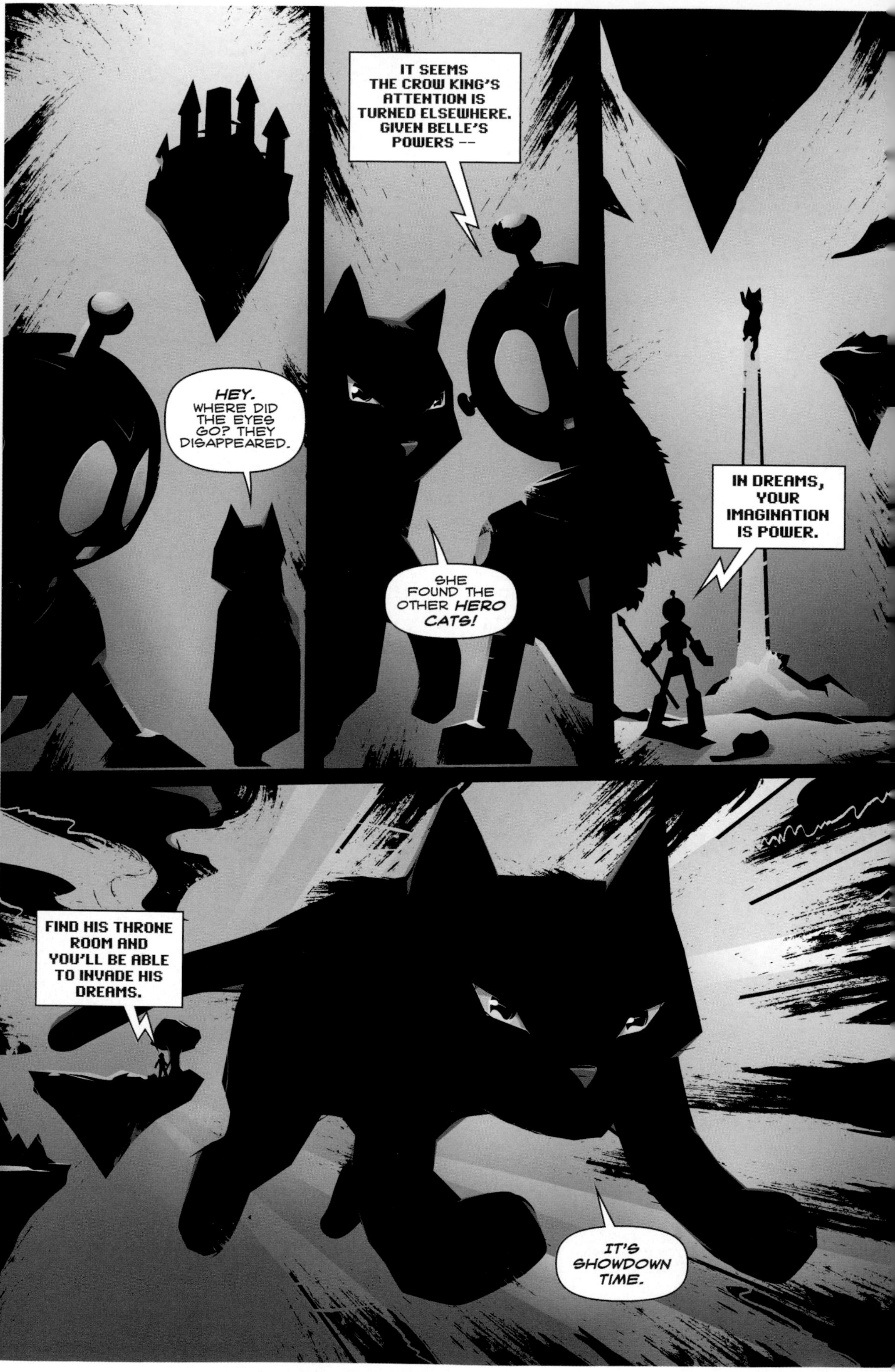

HEY. WHERE DID THE EYES GO? THEY DISAPPEARED.
IT SEEMS THE CROW KING'S ATTENTION IS TURNED ELSEWHERE. GIVEN BELLE'S POWERS --
SHE FOUND THE OTHER HERO CATS!
IN DREAMS, YOUR IMAGINATION IS POWER.
FIND HIS THRONE ROOM AND YOU'LL BE ABLE TO INVADE HIS DREAMS.
IT'S SHOWDOWN TIME.

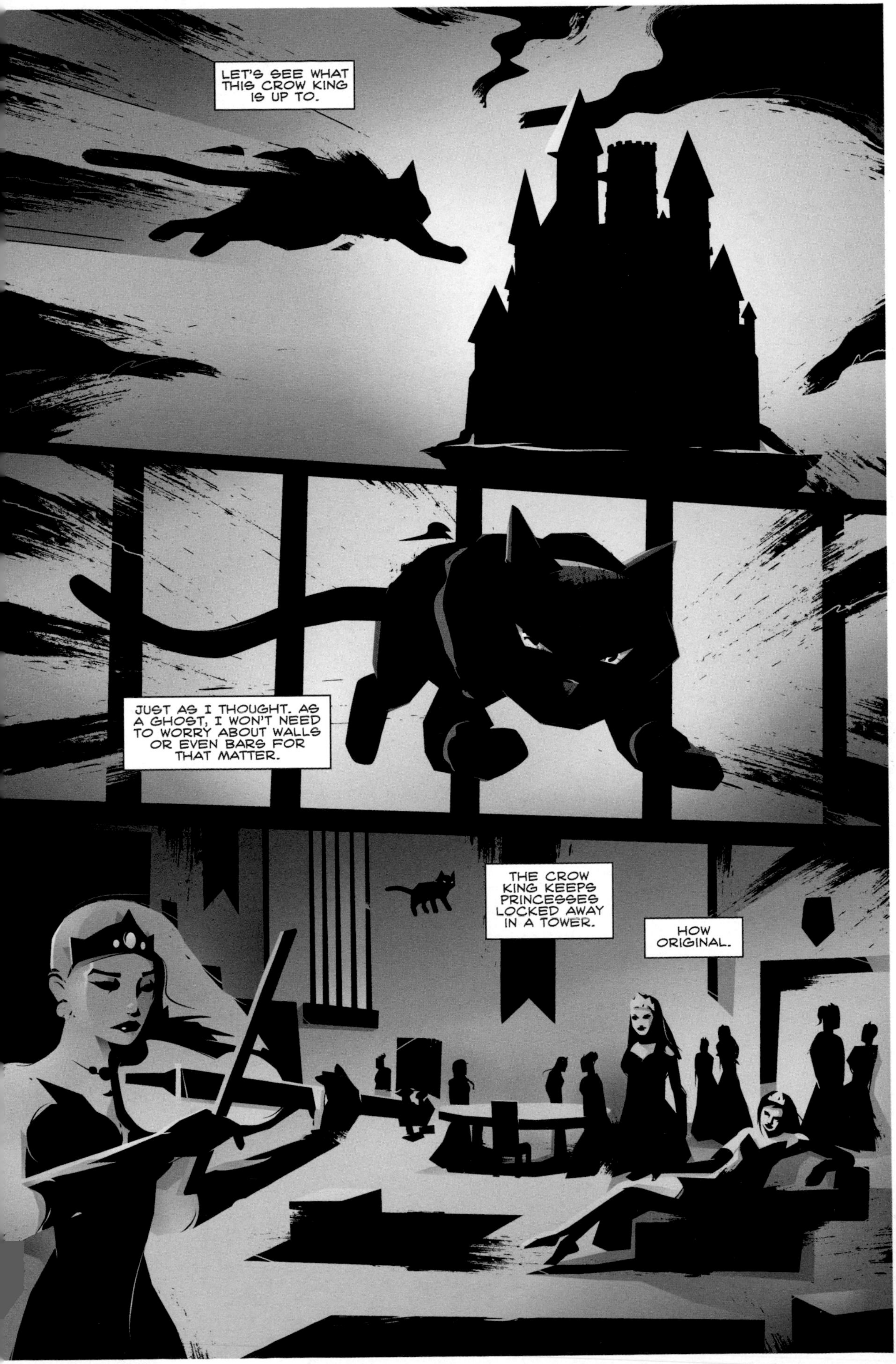
LET'S SEE WHAT THIS CROW KING IS UP TO.
JUST AS I THOUGHT. AS A GHOST, I WON'T NEED TO WORRY ABOUT WALLS OR EVEN BARS FOR THAT MATTER.
THE CROW KING KEEPS PRINCESSES LOCKED AWAY IN A TOWER.
HOW ORIGINAL.

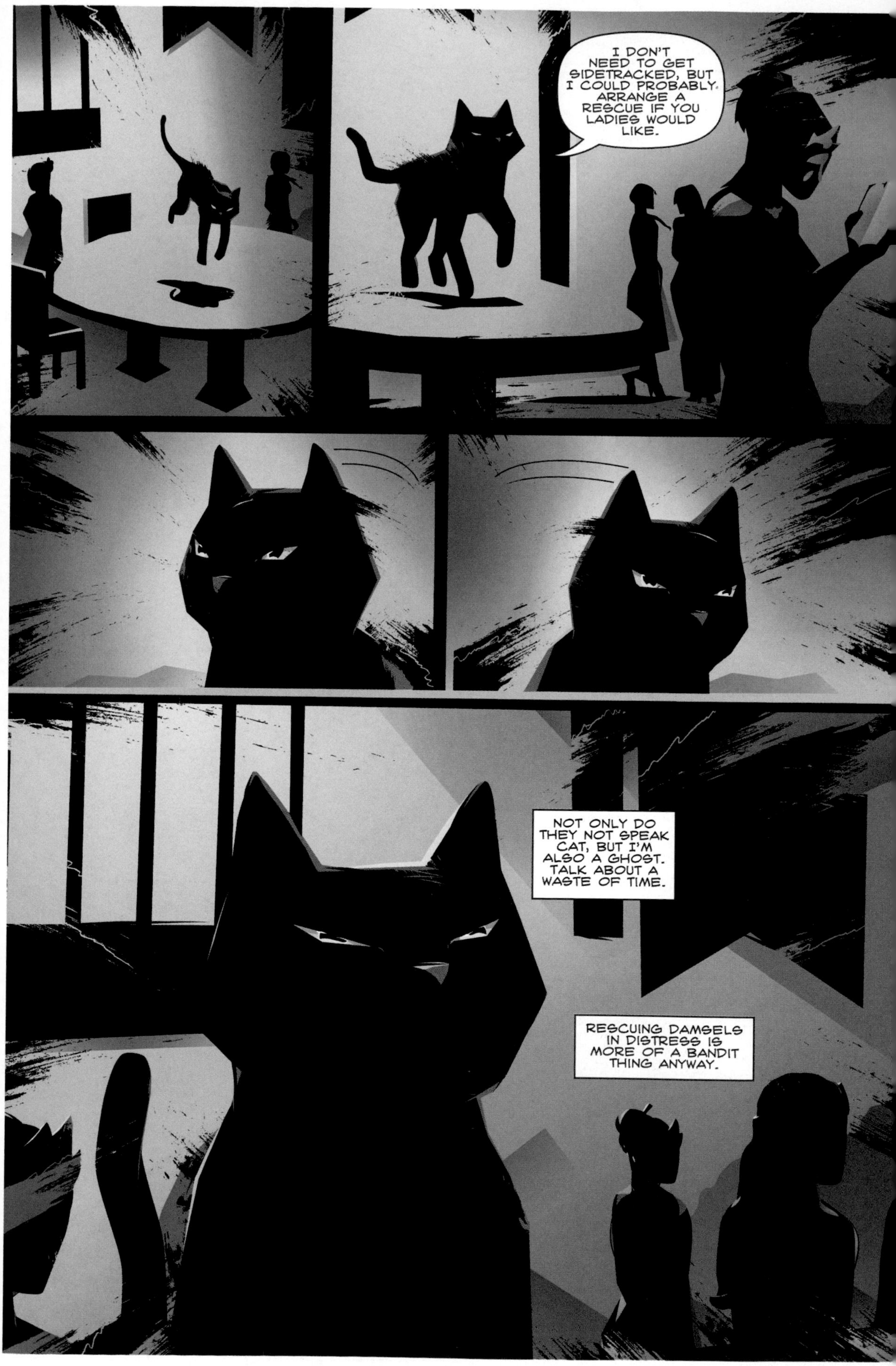
I DON'T NEED TO GET SIDETRACKED, BUT I COULD PROBABLY ARRANGE A RESCUE IF YOU LADIES WOULD LIKE.
NOT ONLY DO THEY NOT SPEAK CAT, BUT I'M ALSO A GHOST. TALK ABOUT A WASTE OF TIME.
RESCUING DAMSELS IN DISTRESS IS MORE OF A BANDIT THING ANYWAY.

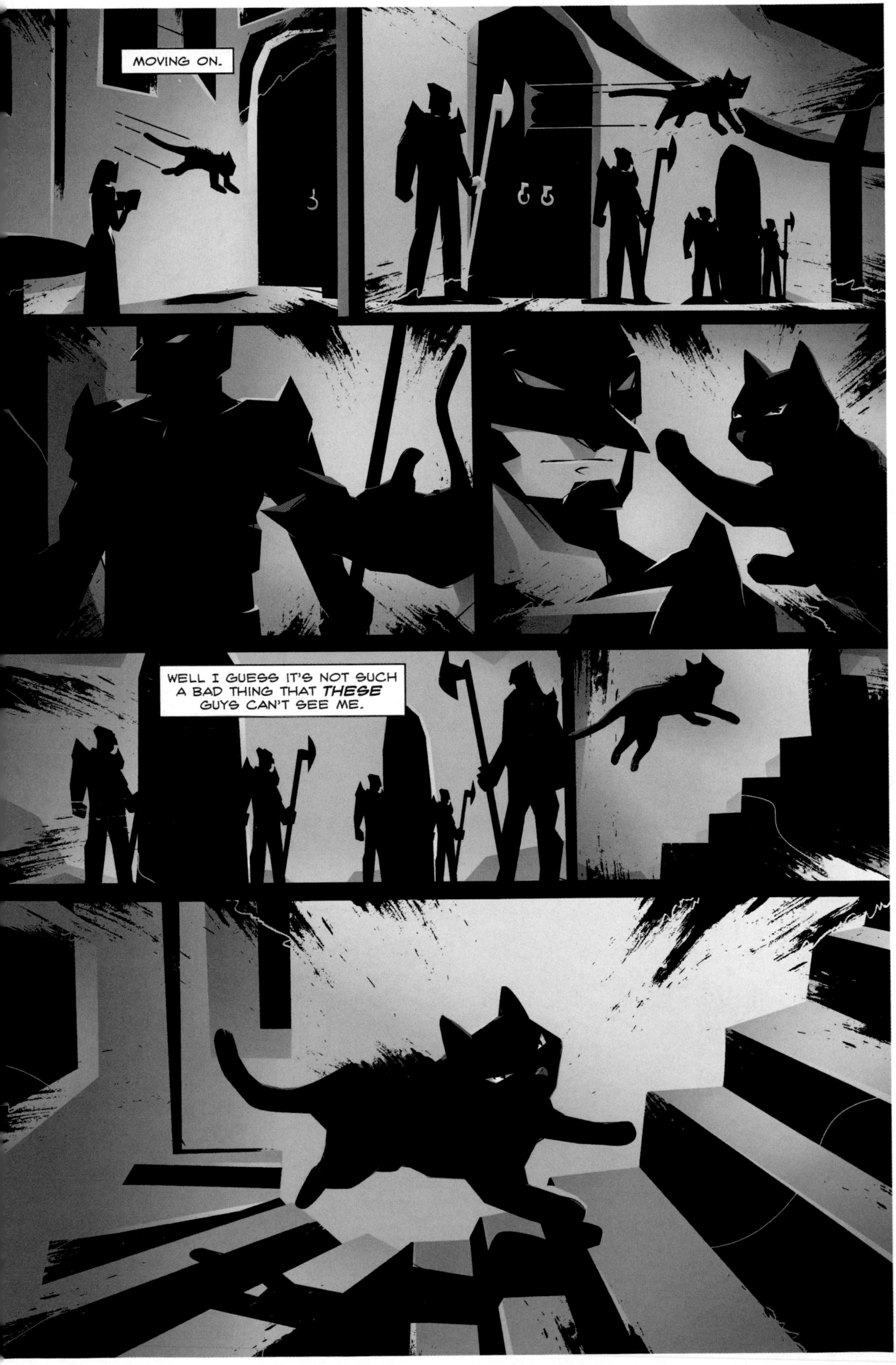
MOVING ON.
WELL I GUESS IT'S NOT SUCH A BAD THING THAT *THESE* GUYS CAN'T SEE ME.

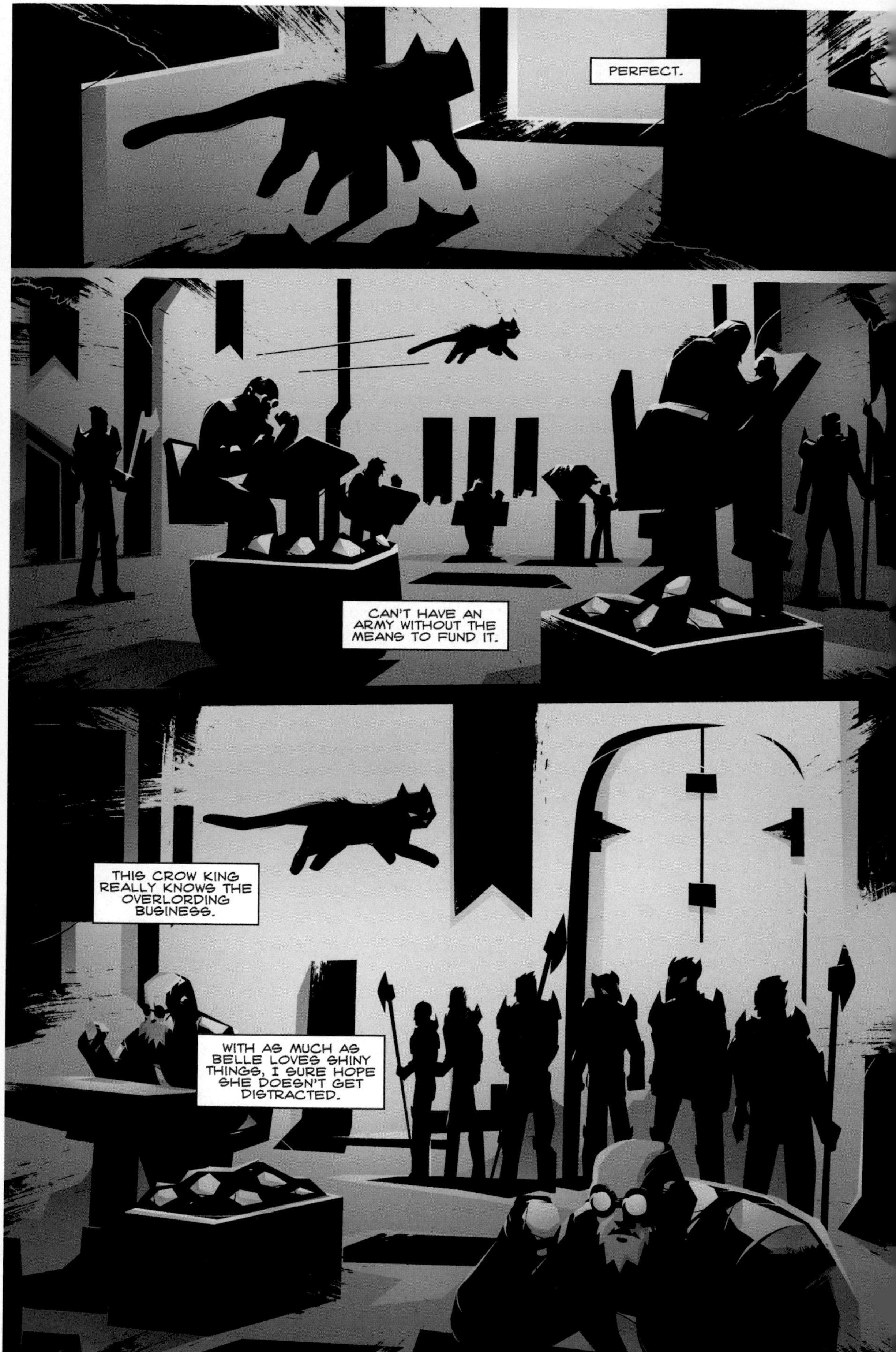
PERFECT.
CAN'T HAVE AN ARMY WITHOUT THE MEANS TO FUND IT.
THIS CROW KING REALLY KNOWS THE OVERLORDING BUSINESS.
WITH AS MUCH AS BELLE LOVES SHINY THINGS, I SURE HOPE SHE DOESN'T GET DISTRACTED.

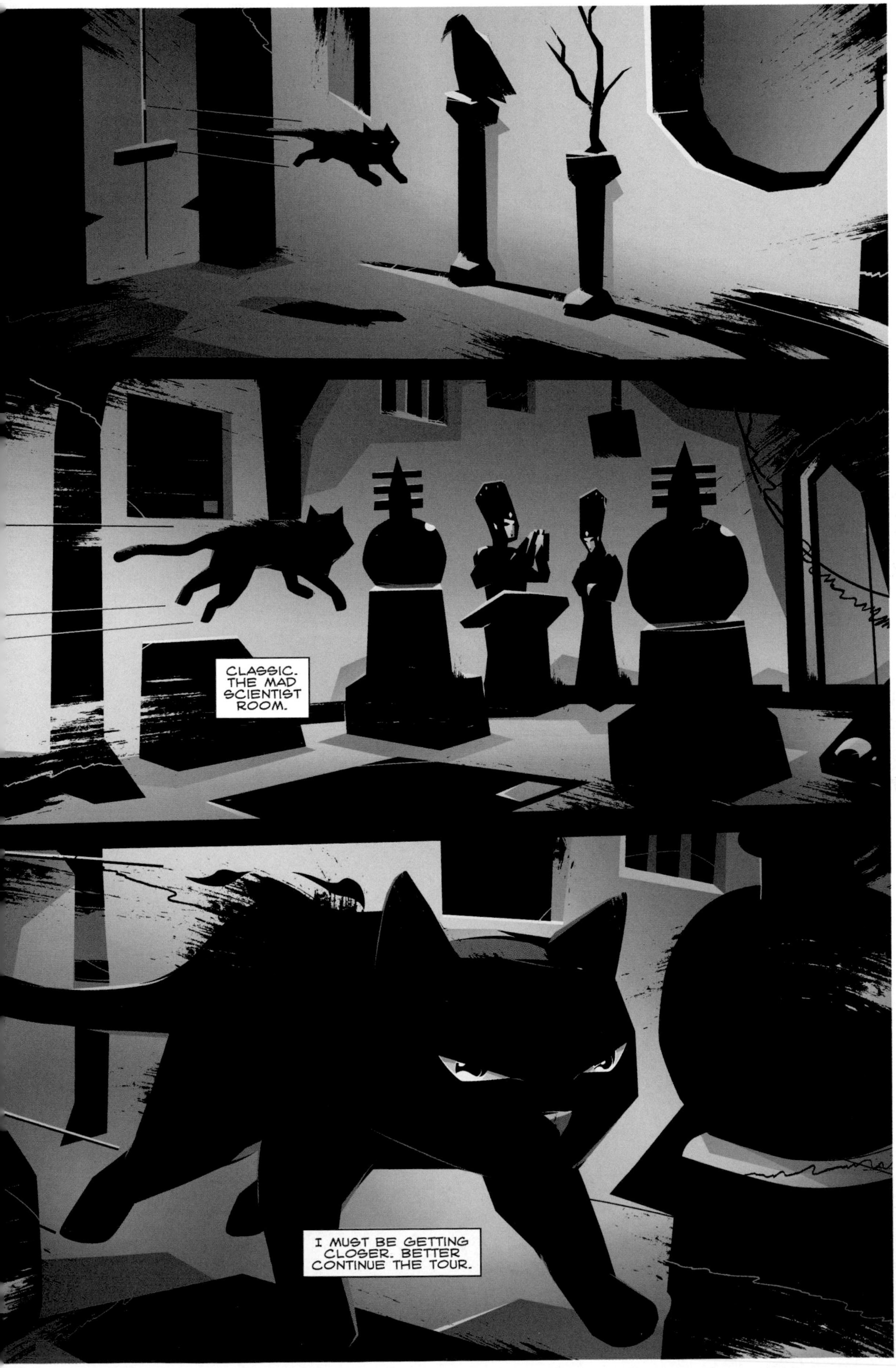
CLASSIC. THE MAD SCIENTIST ROOM.
I MUST BE GETTING CLOSER. BETTER CONTINUE THE TOUR.

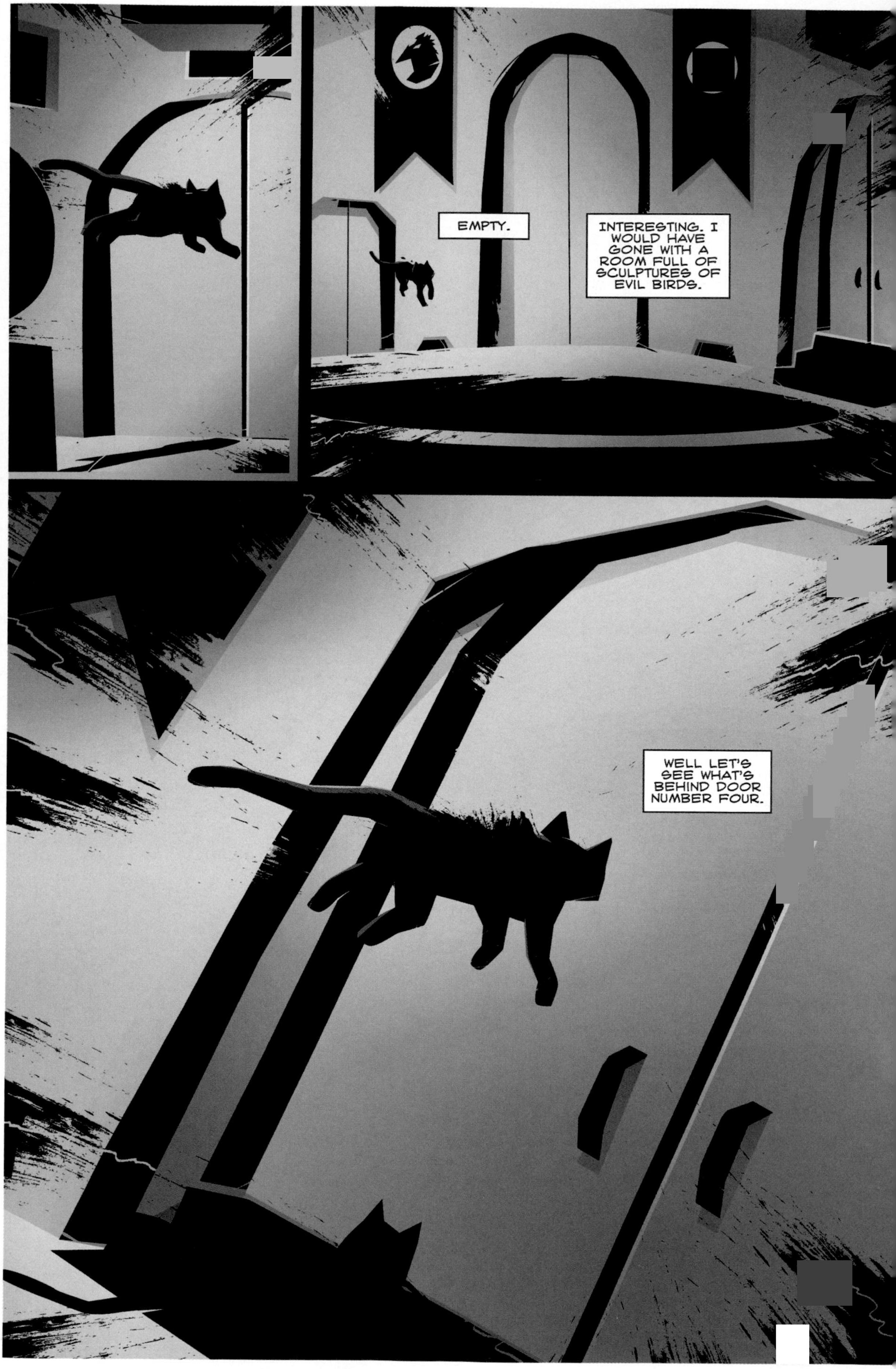
EMPTY.
INTERESTING. I WOULD HAVE GONE WITH A ROOM FULL OF SCULPTURES OF EVIL BIRDS.
WELL LET'S SEE WHAT'S BEHIND DOOR NUMBER FOUR.

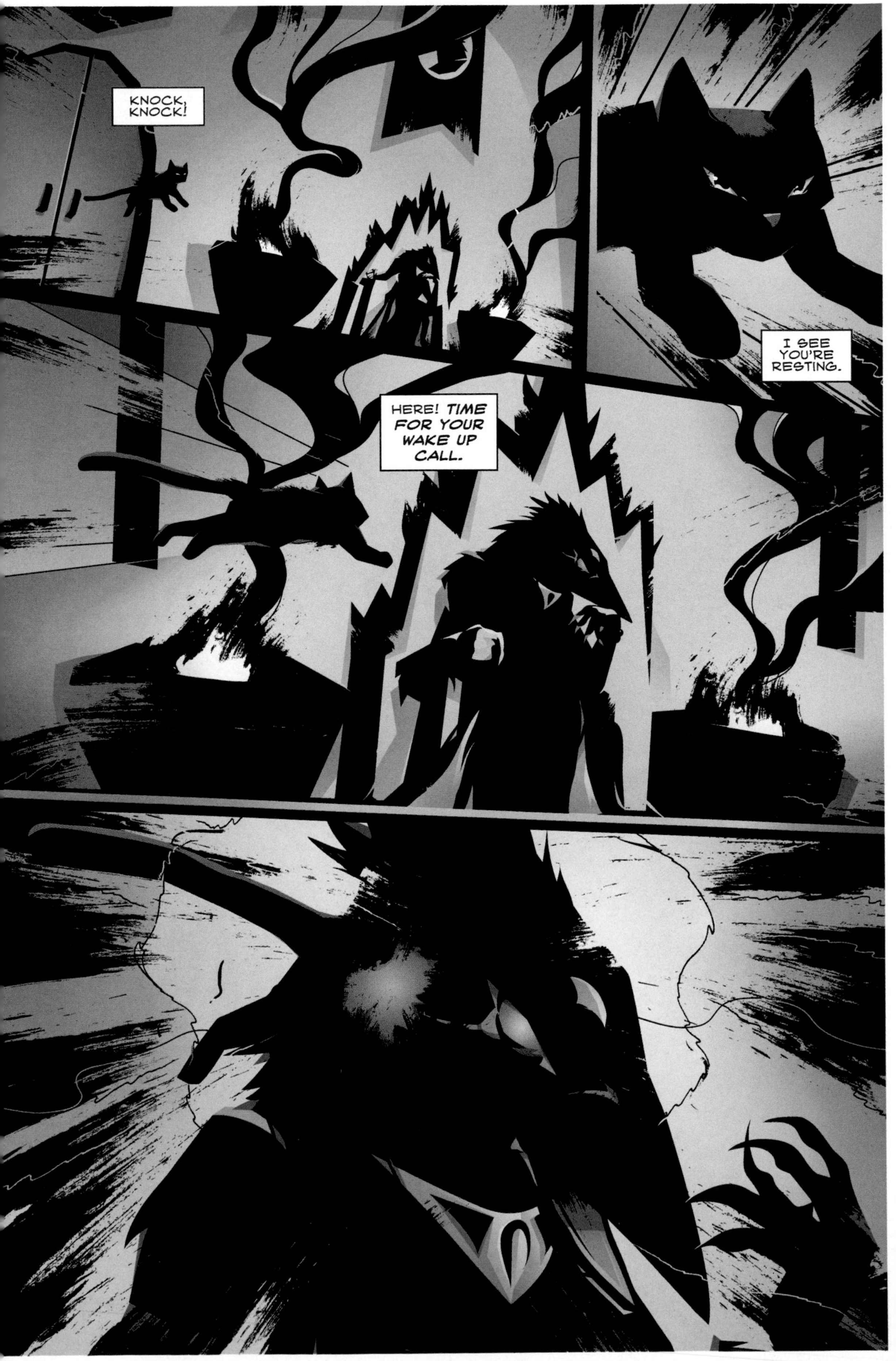

KNOCK, KNOCK!
I SEE YOU'RE RESTING.
HERE! *TIME FOR YOUR WAKE UP CALL.*

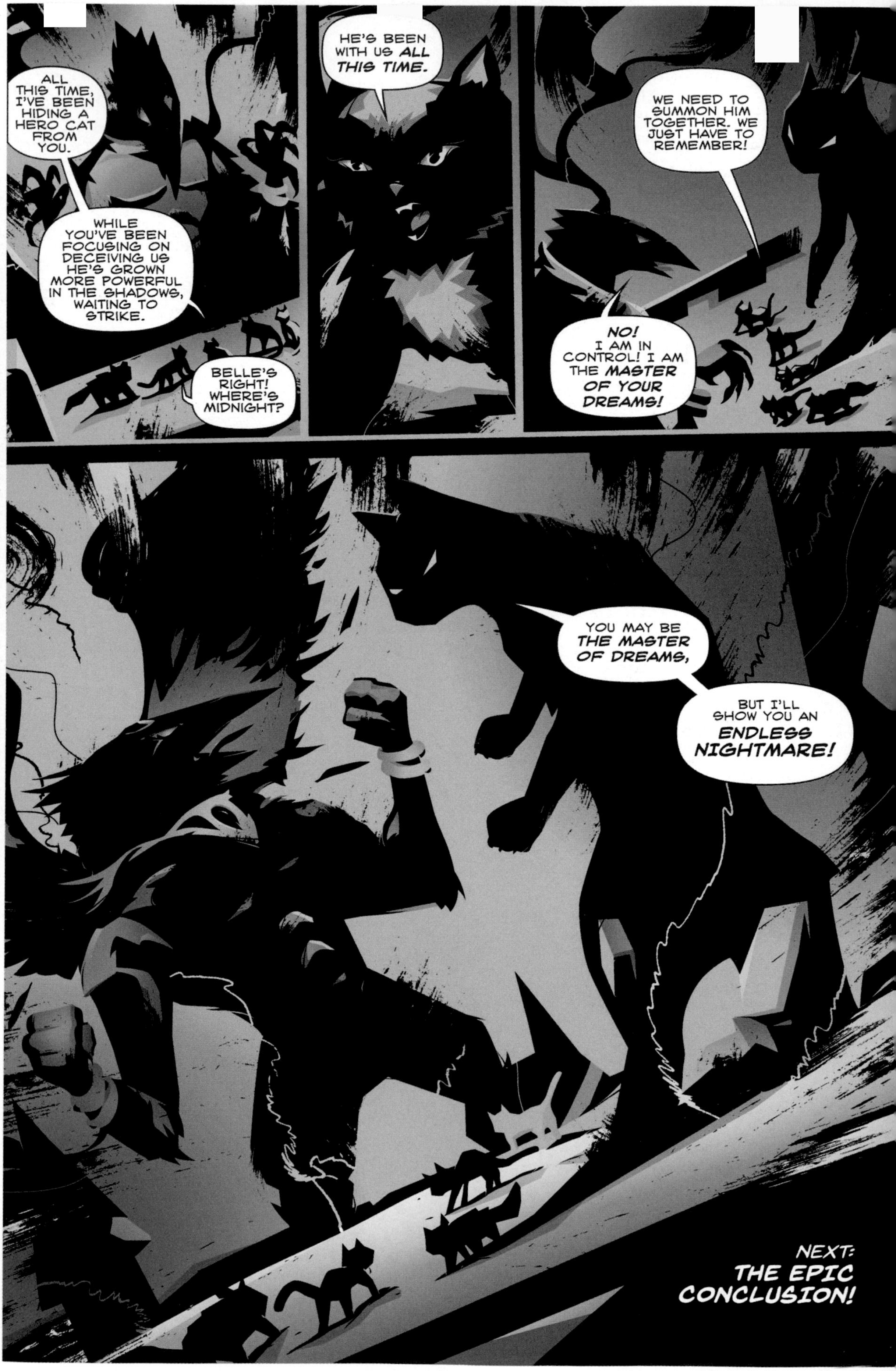
ALL THIS TIME, I'VE BEEN HIDING A HERO CAT FROM YOU.
WHILE YOU'VE BEEN FOCUSING ON DECEIVING US HE'S GROWN MORE POWERFUL IN THE SHADOWS, WAITING TO STRIKE.
BELLE'S RIGHT! WHERE'S MIDNIGHT?
HE'S BEEN WITH US ALL THIS TIME.
WE NEED TO SUMMON HIM TOGETHER. WE JUST HAVE TO REMEMBER!
NO! I AM IN CONTROL! I AM THE MASTER OF YOUR DREAMS!
YOU MAY BE THE MASTER OF DREAMS,
BUT I'LL SHOW YOU AN ENDLESS NIGHTMARE!
NEXT: THE EPIC CONCLUSION!

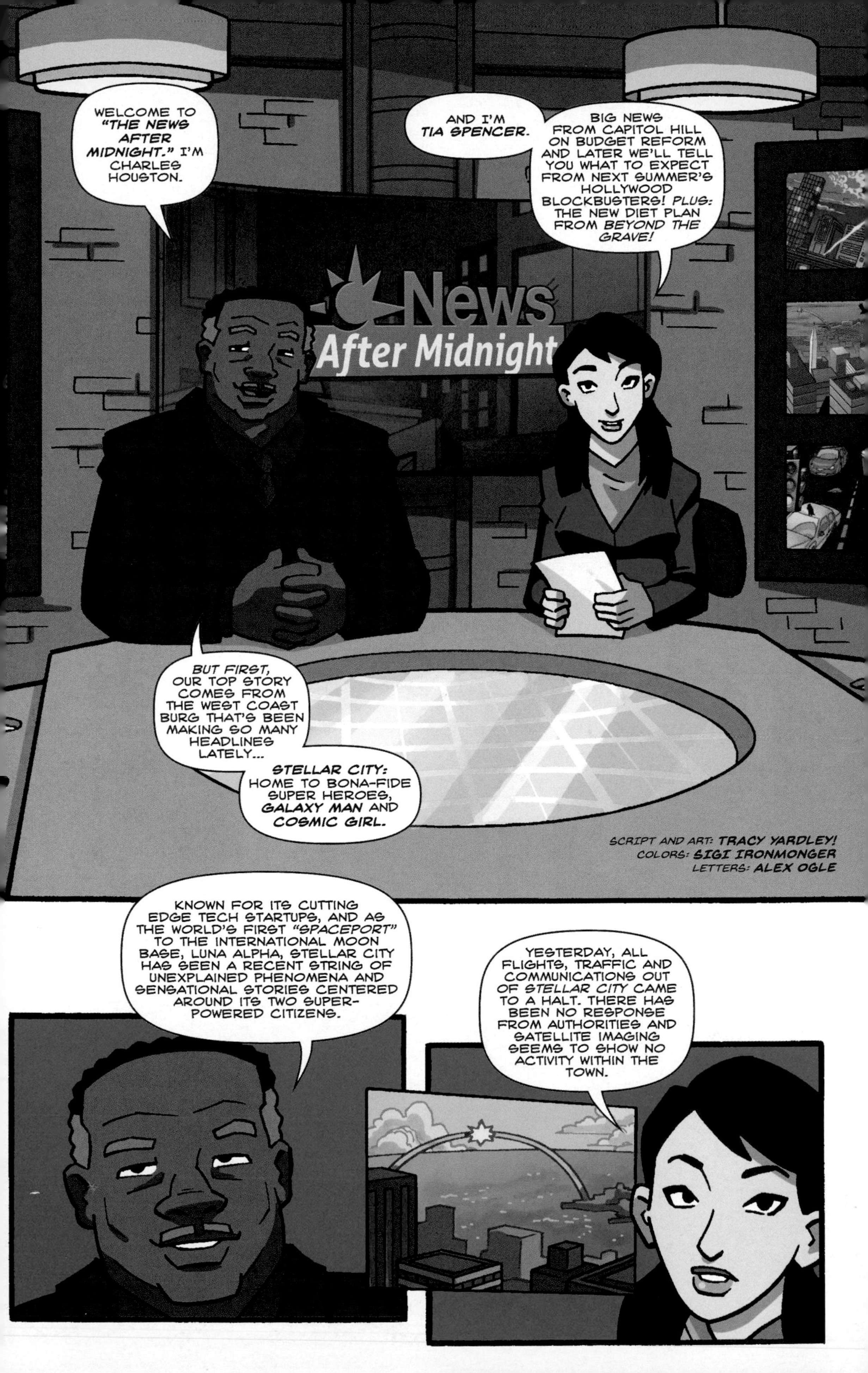
WELCOME TO "THE NEWS AFTER MIDNIGHT." I'M CHARLES HOUSTON.
AND I'M TIA SPENCER.
BIG NEWS FROM CAPITOL HILL ON BUDGET REFORM AND LATER WE'LL TELL YOU WHAT TO EXPECT FROM NEXT SUMMER'S HOLLYWOOD BLOCKBUSTERS! PLUS: THE NEW DIET PLAN FROM BEYOND THE GRAVE!
News After Midnight
BUT FIRST, OUR TOP STORY COMES FROM THE WEST COAST BURG THAT'S BEEN MAKING SO MANY HEADLINES LATELY...
STELLAR CITY: HOME TO BONA-FIDE SUPER HEROES, GALAXY MAN AND COSMIC GIRL.
SCRIPT AND ART: TRACY YARDLEY!
COLORS: SIGI IRONMONGER
LETTERS: ALEX OGLE
KNOWN FOR ITS CUTTING EDGE TECH STARTUPS, AND AS THE WORLD'S FIRST "SPACEPORT" TO THE INTERNATIONAL MOON BASE, LUNA ALPHA, STELLAR CITY HAS SEEN A RECENT STRING OF UNEXPLAINED PHENOMENA AND SENSATIONAL STORIES CENTERED AROUND ITS TWO SUPER-POWERED CITIZENS.
YESTERDAY, ALL FLIGHTS, TRAFFIC AND COMMUNICATIONS OUT OF STELLAR CITY CAME TO A HALT. THERE HAS BEEN NO RESPONSE FROM AUTHORITIES AND SATELLITE IMAGING SEEMS TO SHOW NO ACTIVITY WITHIN THE TOWN.

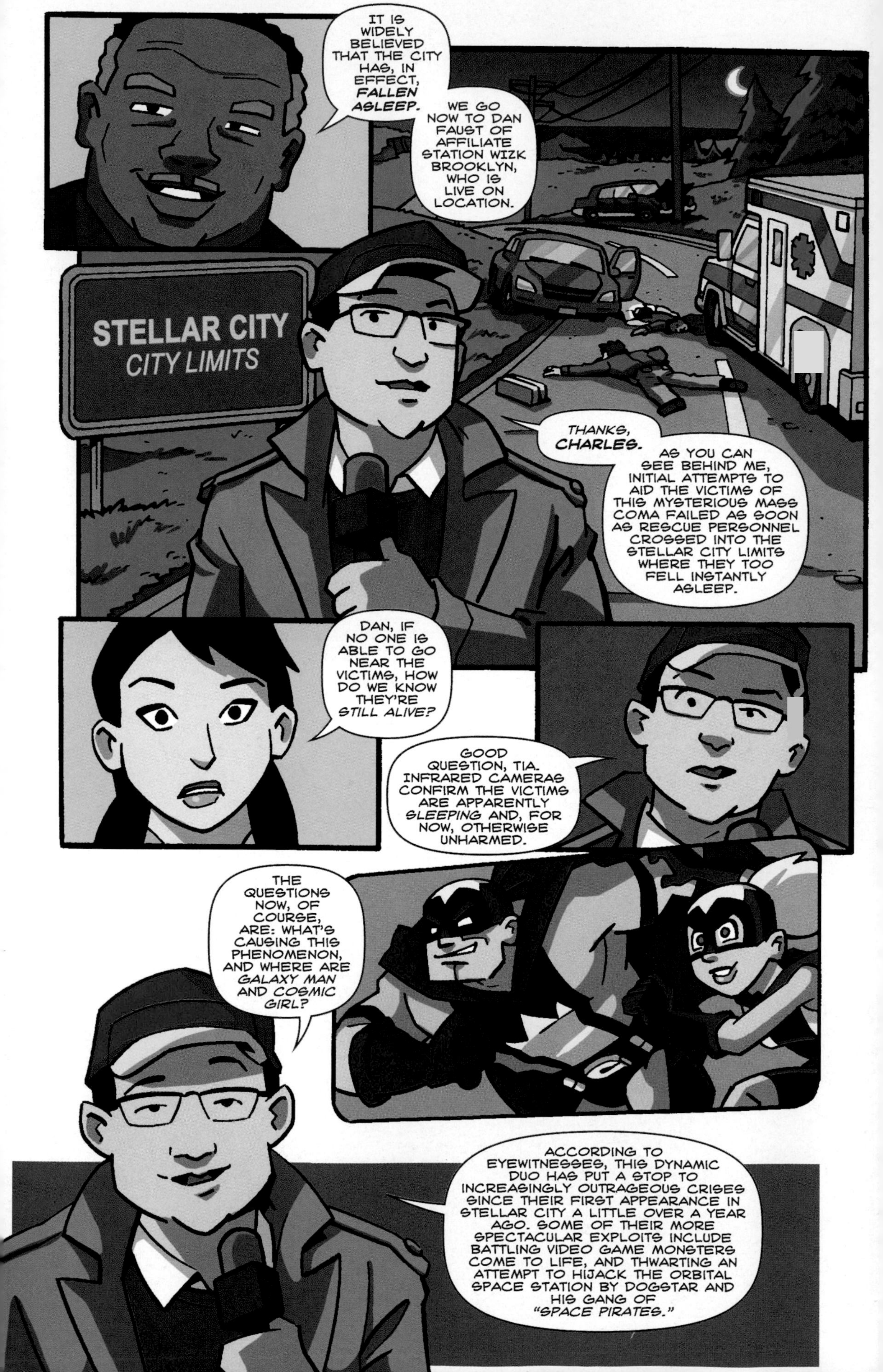
IT IS WIDELY BELIEVED THAT THE CITY HAS, IN EFFECT, FALLEN ASLEEP.
WE GO NOW TO DAN FAUST OF AFFILIATE STATION WIZK BROOKLYN, WHO IS LIVE ON LOCATION.
STELLAR CITY
CITY LIMITS
THANKS, CHARLES.
AS YOU CAN SEE BEHIND ME, INITIAL ATTEMPTS TO AID THE VICTIMS OF THIS MYSTERIOUS MASS COMA FAILED AS SOON AS RESCUE PERSONNEL CROSSED INTO THE STELLAR CITY LIMITS WHERE THEY TOO FELL INSTANTLY ASLEEP.
DAN, IF NO ONE IS ABLE TO GO NEAR THE VICTIMS, HOW DO WE KNOW THEY'RE STILL ALIVE?
GOOD QUESTION, TIA. INFRARED CAMERAS CONFIRM THE VICTIMS ARE APPARENTLY SLEEPING AND, FOR NOW, OTHERWISE UNHARMED.
THE QUESTIONS NOW, OF COURSE, ARE: WHAT'S CAUSING THIS PHENOMENON, AND WHERE ARE GALAXY MAN AND COSMIC GIRL?
ACCORDING TO EYEWITNESSES, THIS DYNAMIC DUO HAS PUT A STOP TO INCREASINGLY OUTRAGEOUS CRISES SINCE THEIR FIRST APPEARANCE IN STELLAR CITY A LITTLE OVER A YEAR AGO. SOME OF THEIR MORE SPECTACULAR EXPLOITS INCLUDE BATTLING VIDEO GAME MONSTERS COME TO LIFE, AND THWARTING AN ATTEMPT TO HIJACK THE ORBITAL SPACE STATION BY DOGSTAR AND HIS GANG OF "SPACE PIRATES."

WE'RE NOW SEEING VIDEO TAKEN JUST DAYS AGO AS THE LOCAL HEROES DID BATTLE WITH AN APPARENT "SUPER VILLAIN" DUBBED "THE BEEKEEPER."

THOUGH THERE WAS A FAIR AMOUNT OF PROPERTY DAMAGE, AN OVERWHELMING MAJORITY OF RESIDENTS APPROVE OF GALAXY MAN AND COSMIC GIRL'S EFFORTS ON THEIR BEHALF, DESPITE THE GROWING RISK OF DANGEROUS SUPER SCUFFLES BECOMING A FREQUENT PART OF LIFE IN STELLAR CITY.

HOWEVER, NEITHER GALAXY MAN NOR COSMIC GIRL HAVE MADE AN APPEARANCE, LEAVING MANY TO ASSUME THAT THEY TOO HAVE FALLEN VICTIM TO THE CITY-WIDE SLUMBER.

IS THIS THE WORK OF SOME *NEW* SUPER VILLAIN? WHAT UNKNOWN FORCES ARE AT WORK? HOW LONG CAN THE CITIZENS LAST AS THEY ARE? AND, WITH *GALAXY MAN* AND *COSMIC GIRL* SEEMINGLY PUT OUT OF ACTION, WHO WILL SAVE STELLAR CITY?

GRIPPING STUFF! THANKS TO DAN FAUST FOR THAT REPORT. WE'LL KEEP YOU UPDATED ON THE LATEST.

UP NEXT: CORPORATE COVER UP AT REGAL EMPIRE ENTERPRISES AND REPORTS OF A REAL LIFE "CAT" BURGLAR.

ACTION LAB ENTERTAINMENT

Bryan Seaton - Publisher
Kevin Freeman - President
Dave Dwonch - Creative Director
Shawn Gabborin - Editor in Chief
Jamal Igle - Director of Marketing
Jim Dietz - Social Media Director
Jeremy Whitley - Education Outreach Director
Chad Cicceni & Colleen Boyd - Associate Editors

THE STORY CONTINUES IN
MIDNIGHT OVER STELLAR CITY #3
AND HERO CATS OF STELLAR CITY #9

After the tragic events of last issue, Cyrus Perkins has gone from aimless Taxi Cab Driver to amateur Detective. Teaming with Michael, the ghost boy trapped in his car, Cyrus speeds into mystery, danger, and a conspiracy too twisted for words!

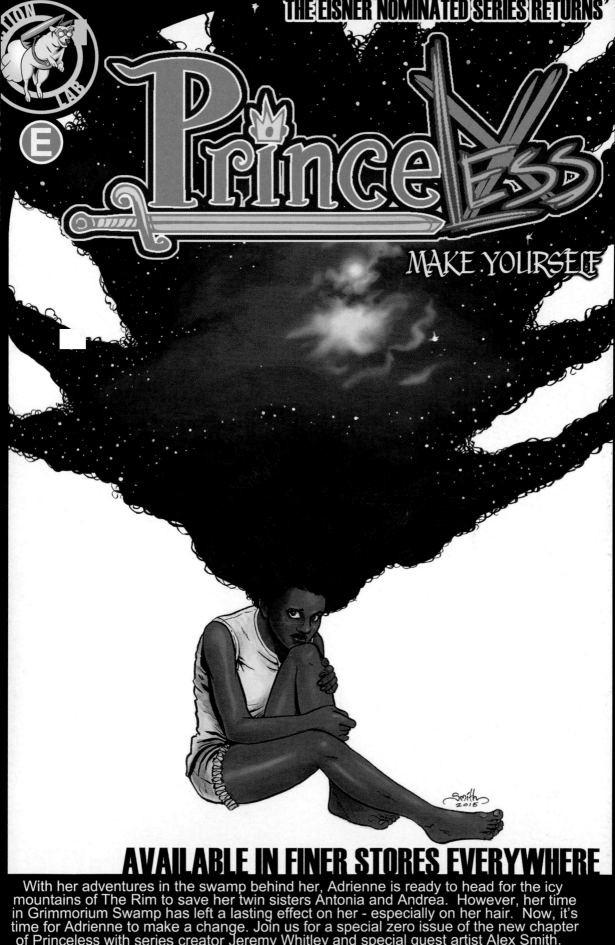

ACTION LAB

READ MORE NOW

Hero Cats: Midnight Over Stellar City - Action Lab
www.actionlabcomics.com

00211

7 02382 69112 7

ACTIONLABCOMICS.COM

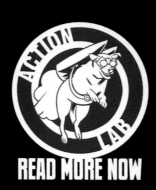

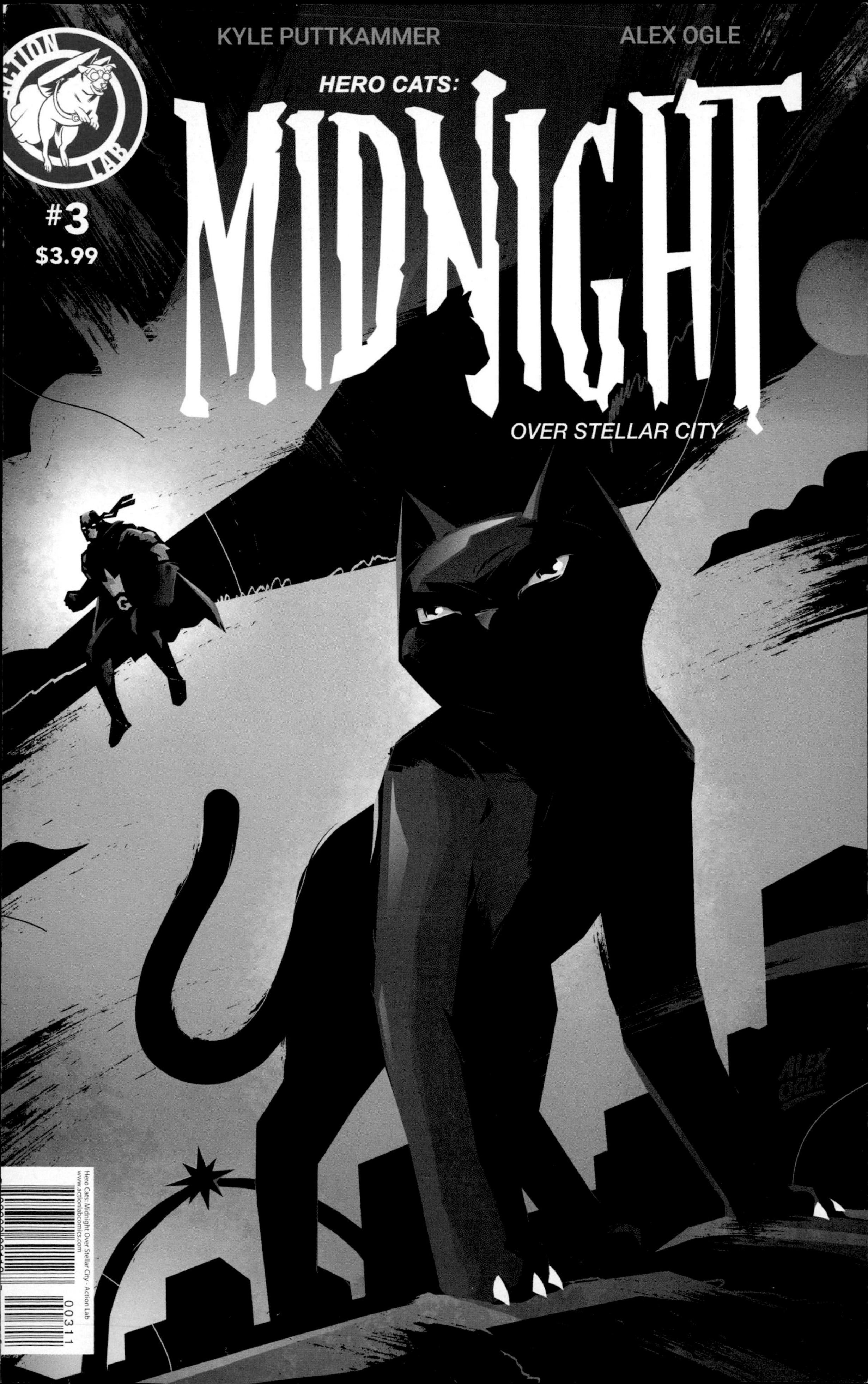
KYLE PUTTKAMMER
ALEX OGLE
ACTION LAB
HERO CATS:
MIDNIGHT
OVER STELLAR CITY
#3
$3.99
Hero Cats: Midnight Over Stellar City · Action Lab
www.actionlabcomics.com

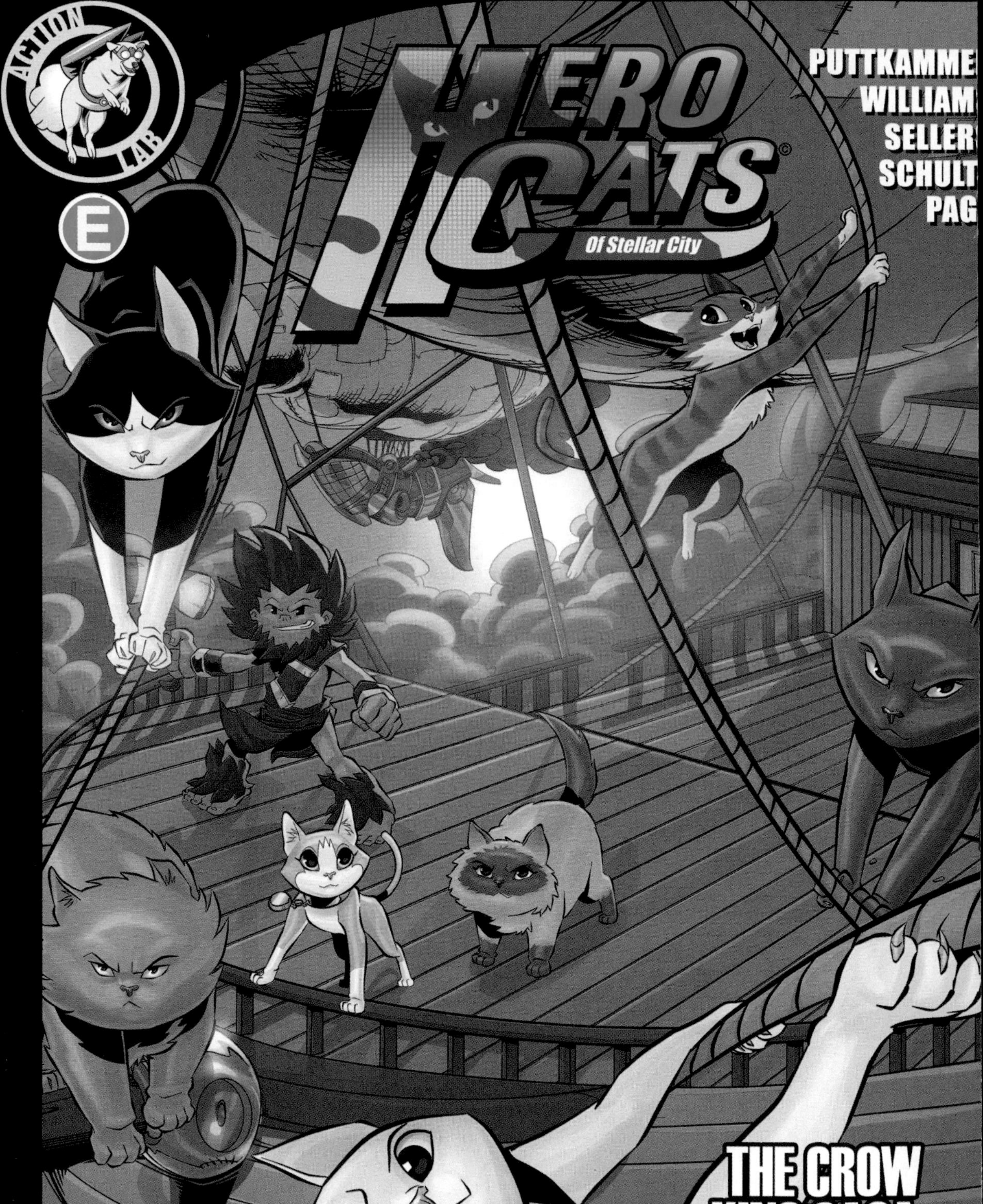
ACTION LAB
E
HERO CATS
Of Stellar City
PUTTKAMME
WILLIAM
SELLER
SCHULT
PAG
THE CROW KING SAGA...
COLLECTED!
AVAILABLE IN FINER STORES EVERYWHER

The Crow King Saga. Worlds collide and heroes unite as the cats face their biggest challenge yet! Meet Bandit as he joins the Hero Cats on a fantastical journey to save Stellar City. Collects Hero Cats of Stellar City 7-9.

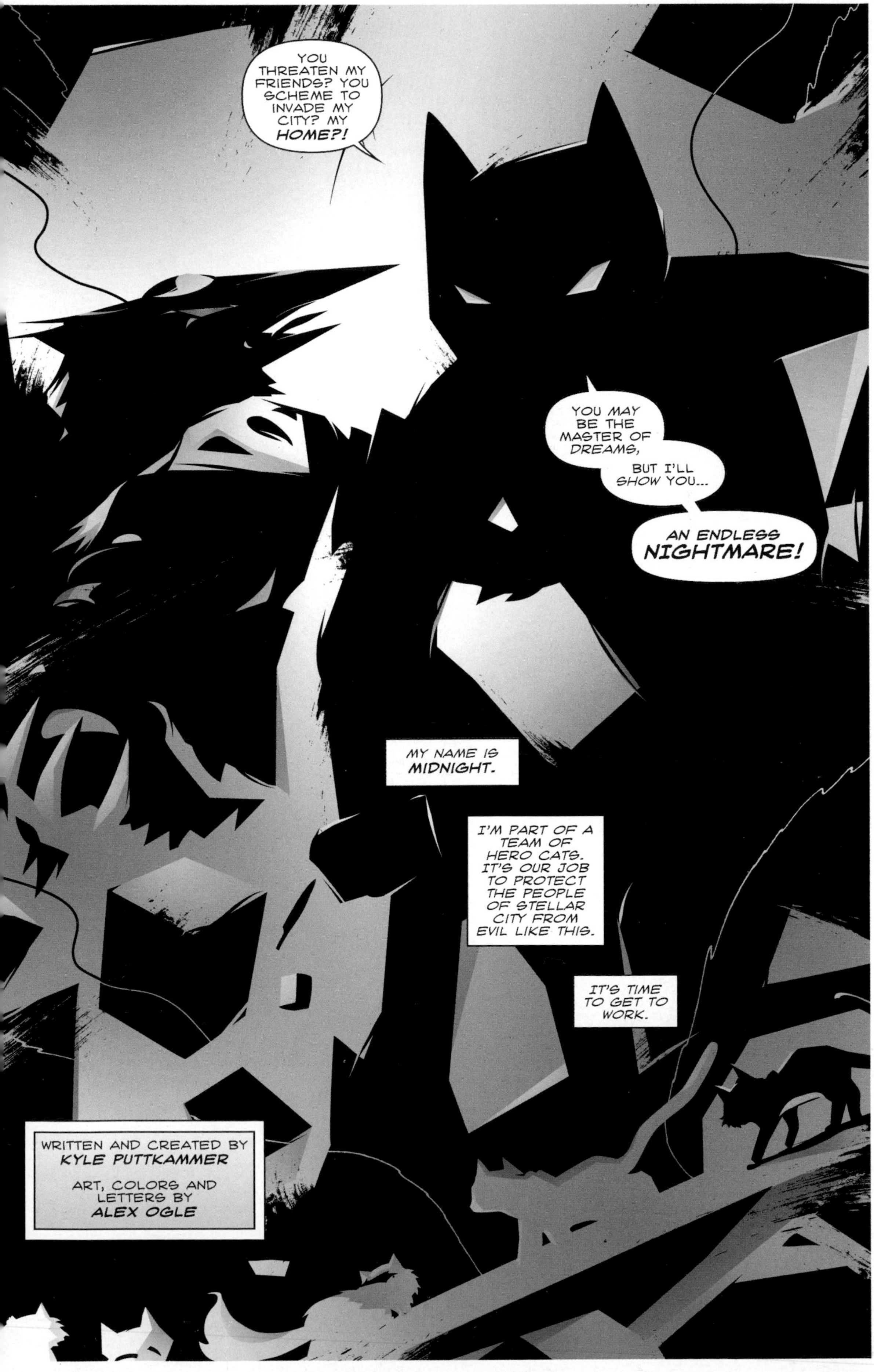
YOU THREATEN MY FRIENDS? YOU SCHEME TO INVADE MY CITY? MY HOME?!
YOU MAY BE THE MASTER OF DREAMS,
BUT I'LL SHOW YOU...
AN ENDLESS NIGHTMARE!
MY NAME IS MIDNIGHT.
I'M PART OF A TEAM OF HERO CATS. IT'S OUR JOB TO PROTECT THE PEOPLE OF STELLAR CITY FROM EVIL LIKE THIS.
IT'S TIME TO GET TO WORK.
WRITTEN AND CREATED BY KYLE PUTTKAMMER
ART, COLORS AND LETTERS BY ALEX OGLE

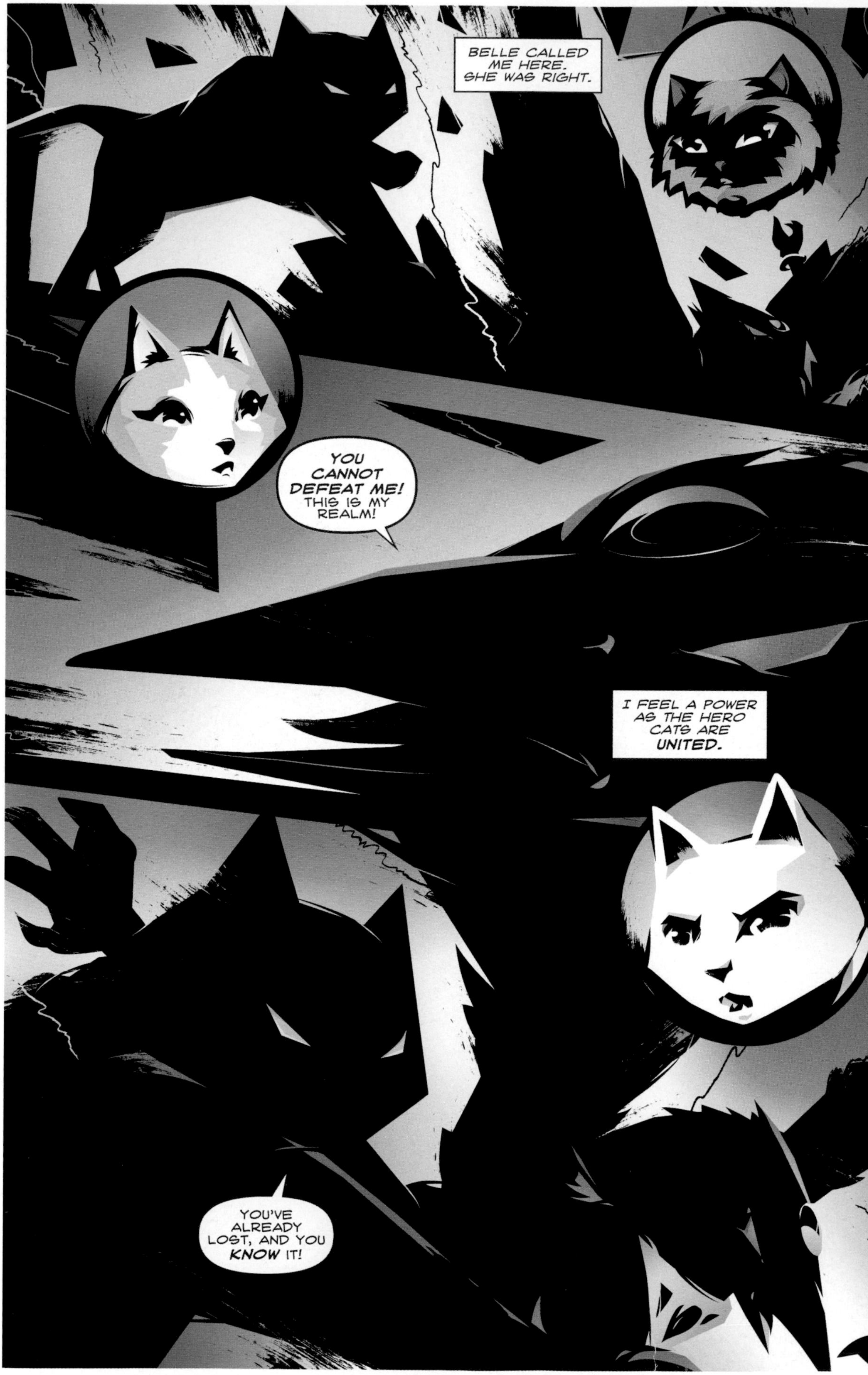
BELLE CALLED ME HERE. SHE WAS RIGHT.
YOU CANNOT DEFEAT ME! THIS IS MY REALM!
I FEEL A POWER AS THE HERO CATS ARE UNITED.
YOU'VE ALREADY LOST, AND YOU KNOW IT!

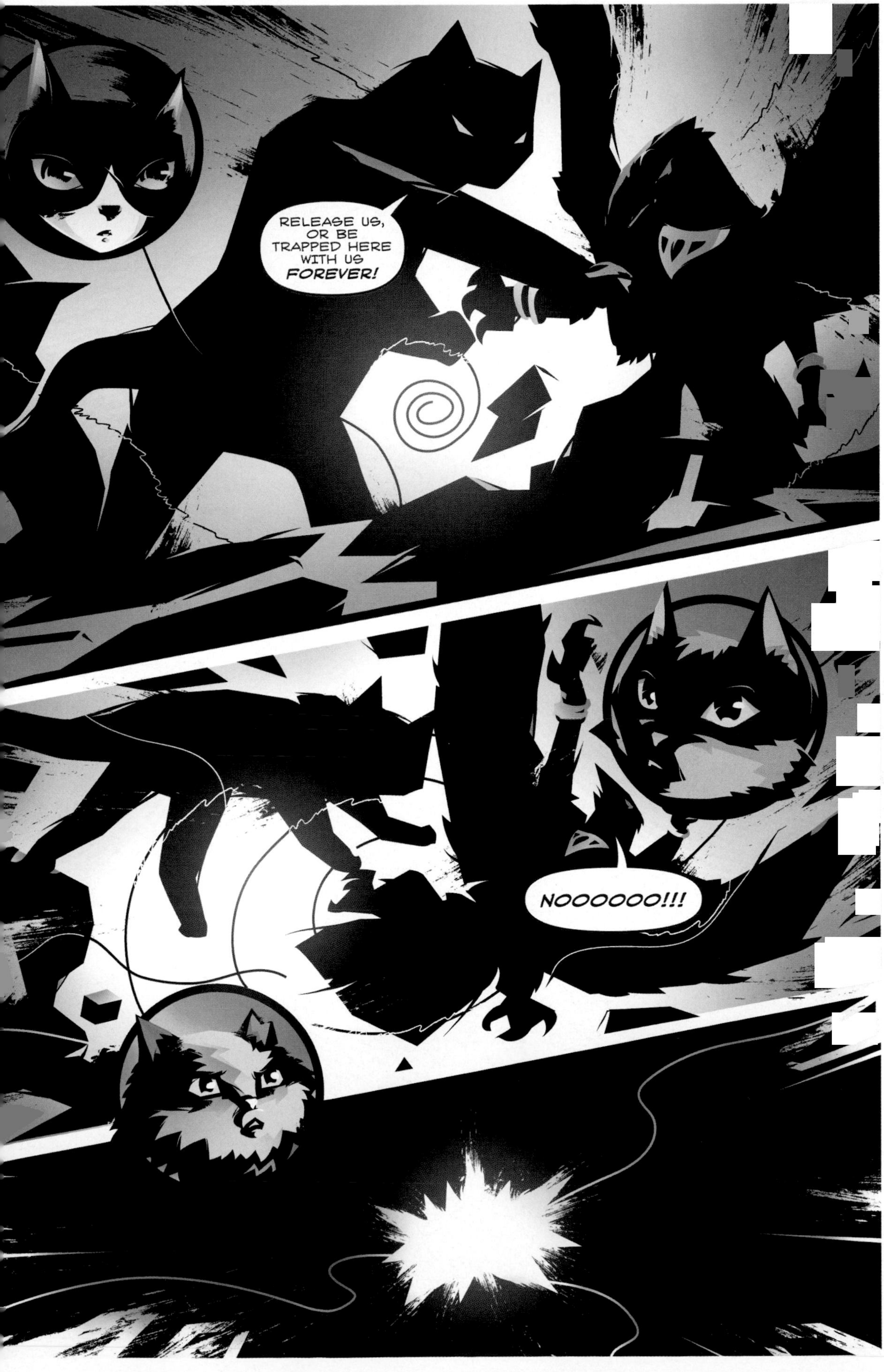
RELEASE US, OR BE TRAPPED HERE WITH US FOREVER!
NOOOOOO!!!

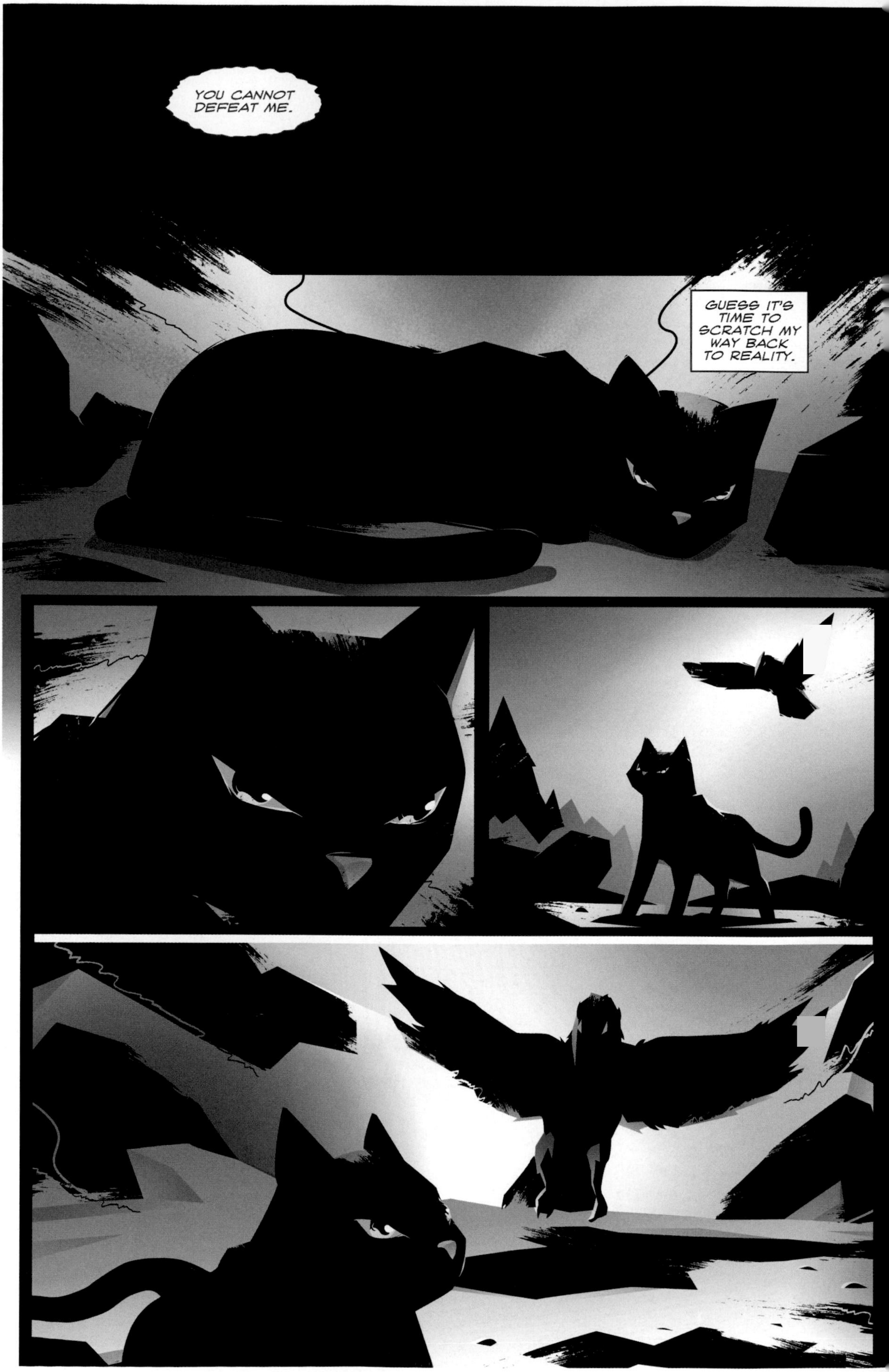
YOU CANNOT DEFEAT ME.
GUESS IT'S TIME TO SCRATCH MY WAY BACK TO REALITY.

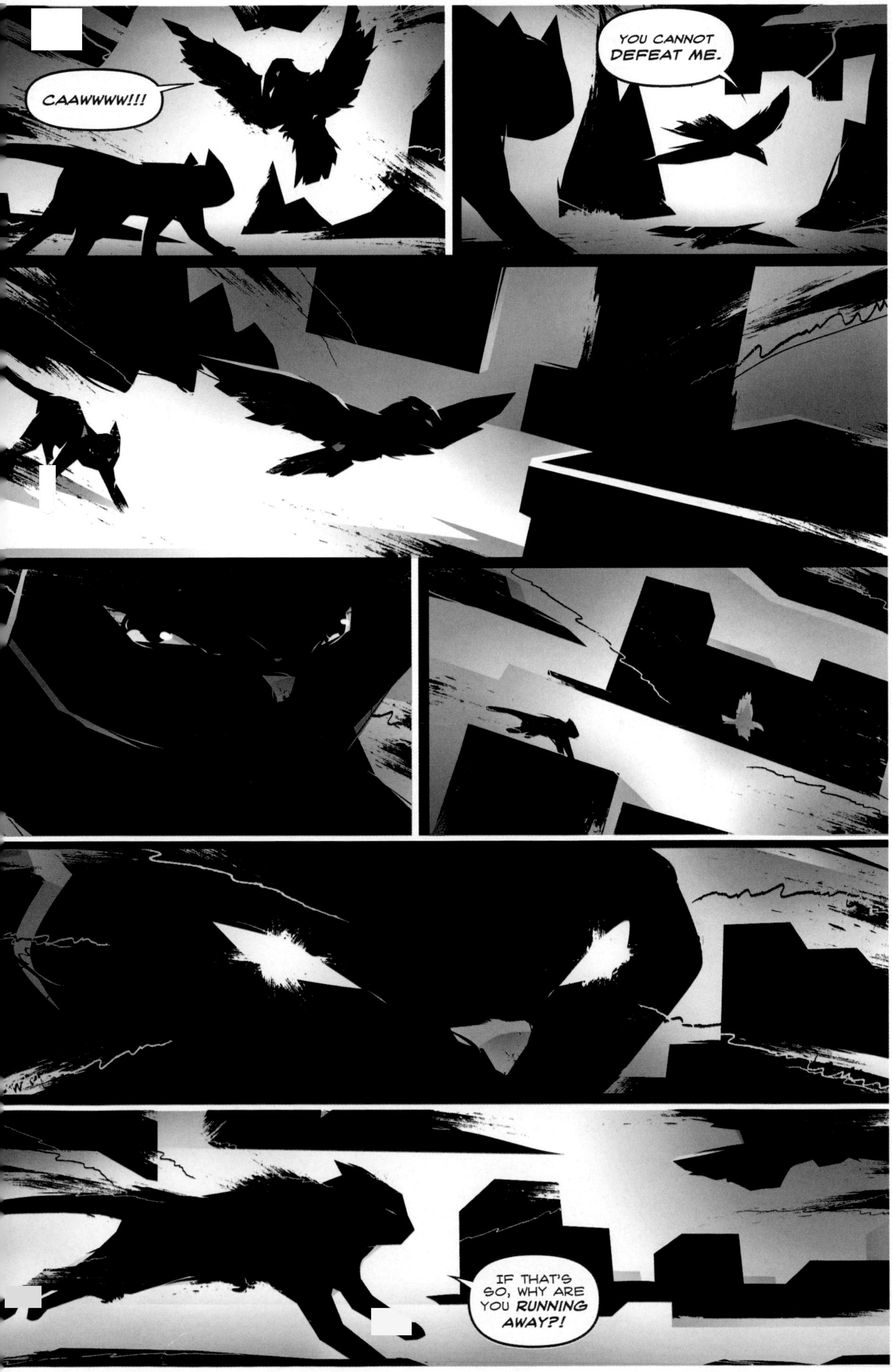
CAAWWWW!!!
YOU CANNOT DEFEAT ME.
IF THAT'S SO, WHY ARE YOU RUNNING AWAY?!

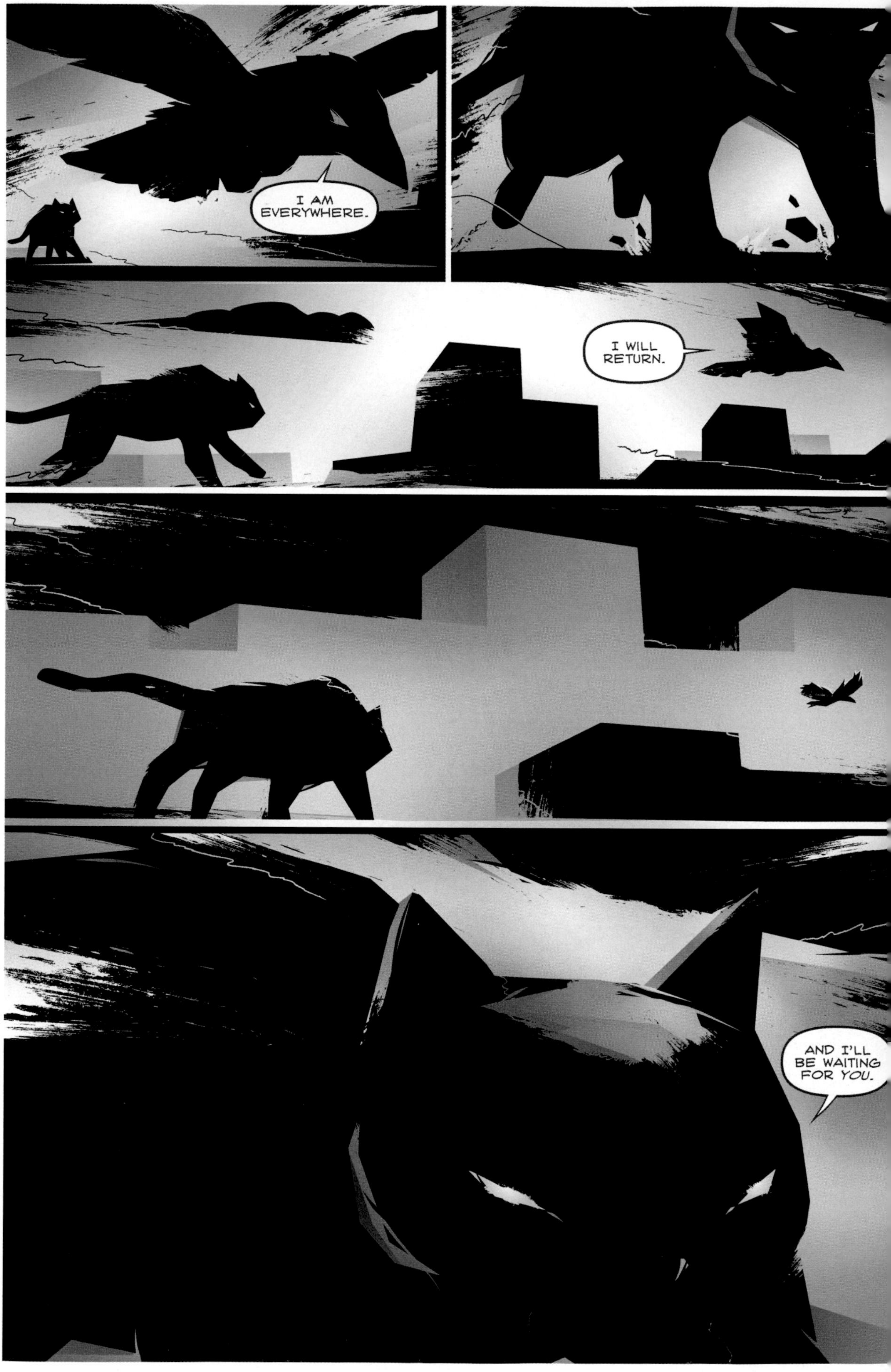
I AM EVERYWHERE.
I WILL RETURN.
AND I'LL BE WAITING FOR *YOU*.

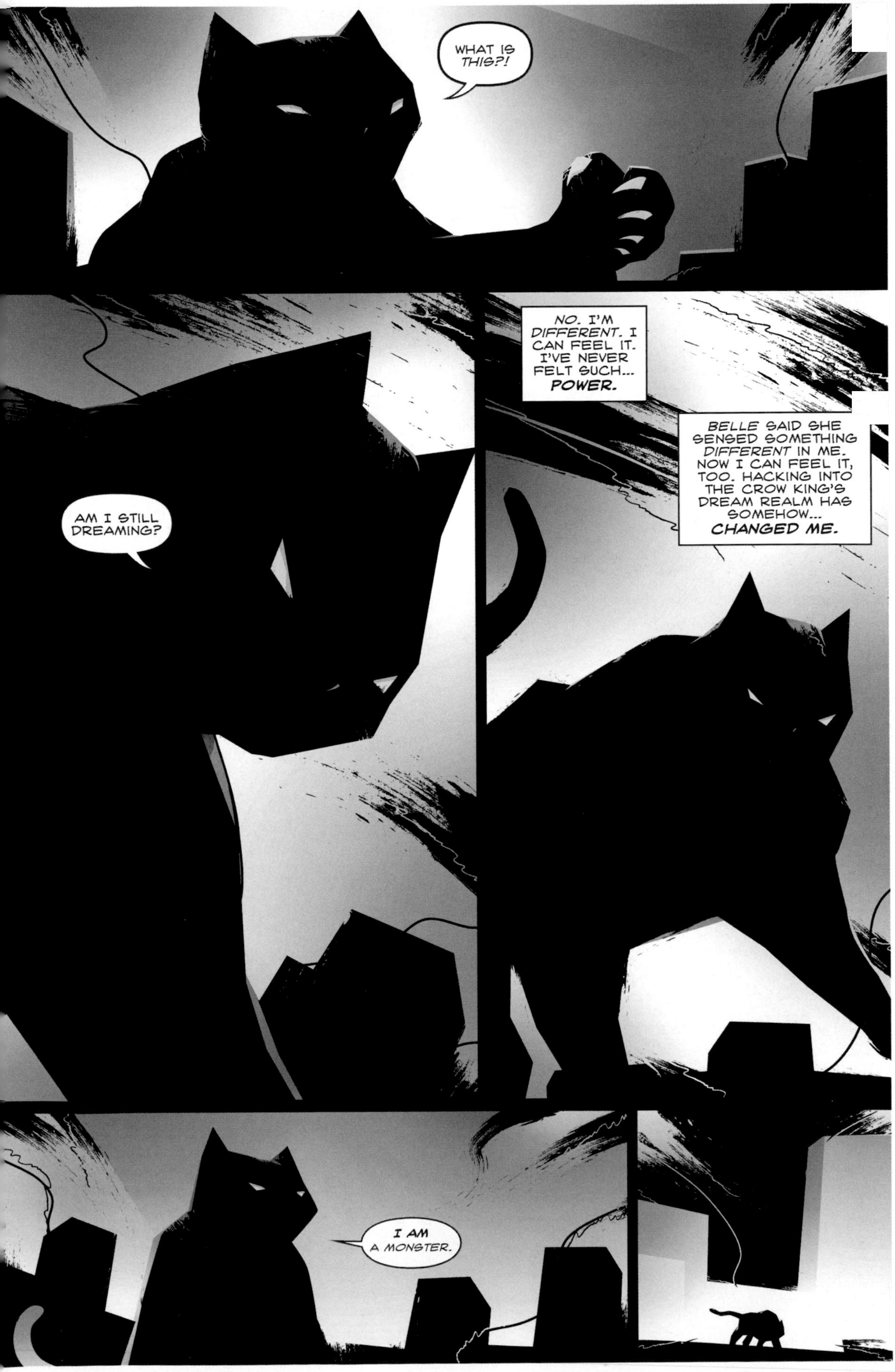
WHAT IS THIS?!
AM I STILL DREAMING?
NO. I'M DIFFERENT. I CAN FEEL IT. I'VE NEVER FELT SUCH... POWER.
BELLE SAID SHE SENSED SOMETHING DIFFERENT IN ME. NOW I CAN FEEL IT, TOO. HACKING INTO THE CROW KING'S DREAM REALM HAS SOMEHOW... CHANGED ME.
I AM A MONSTER.

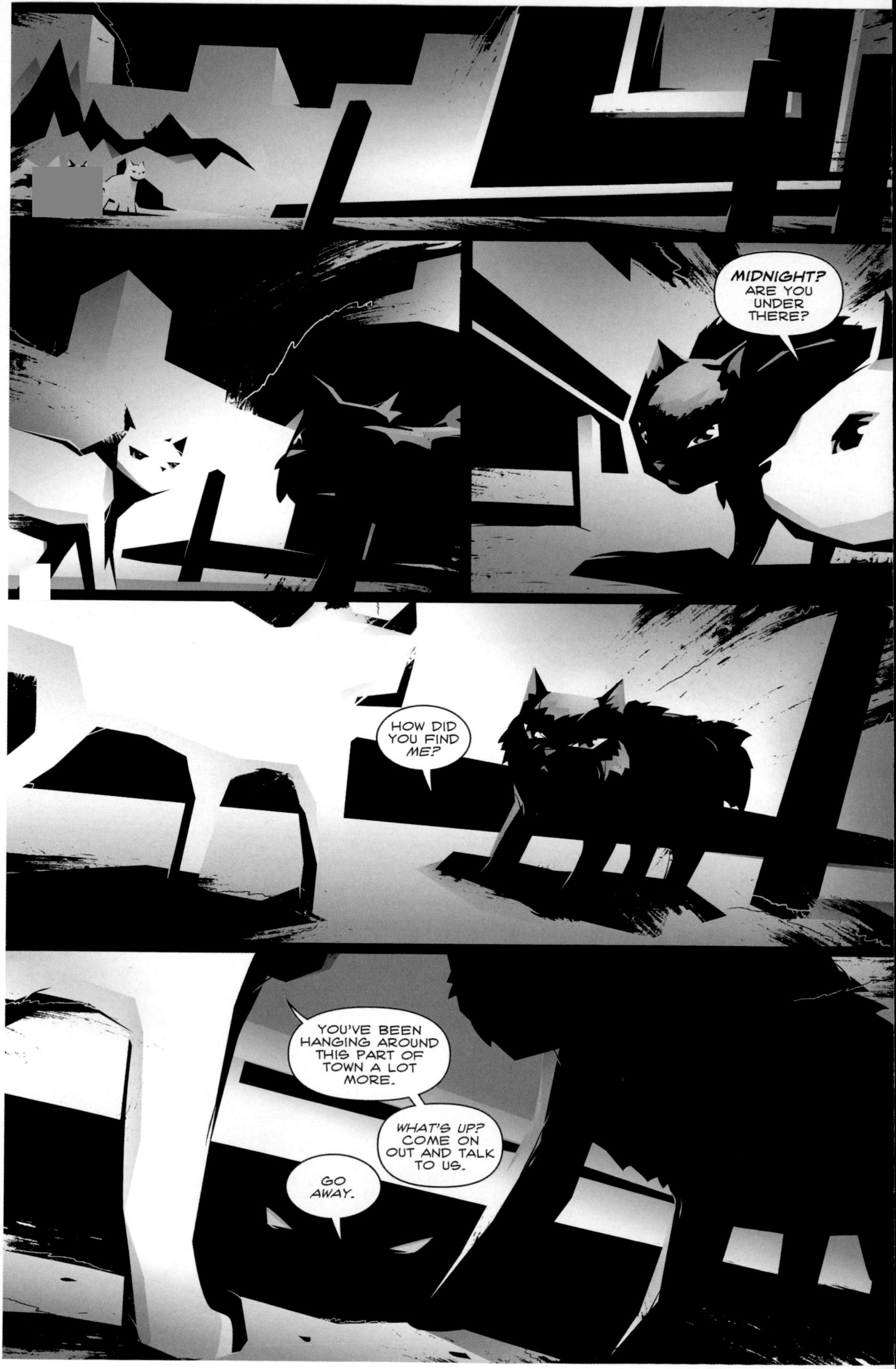
MIDNIGHT? ARE YOU UNDER THERE?
HOW DID YOU FIND ME?
YOU'VE BEEN HANGING AROUND THIS PART OF TOWN A LOT MORE.
WHAT'S UP? COME ON OUT AND TALK TO US.
GO AWAY.

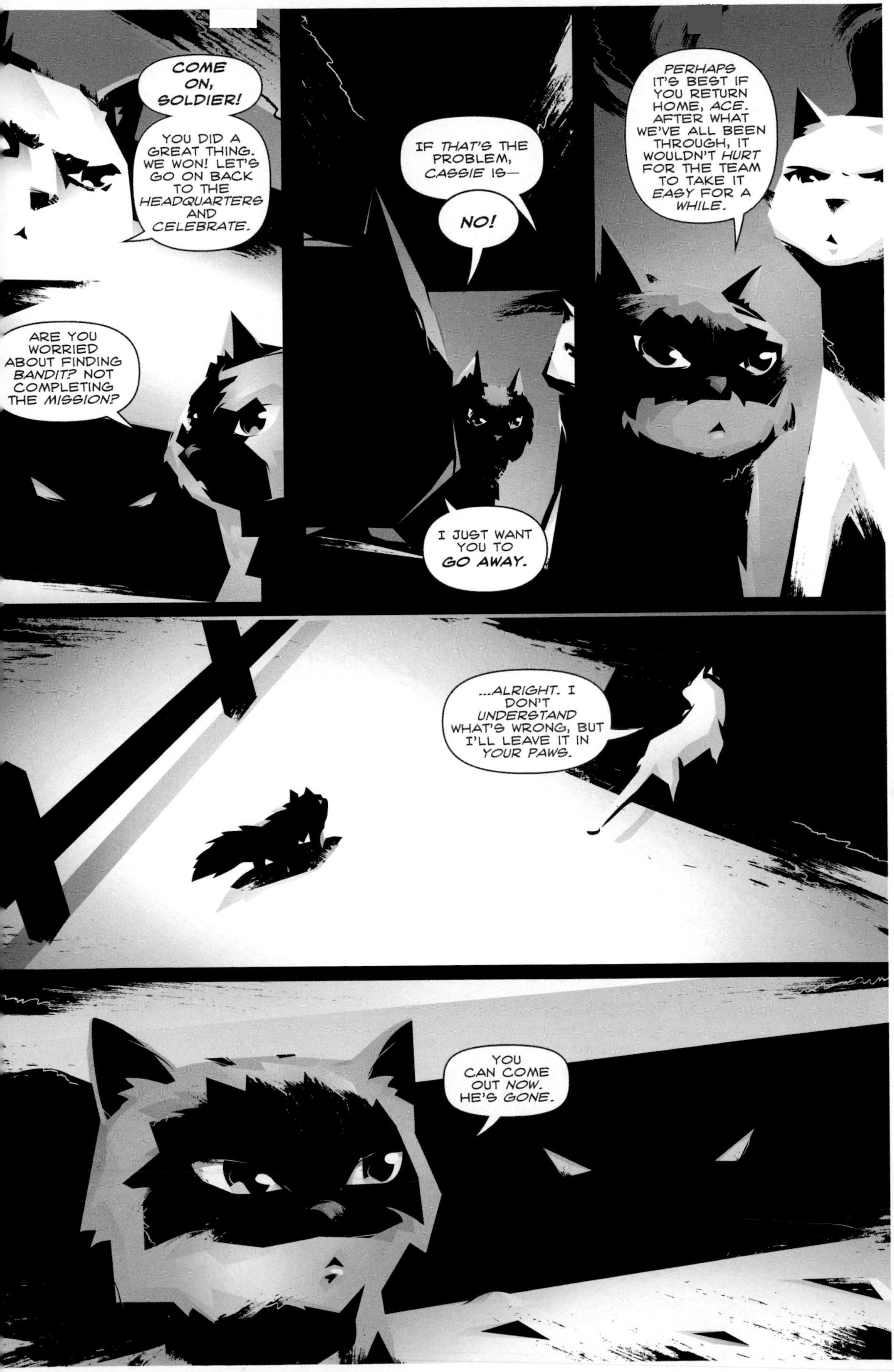
COME ON, SOLDIER!
YOU DID A GREAT THING. WE WON! LET'S GO ON BACK TO THE HEADQUARTERS AND CELEBRATE.
ARE YOU WORRIED ABOUT FINDING BANDIT? NOT COMPLETING THE MISSION?
IF THAT'S THE PROBLEM, CASSIE IS—
NO!
I JUST WANT YOU TO GO AWAY.
PERHAPS IT'S BEST IF YOU RETURN HOME, ACE. AFTER WHAT WE'VE ALL BEEN THROUGH, IT WOULDN'T HURT FOR THE TEAM TO TAKE IT EASY FOR A WHILE.
...ALRIGHT. I DON'T UNDERSTAND WHAT'S WRONG, BUT I'LL LEAVE IT IN YOUR PAWS.
YOU CAN COME OUT NOW. HE'S GONE.

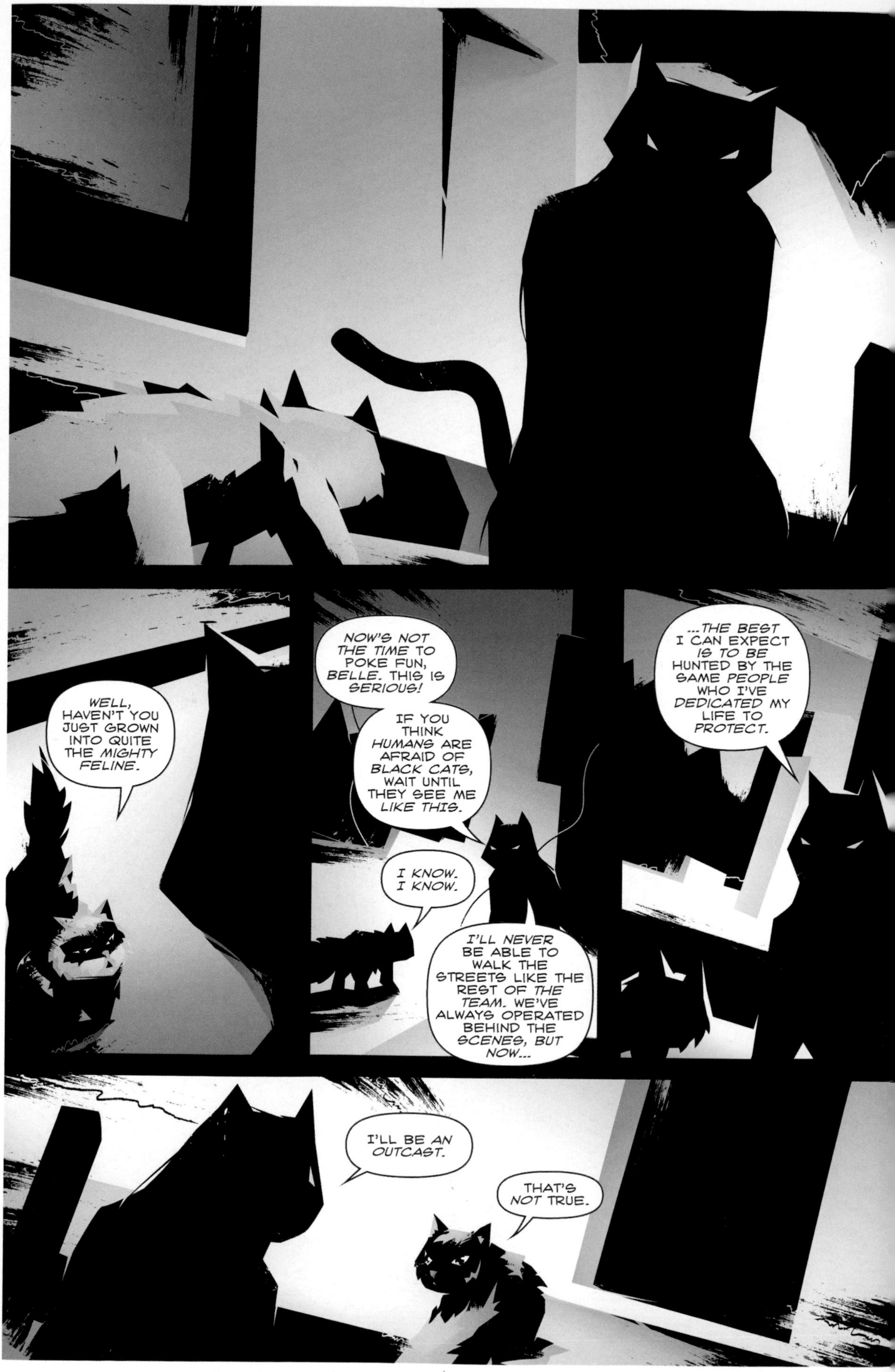
WELL, HAVEN'T YOU JUST GROWN INTO QUITE THE MIGHTY FELINE.
NOW'S NOT THE TIME TO POKE FUN, BELLE. THIS IS SERIOUS!
IF YOU THINK HUMANS ARE AFRAID OF BLACK CATS, WAIT UNTIL THEY SEE ME LIKE THIS.
I KNOW. I KNOW.
I'LL NEVER BE ABLE TO WALK THE STREETS LIKE THE REST OF THE TEAM. WE'VE ALWAYS OPERATED BEHIND THE SCENES, BUT NOW...
...THE BEST I CAN EXPECT IS TO BE HUNTED BY THE SAME PEOPLE WHO I'VE DEDICATED MY LIFE TO PROTECT.
I'LL BE AN OUTCAST.
THAT'S NOT TRUE.

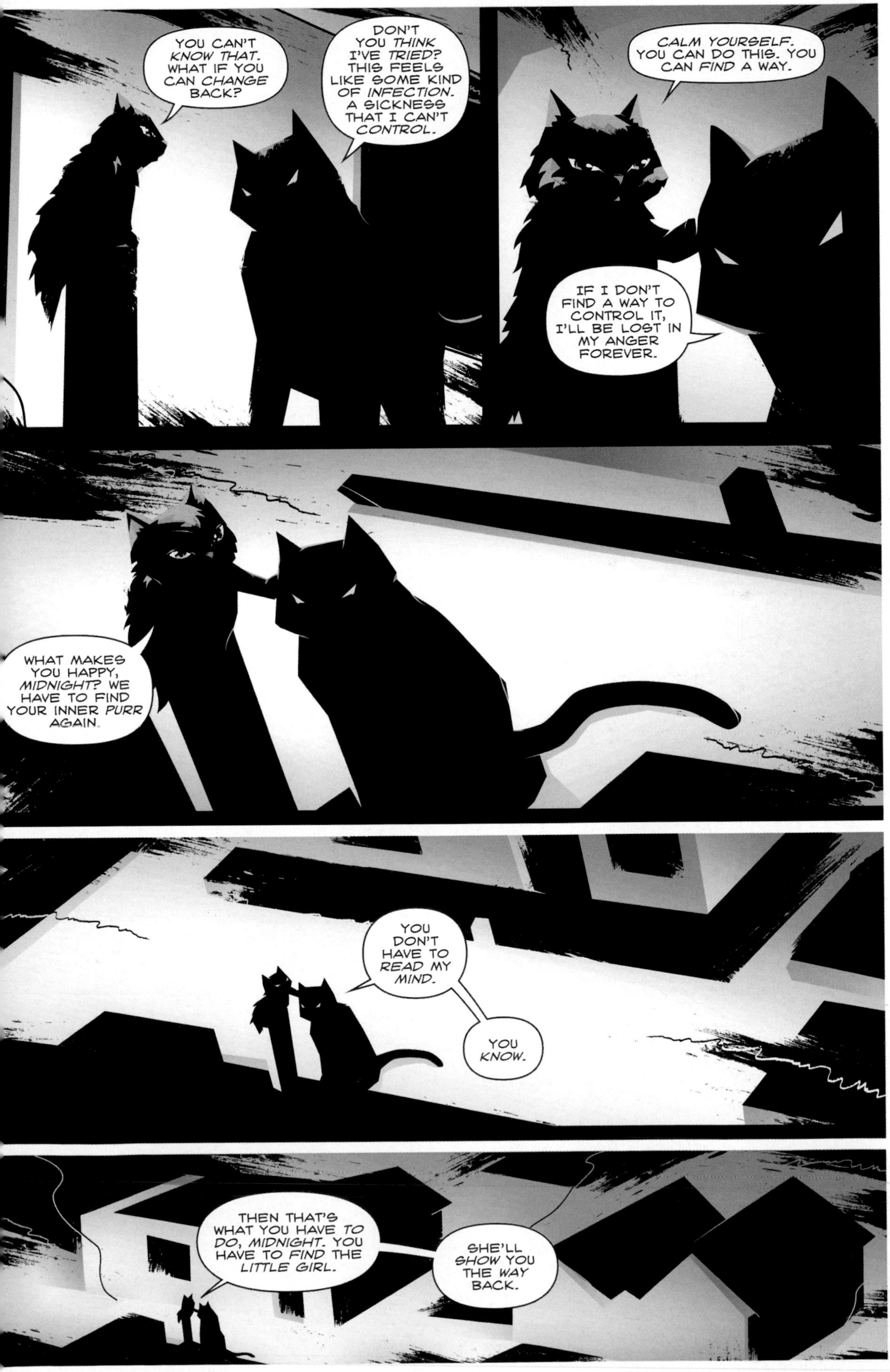
YOU CAN'T KNOW THAT. WHAT IF YOU CAN CHANGE BACK?
DON'T YOU THINK I'VE TRIED? THIS FEELS LIKE SOME KIND OF INFECTION. A SICKNESS THAT I CAN'T CONTROL.
CALM YOURSELF. YOU CAN DO THIS. YOU CAN FIND A WAY.
IF I DON'T FIND A WAY TO CONTROL IT, I'LL BE LOST IN MY ANGER FOREVER.
WHAT MAKES YOU HAPPY, MIDNIGHT? WE HAVE TO FIND YOUR INNER PURR AGAIN.
YOU DON'T HAVE TO READ MY MIND.
YOU KNOW.
THEN THAT'S WHAT YOU HAVE TO DO, MIDNIGHT. YOU HAVE TO FIND THE LITTLE GIRL.
SHE'LL SHOW YOU THE WAY BACK.

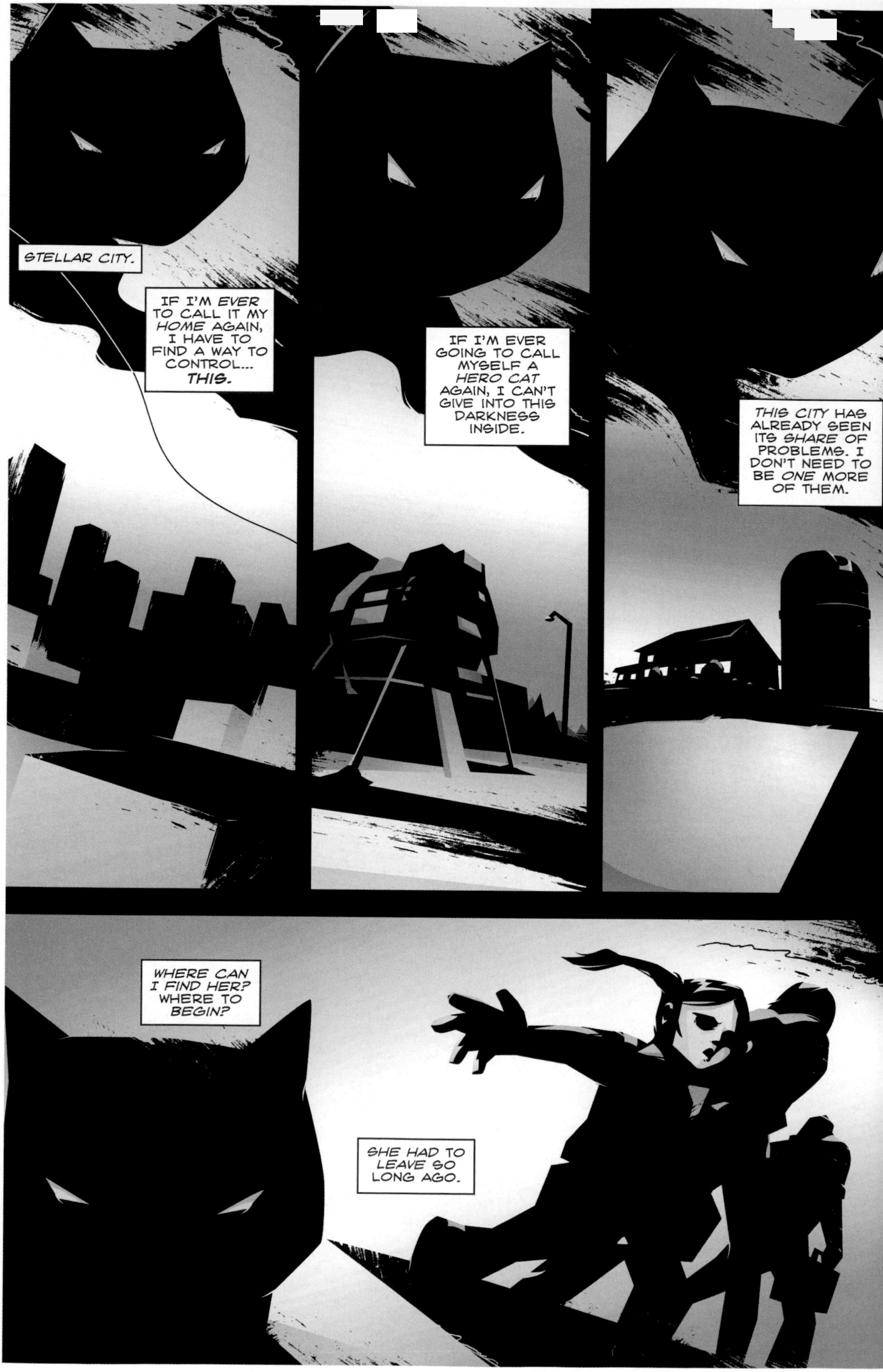
STELLAR CITY.
IF I'M EVER TO CALL IT MY HOME AGAIN, I HAVE TO FIND A WAY TO CONTROL... THIS.
IF I'M EVER GOING TO CALL MYSELF A HERO CAT AGAIN, I CAN'T GIVE INTO THIS DARKNESS INSIDE.
THIS CITY HAS ALREADY SEEN ITS SHARE OF PROBLEMS. I DON'T NEED TO BE ONE MORE OF THEM.
WHERE CAN I FIND HER? WHERE TO BEGIN?
SHE HAD TO LEAVE SO LONG AGO.

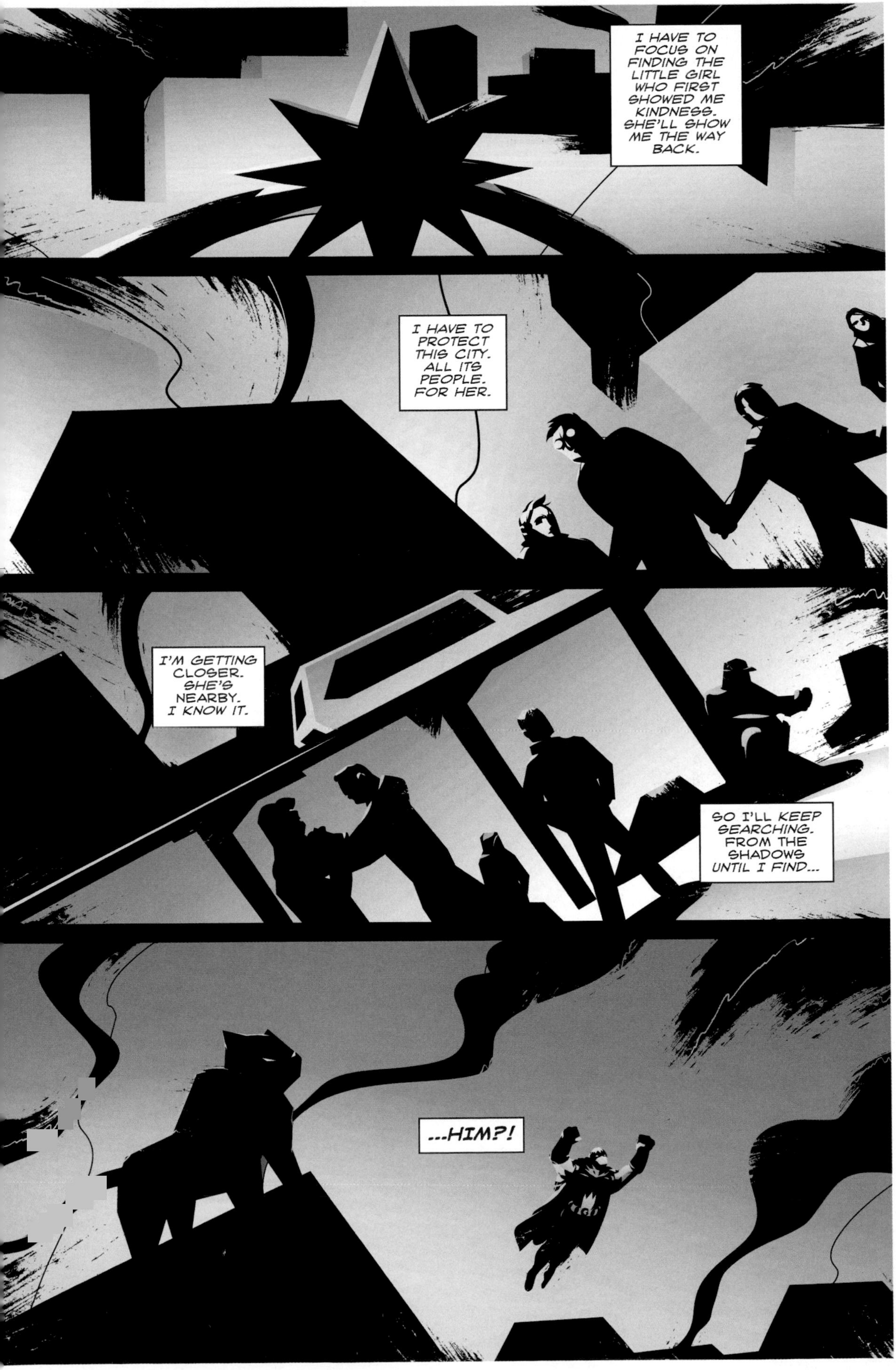
I HAVE TO FOCUS ON FINDING THE LITTLE GIRL WHO FIRST SHOWED ME KINDNESS. SHE'LL SHOW ME THE WAY BACK.
I HAVE TO PROTECT THIS CITY. ALL ITS PEOPLE. FOR HER.
I'M GETTING CLOSER. SHE'S NEARBY. I KNOW IT.
SO I'LL KEEP SEARCHING. FROM THE SHADOWS UNTIL I FIND...
...HIM?!

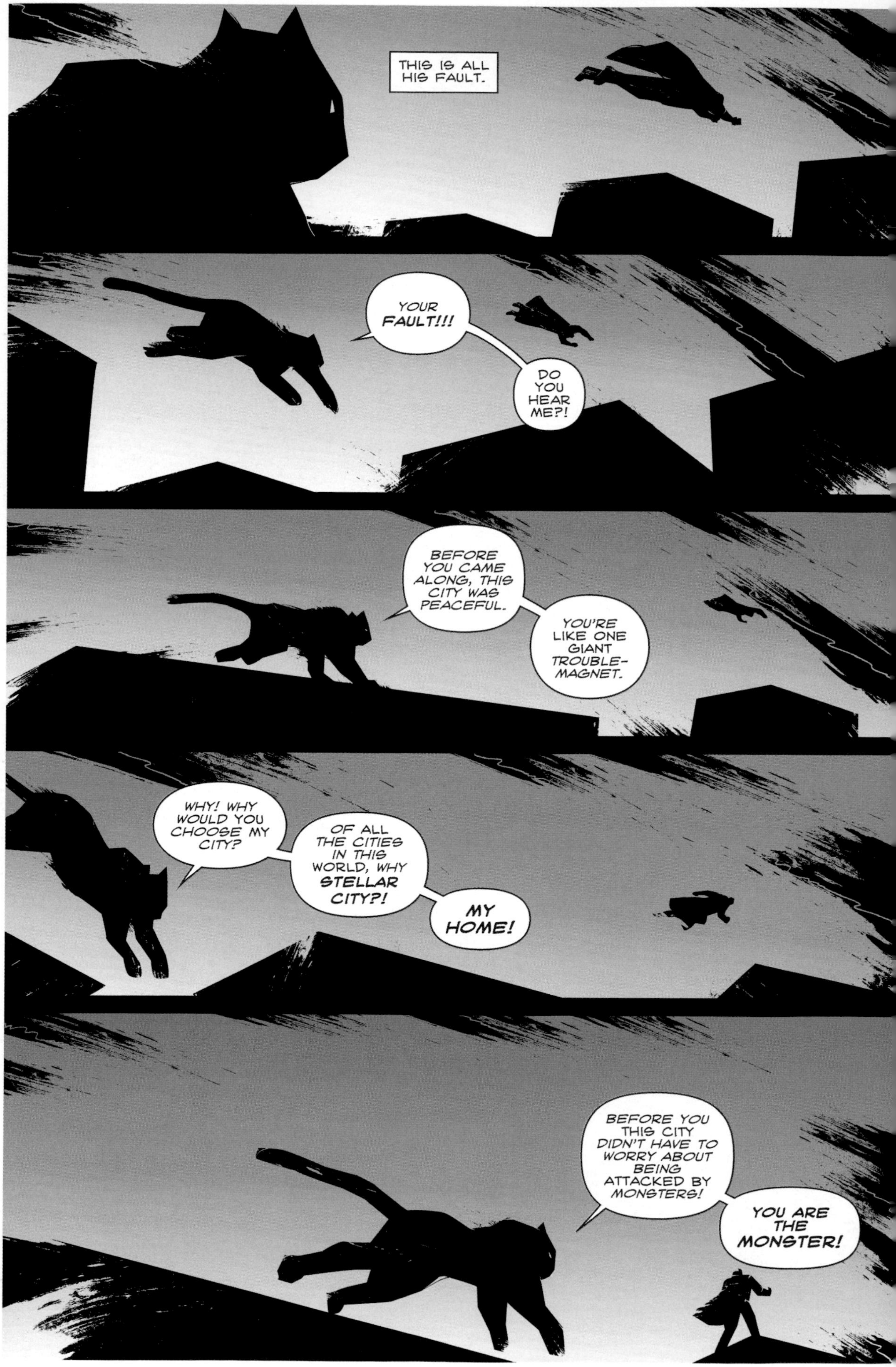
THIS IS ALL HIS FAULT.
YOUR FAULT!!!
DO YOU HEAR ME?!
BEFORE YOU CAME ALONG, THIS CITY WAS PEACEFUL.
YOU'RE LIKE ONE GIANT TROUBLE-MAGNET.
WHY! WHY WOULD YOU CHOOSE MY CITY?
OF ALL THE CITIES IN THIS WORLD, WHY STELLAR CITY?!
MY HOME!
BEFORE YOU THIS CITY DIDN'T HAVE TO WORRY ABOUT BEING ATTACKED BY MONSTERS!
YOU ARE THE MONSTER!

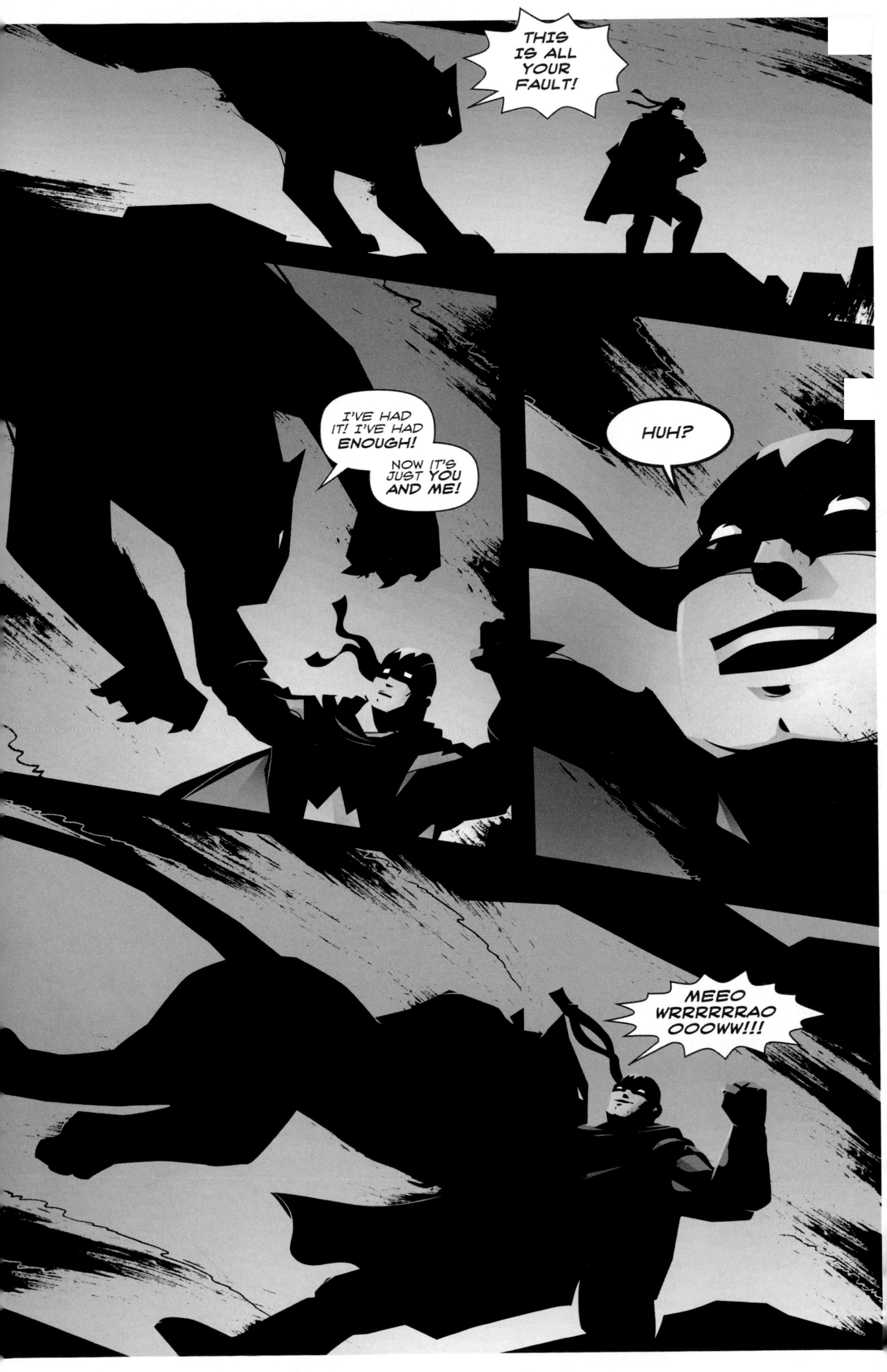
THIS IS ALL YOUR FAULT!
I'VE HAD IT! I'VE HAD ENOUGH!
NOW IT'S JUST YOU AND ME!
HUH?
MEEO WRRRRRRAO OOOWW!!!

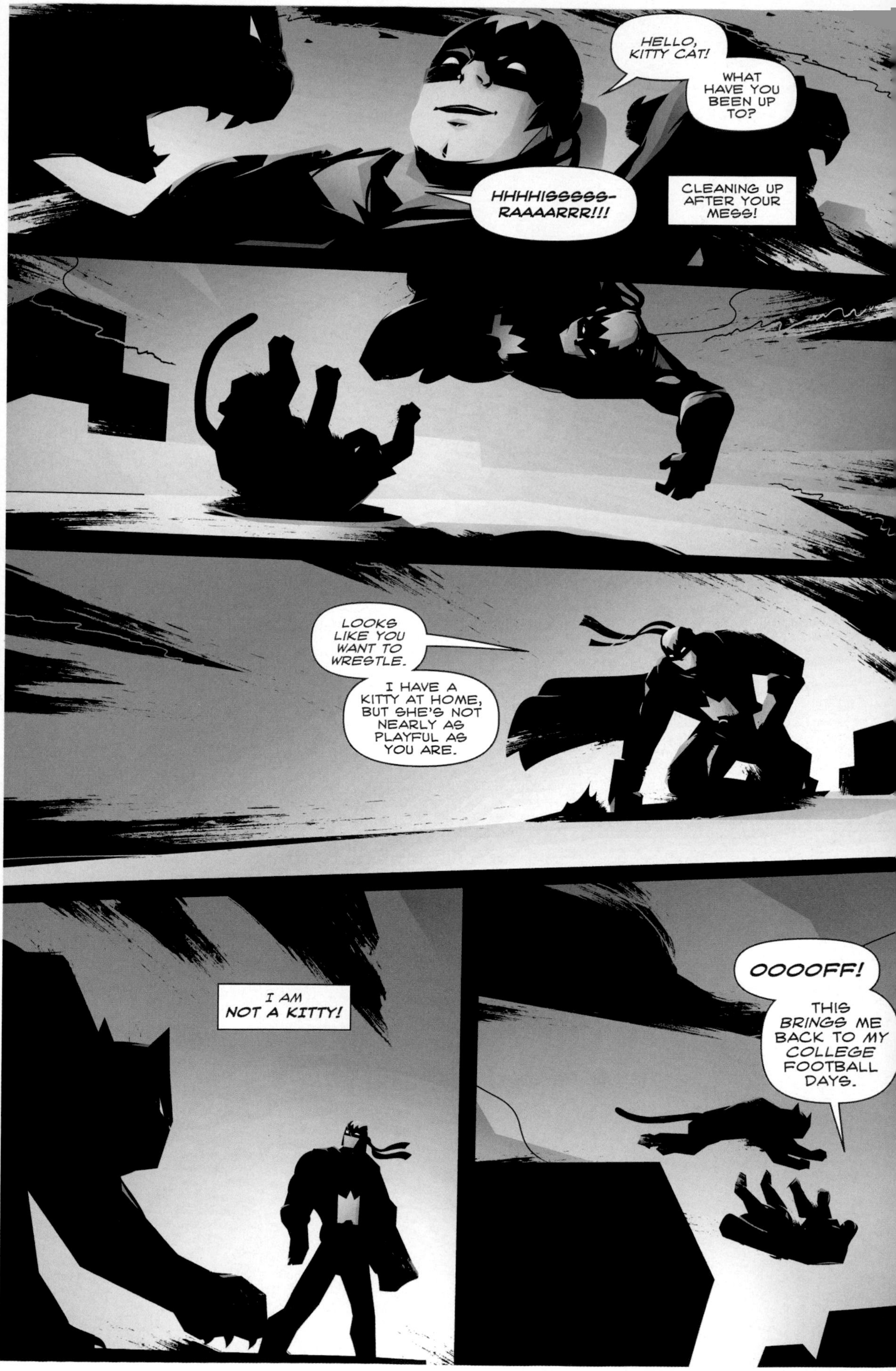

HELLO, KITTY CAT!
WHAT HAVE YOU BEEN UP TO?
HHHHISSSSS-RAAAARRR!!!
CLEANING UP AFTER YOUR MESS!
LOOKS LIKE YOU WANT TO WRESTLE.
I HAVE A KITTY AT HOME, BUT SHE'S NOT NEARLY AS PLAYFUL AS YOU ARE.
I AM NOT A KITTY!
OOOOFF!
THIS BRINGS ME BACK TO MY COLLEGE FOOTBALL DAYS.

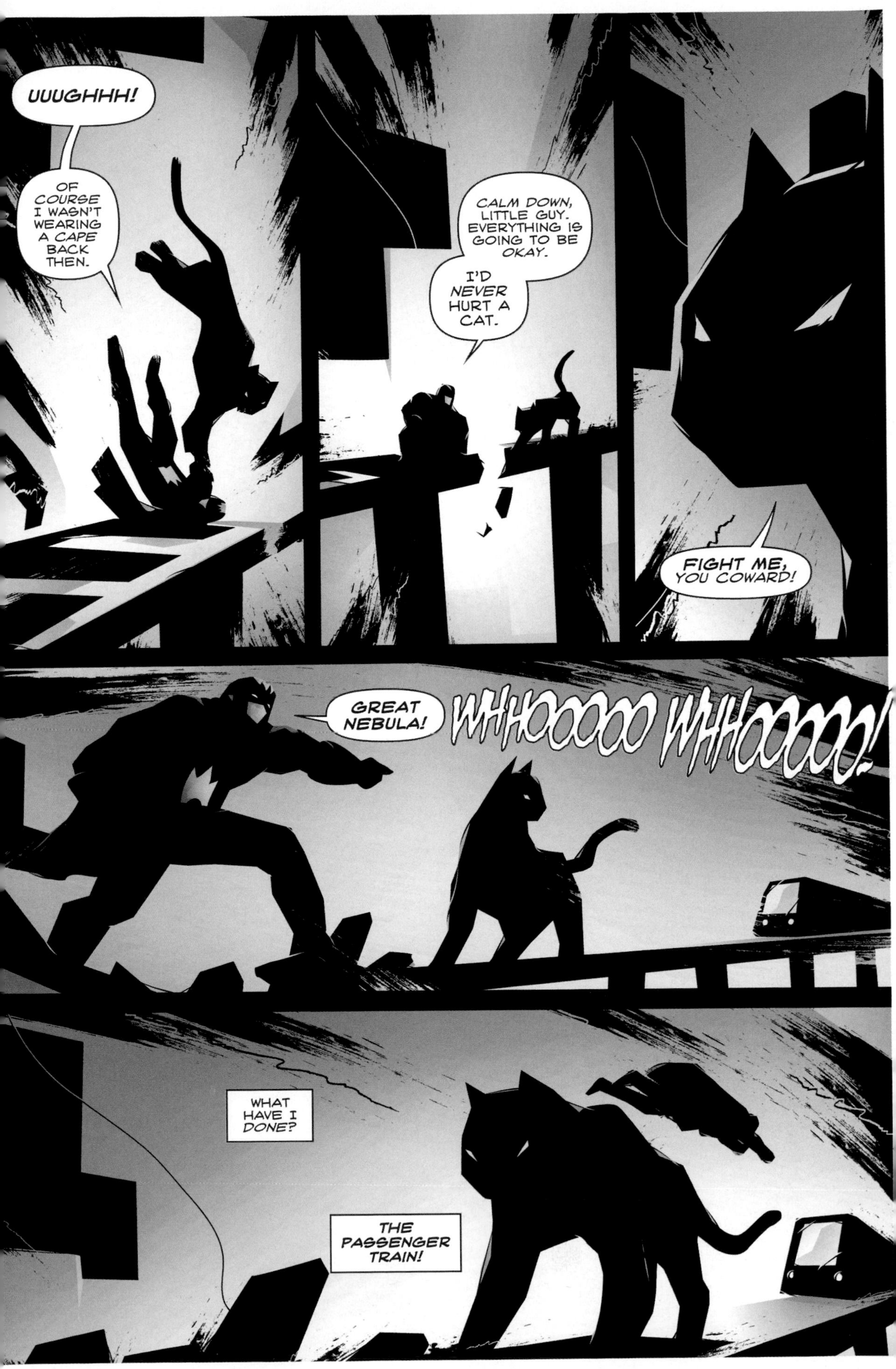
UUUGHHH!
OF COURSE I WASN'T WEARING A CAPE BACK THEN.
CALM DOWN, LITTLE GUY. EVERYTHING IS GOING TO BE OKAY.
I'D NEVER HURT A CAT.
FIGHT ME, YOU COWARD!
GREAT NEBULA!
WHHOOOOO WHHOOOOO!
WHAT HAVE I DONE?
THE PASSENGER TRAIN!

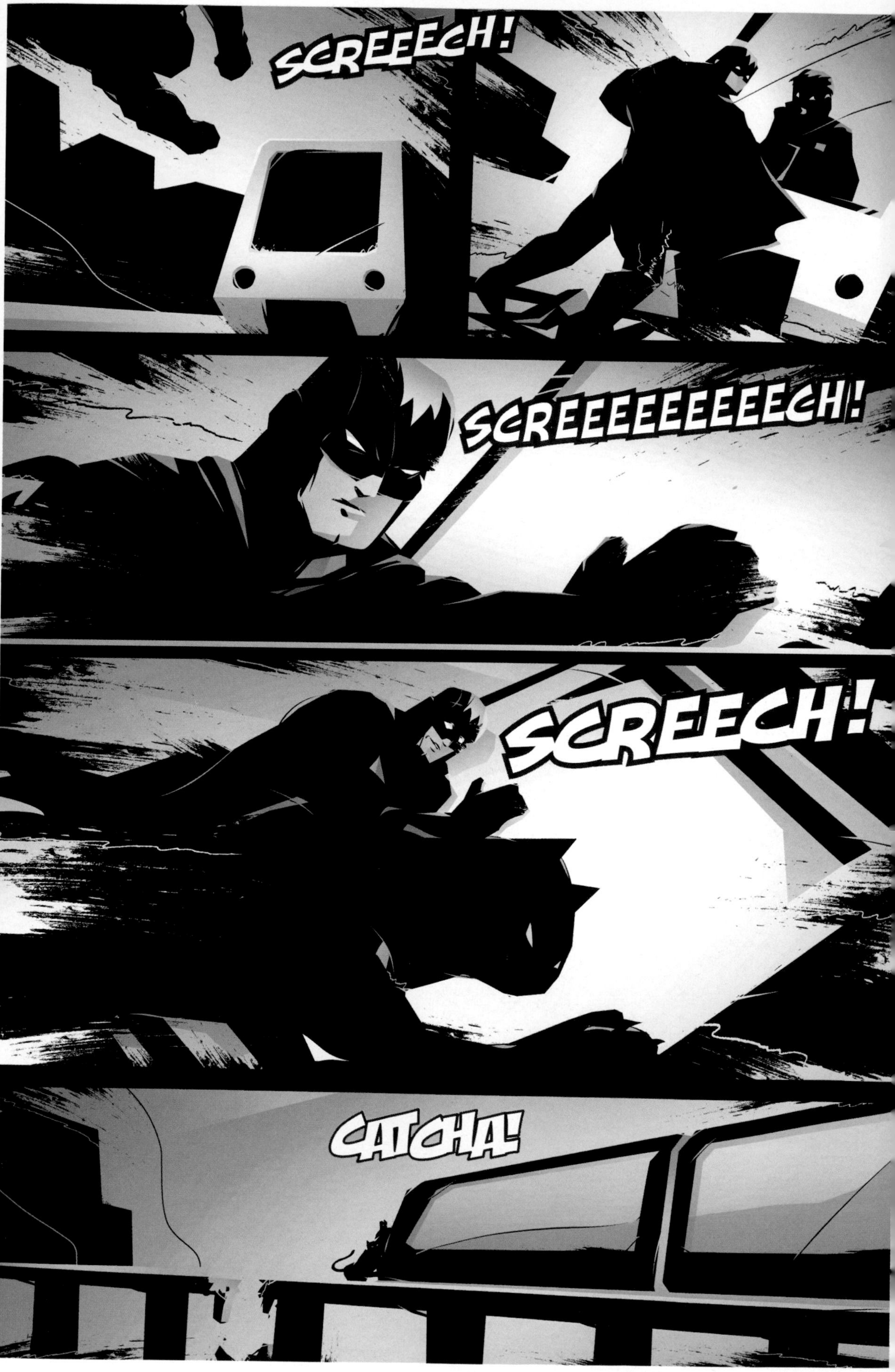
SCREEECH!
SCREEEEEEEEEECH!
SCREECH!
CATCHA!

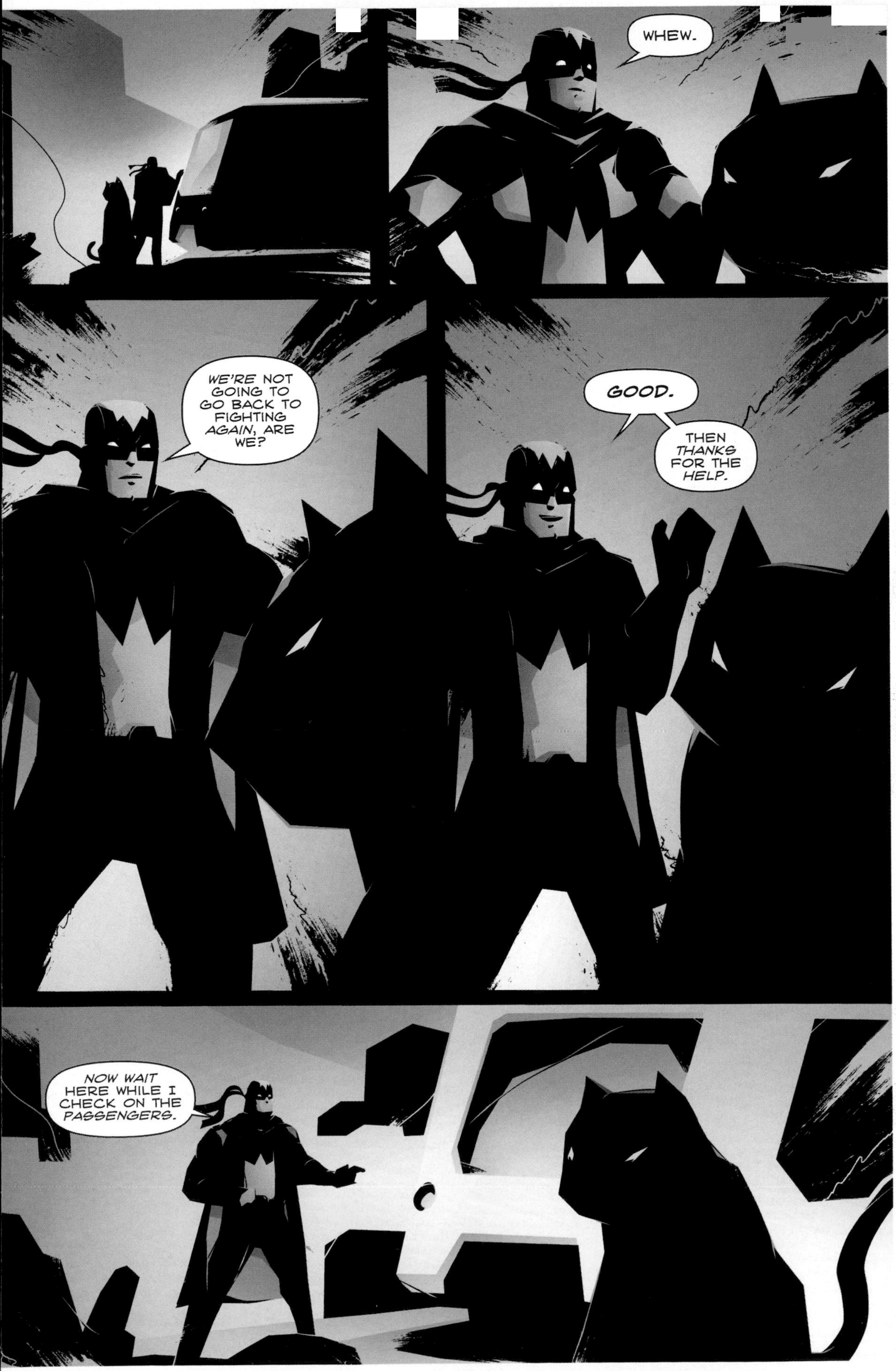
WHEW.
WE'RE NOT GOING TO GO BACK TO FIGHTING AGAIN, ARE WE?
GOOD.
THEN THANKS FOR THE HELP.
NOW WAIT HERE WHILE I CHECK ON THE PASSENGERS.

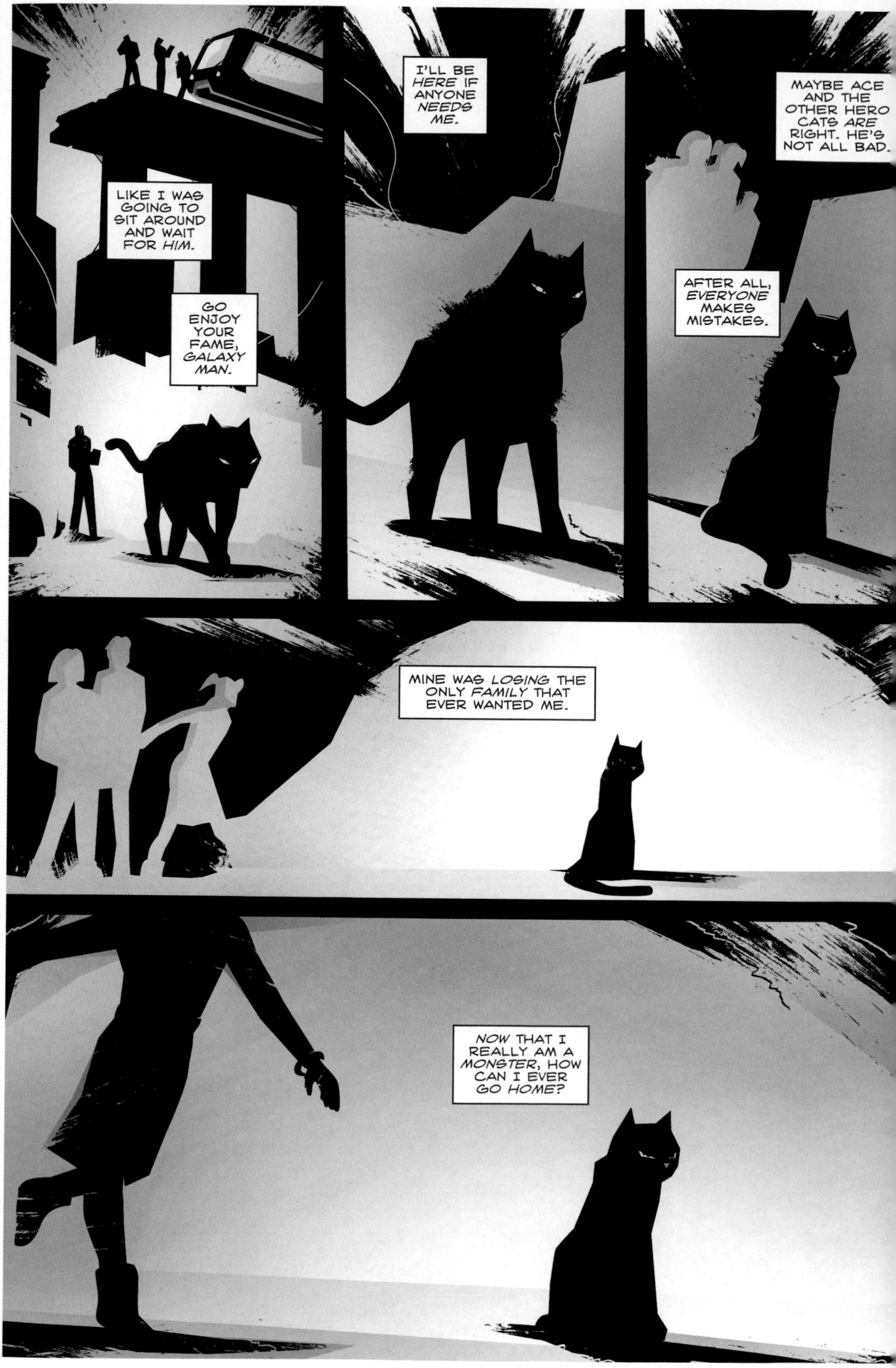
LIKE I WAS GOING TO SIT AROUND AND WAIT FOR *HIM*.
GO ENJOY YOUR FAME, *GALAXY MAN*.
I'LL BE *HERE* IF ANYONE *NEEDS ME*.
MAYBE ACE AND THE OTHER HERO CATS *ARE* RIGHT. HE'S NOT ALL BAD.
AFTER ALL, *EVERYONE* MAKES MISTAKES.
MINE WAS *LOSING* THE ONLY *FAMILY* THAT EVER WANTED ME.
NOW THAT I REALLY AM A *MONSTER*, HOW CAN I EVER GO *HOME*?

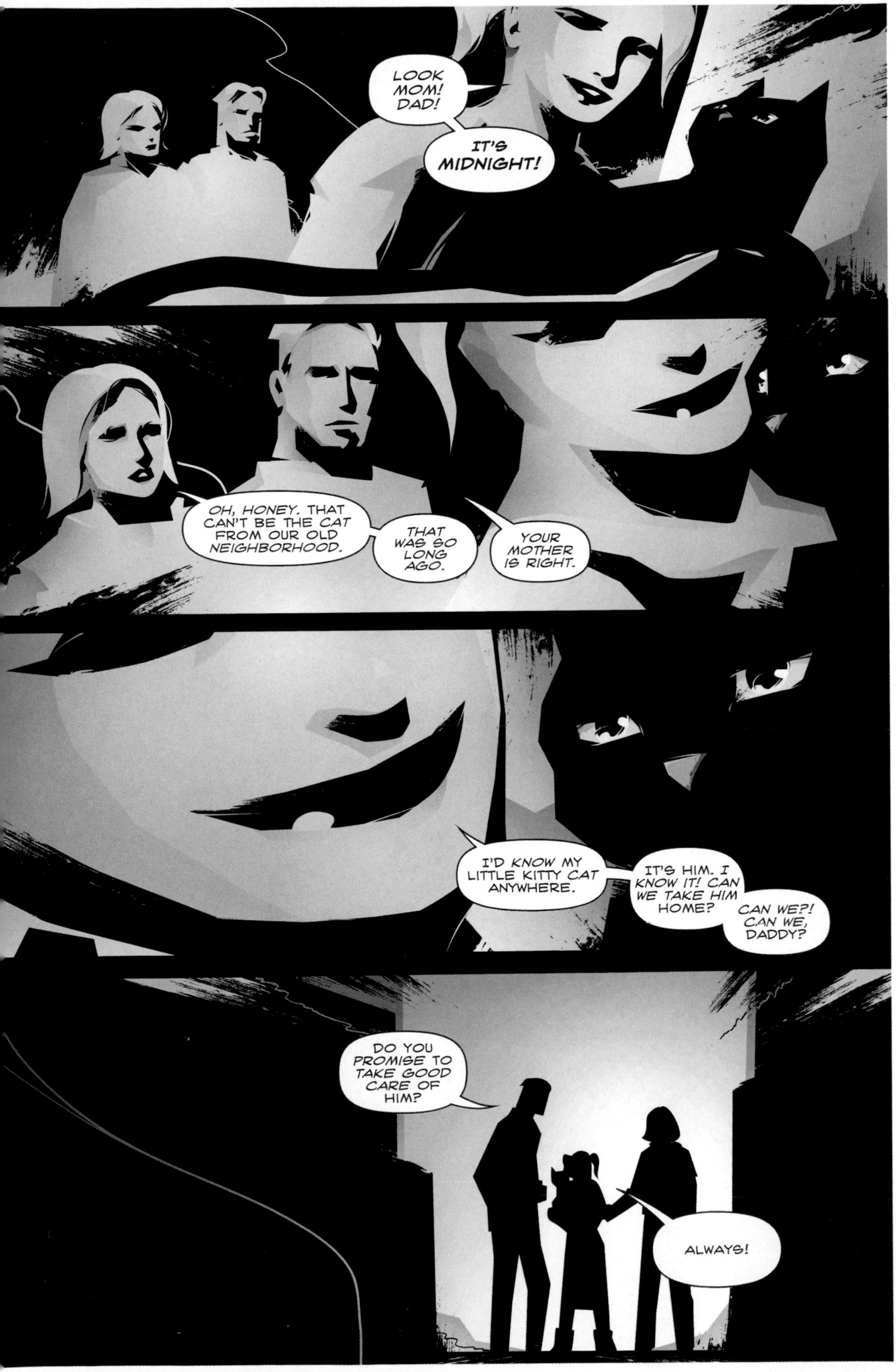
LOOK MOM! DAD!
IT'S MIDNIGHT!
OH, HONEY. THAT CAN'T BE THE CAT FROM OUR OLD NEIGHBORHOOD.
THAT WAS SO LONG AGO.
YOUR MOTHER IS RIGHT.
I'D KNOW MY LITTLE KITTY CAT ANYWHERE.
IT'S HIM. I KNOW IT! CAN WE TAKE HIM HOME?
CAN WE?! CAN WE, DADDY?
DO YOU PROMISE TO TAKE GOOD CARE OF HIM?
ALWAYS!

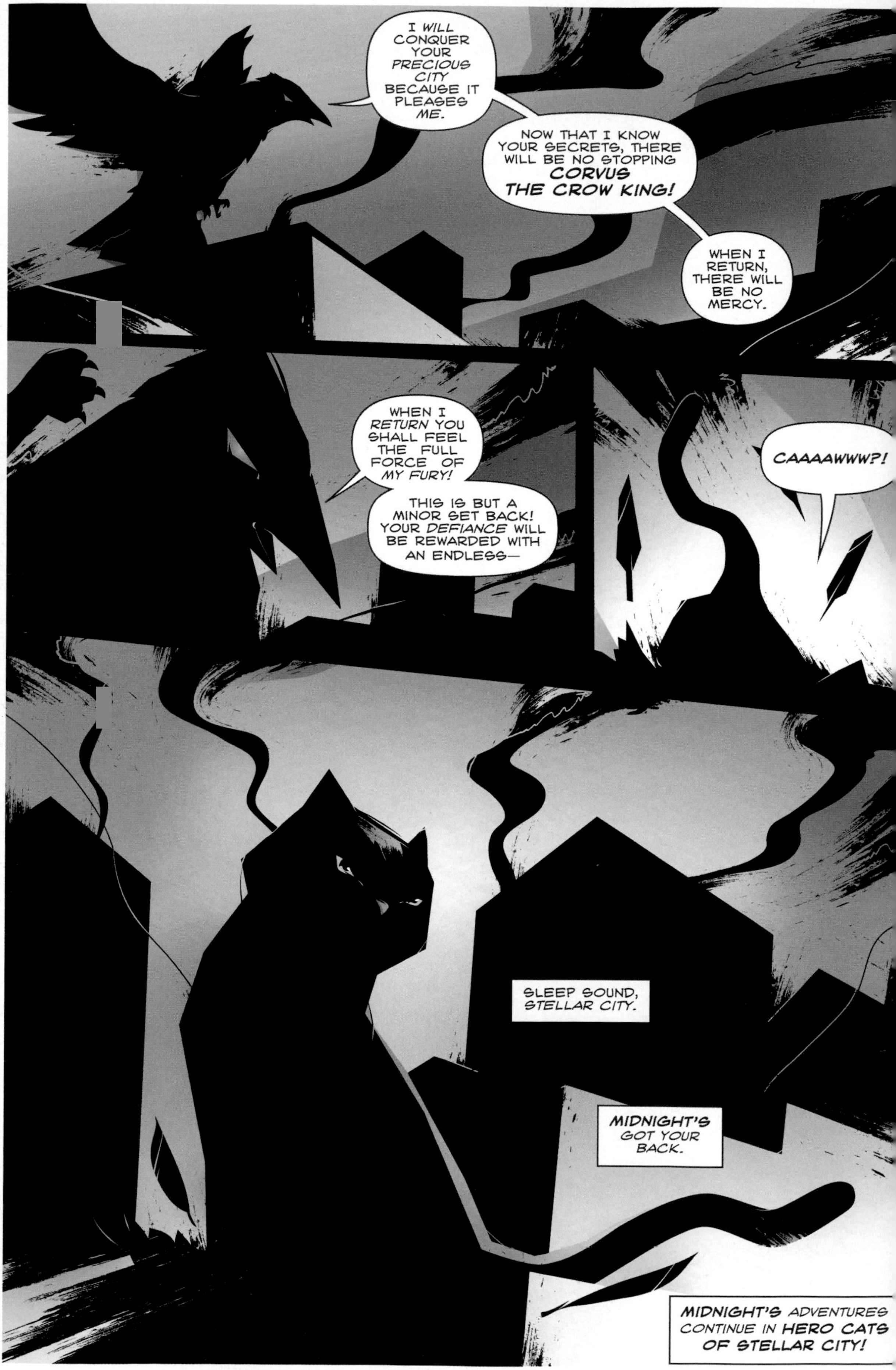
I WILL CONQUER YOUR PRECIOUS CITY BECAUSE IT PLEASES ME.
NOW THAT I KNOW YOUR SECRETS, THERE WILL BE NO STOPPING CORVUS THE CROW KING!
WHEN I RETURN, THERE WILL BE NO MERCY.
WHEN I RETURN YOU SHALL FEEL THE FULL FORCE OF MY FURY!
THIS IS BUT A MINOR SET BACK! YOUR DEFIANCE WILL BE REWARDED WITH AN ENDLESS—
CAAAAWWW?!
SLEEP SOUND, STELLAR CITY.
MIDNIGHT'S GOT YOUR BACK.
MIDNIGHT'S ADVENTURES CONTINUE IN HERO CATS OF STELLAR CITY!

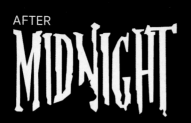

AFTER MIDNIGHT

TIPS FOR **DRAWING COMICS**

WITH ALEX OGLE

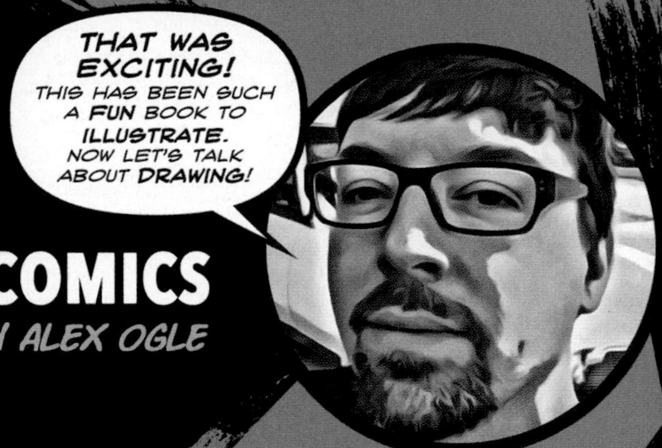
THAT WAS EXCITING! THIS HAS BEEN SUCH A FUN BOOK TO ILLUSTRATE. NOW LET'S TALK ABOUT DRAWING!

GET STARTED!

WE ALL BEGIN SOMEWHERE. TRY STARTING BY FOLLOWING STEP BY STEP GUIDES.

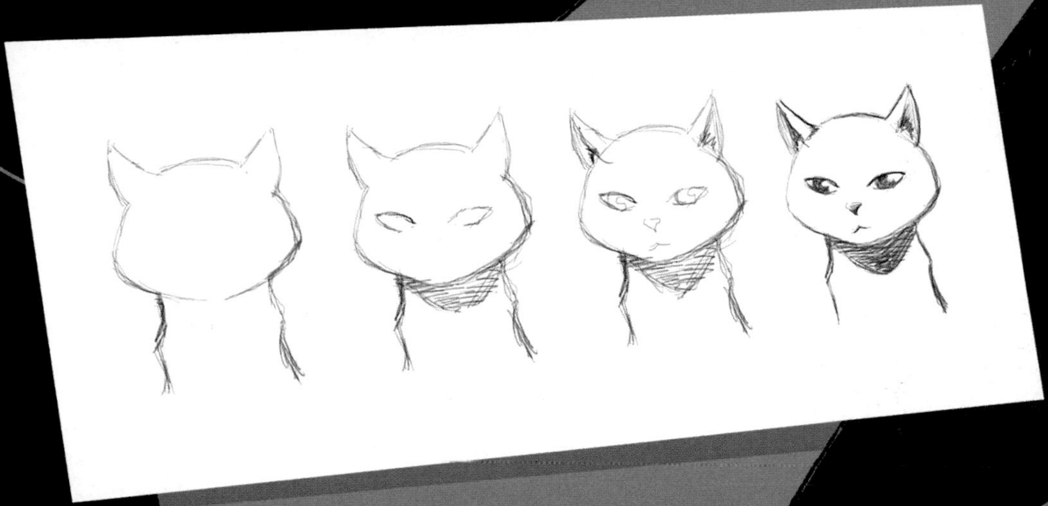

MAKE IT 3D!

THINK ABOUT THE 3D SHAPES THAT MAKE UP YOUR FIGURES AS YOU DRAW. SKETCH THE FORMS LIGHTLY AND DRAW DARKER CLEAN LINES OVER THEM.

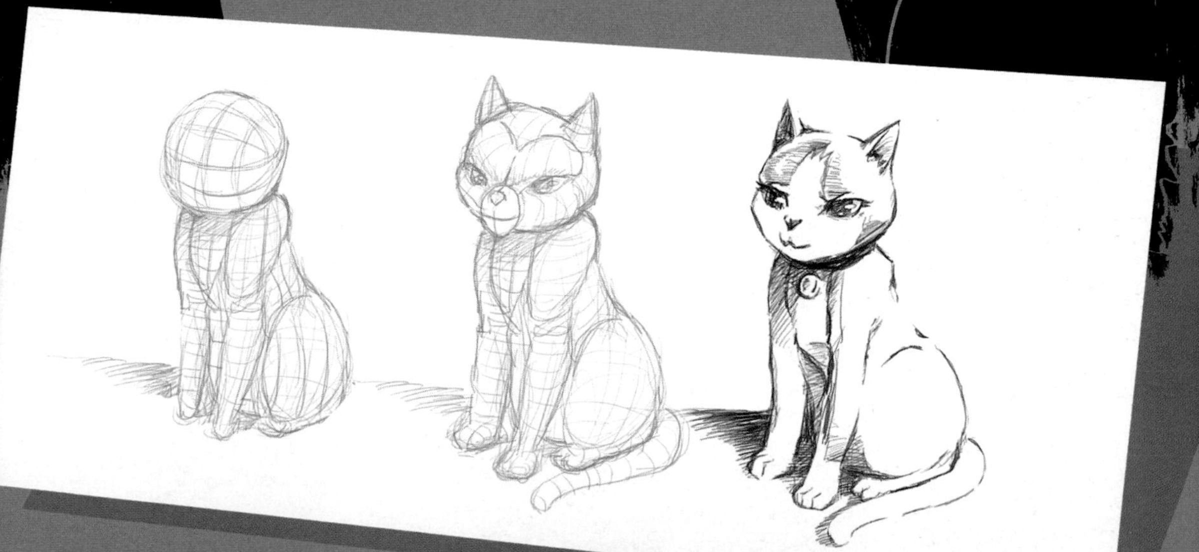

STAY MOTIVATED!

IT CAN TAKE A LONG TIME TO DEVELOP YOUR TALENT. JUST REMEMBER IT IS FUN TO TELL STORIES NO MATTER WHAT YOUR SKILL LEVEL. HAVE FUN AND EACH COMIC YOU MAKE WILL BE BETTER THAN YOUR LAST.

PRACTICE DRAWING PAGES!

COMICS ARE MADE OF PANELS. MOST PAGES HAVE FOUR TO FIVE PANELS. DRAW SOME PAGES AND TRY TO SPACE YOUR CHARACTERS EVENLY.

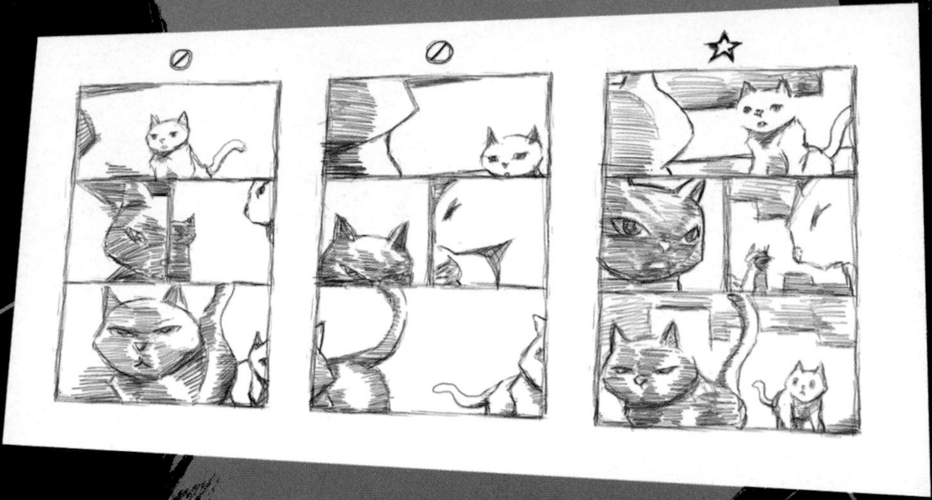

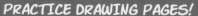

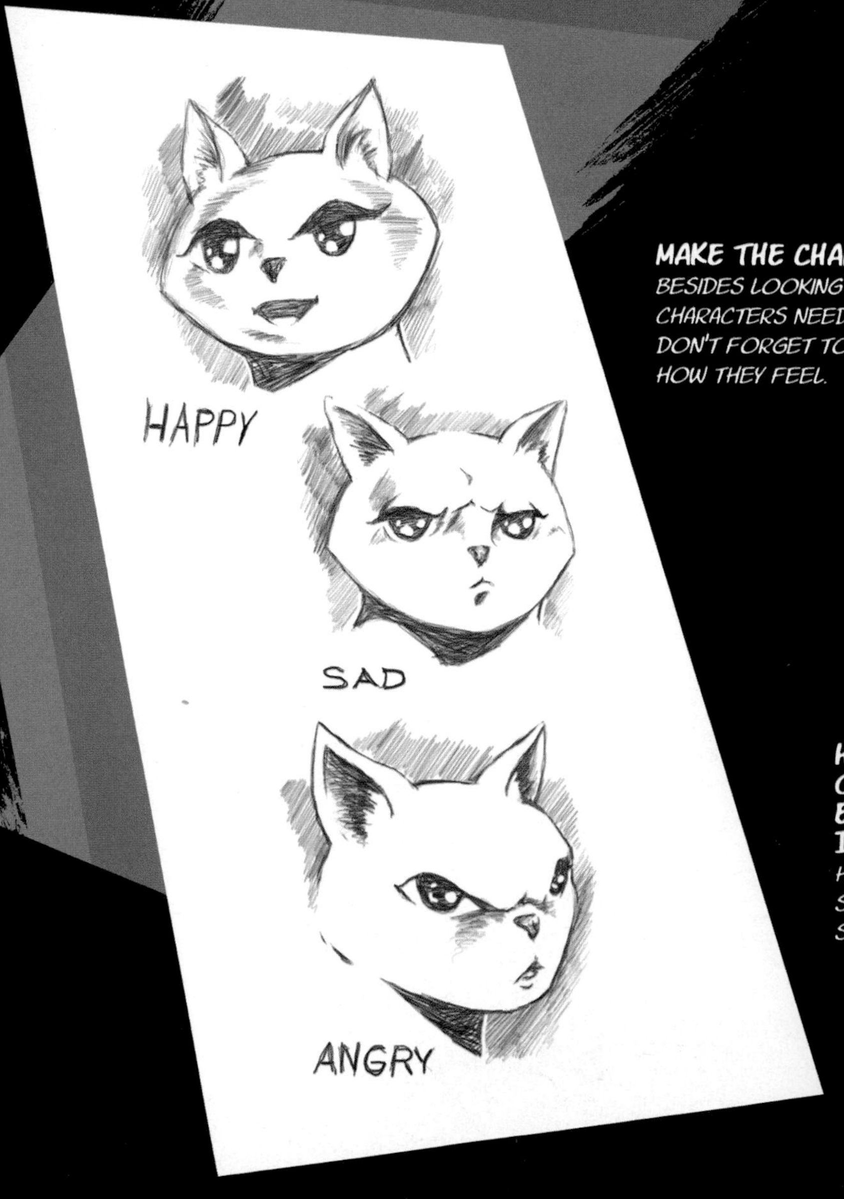
HAPPY
SAD
ANGRY

MAKE THE CHARACTERS ACT!

BESIDES LOOKING COOL YOUR CHARACTERS NEED PERSONALITES. DON'T FORGET TO LET THEM EXPRESS HOW THEY FEEL.

HERE IS A LIST OF SOME COMMON EMOTIONS USED IN COMICS:

HAPPY, SAD, ANGRY, SHOCKED, CONFUSED, SHY, AND CONFIDENT.

DRAW FASTER!

AS A COMIC ARTIST YOU HAVE TO DRAW MANY PANELS QUICKLY. TRY TIMING YOURSELF. SEE HOW WELL YOU CAN DRAW A PANEL IN 20 MINUTES.

SHARE WHAT YOU'VE MADE!

COMICS ARE A FORM OF ENTERTAINMENT. LET YOUR FRIENDS AND FAMILY READ YOUR WORK. TRY TO MAKE STORIES THAT THEY WILL ENJOY!

WE WOULD LOVE TO SEE YOUR ART!

EMAIL US AT:
KYLE@GALACTICQUEST.COM
WWW.HEROCATSCOMIC.COM

CTION LAB ENTERTAINMENT

ryan Seaton - Publisher
ave Dwonch - President
hawn Gabborin - Editor in Chief
amal Igle - Director of Marketing
m Dietz - Social Media Director
eremy Whitley - Education Outreach Director
had Cicceni & Colleen Boyd - Associate Editors

THE STORY CONTINUES IN
HERO CATS OF STELLAR CITY #10

FROM GARY TURNER
CARLOS GOMEZ AND TEODORO GONZALE

Mage

AVAILABLE IN FINER STORES EVERYWHER

Into a realm of magic and savagery comes a mysterious boy washed ashore. His is a lone survivor. Befriended by an apprentice magi, her quirky mentor, and a metal golem, together they are Kai's only hope to stay alive long enough for rescue. Prepare yourself for a d20 RPG adventure with an all new twist.

FROM DAVE DWONCH & ANNA LENCIONI

CYRUS PERKINS
AND THE HAUNTED TAXI CAB

AVAILABLE IN FINER STORES EVERYWHERE

The stunning conclusion to the most innovative crime noir in comics! Will Cyrus solve Michael's murder? Will Michael finally get the peace he deserves? If you think you know how the story ends, you are DEAD WRONG.

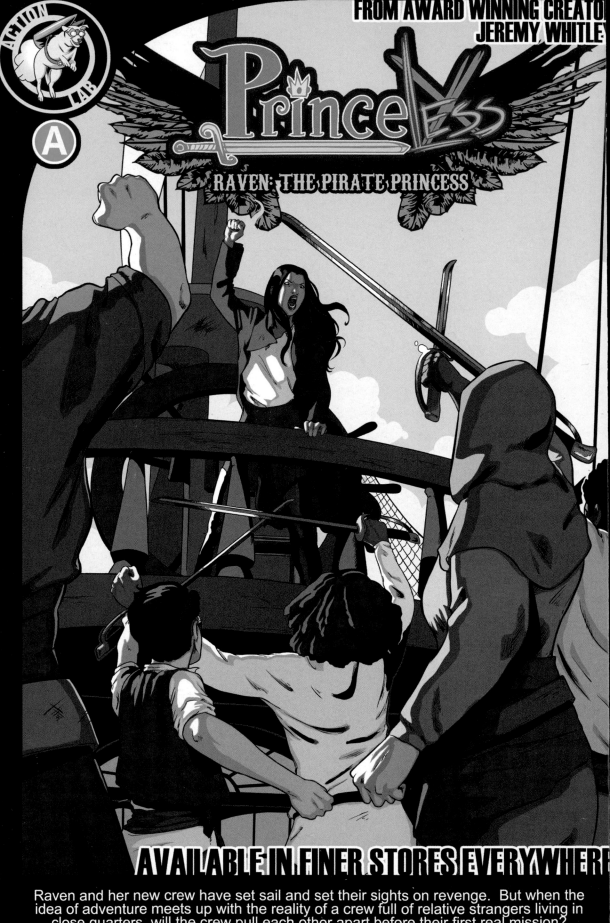

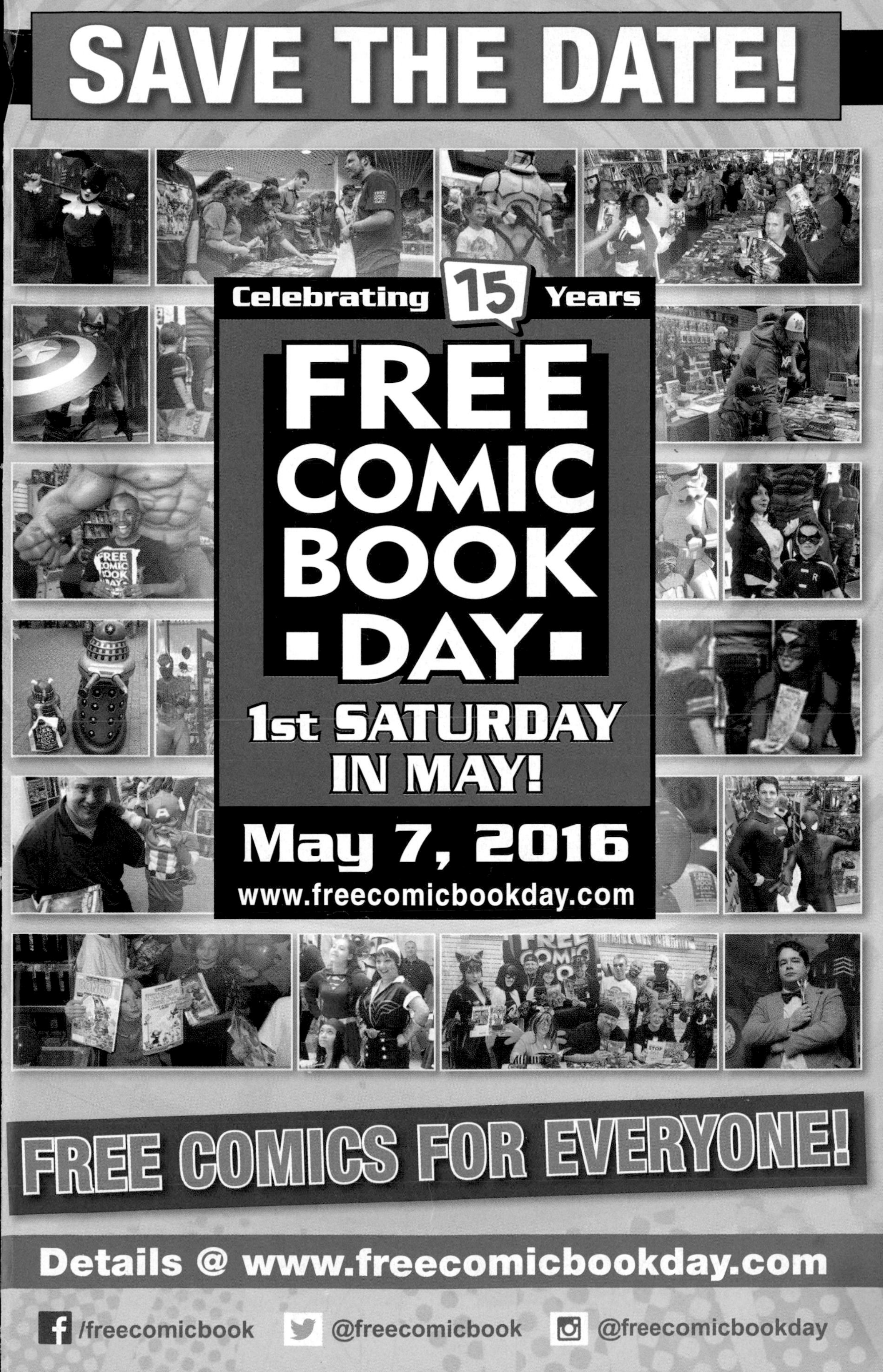
SAVE THE DATE!
Celebrating 15 Years
FREE COMIC BOOK DAY
1st SATURDAY IN MAY!
May 7, 2016
www.freecomicbookday.com
FREE COMICS FOR EVERYONE!
Details @ www.freecomicbookday.com
/freecomicbook
@freecomicbook
@freecomicbookday